D1021330

Born in Dublin, **Oisín McGann** spent his childhood there and in Drogheda, County Louth. He studied at Dún Laoghaire School of Art and Design, and then worked in advertising, design and film animation. He now lives in Drogheda and works as a freelance illustrator and artist. He is the author of *The Gods and Their Machines* and a number of other books for younger readers. *The Harvest Tide Project* is the first book in **The Archisan Tales** and Oisín is currently finalising the second book in the series, *Under Fragile Stone*.

# THE HARVEST TIDE PROJECT

## THE ARCHISAN TALES

Oisín McGann

THE O'BRIEN PRESS
DUBLIN

First published 2004 by The O'Brien Press Ltd.,
20 Victoria Road, Dublin 6, Ireland.
Tel: +353 1 4923333; Fax: +353 1 4922777
E-mail: books@obrien.ie
Website: www.obrien.ie

ISBN: 0-86278-834-X

British Library Cataloguing-in-Publication Data
A catalogue record for this title is available from the British Library

The O'Brien Press receives assistance from

1 2 3 4 5 6
04 05 06 07 08

Editing, typesetting and design:
The O'Brien Press Ltd
Printing: AIT Nørhaven A/S

Cover image of Sea lions courtesy of Science Photo Library

*This is for my brother, Marek – for being there to talk stories when we were young.*

# ACKNOWLEDGEMENTS

While *The Gods And Their Machines* was my first novel to be published, this was the first one I wrote. I want to thank my family, friends and all those who offered input and encouragement while I struggled to get it right. The first couple of drafts of *The Harvest Tide Project* were written while I was in England, and I owe a debt to my aunt, Margaret Summers, and my cousins Sinéad, David and Mary for making me feel welcome in London, and helping me get settled. I'm grateful to the people at O'Brien Press – particularly my editor, Susan Houlden – for their expertise and support, and for taking the risk with my books. I'd also like to thank the world of advertising, for making me want to quit and find a better life. And a special thanks to my Mum ... for everything.

# CONTENTS

# PROLOGUE

If Taya and Lorkrin Archisan had known how much trouble their curiosity would cause, they might have thought twice about searching for that door. But they would probably have gone and done it anyway.

It was Lorkrin who had first discovered that two of the rooms were too small for the house. The combined length of the two rooms that lay within the west side of their uncle's farmhouse was four paces shorter than the outside of the house. Walls just weren't that thick. So, like anyone else with an imagination, they had come to the conclusion that they had found a secret room. All that remained was to find the door and figure out how to open it.

While Taya searched the dividing wall in each room, Lorkrin started pushing and pulling things in the hope of finding a hidden lever. He was disappointed with the lack of results. Not one of the candlesticks, books or pieces of sculpture caused any movement in the stone wall. But Taya did find something, a small gap between two of the stone blocks, hidden from sight behind a small tapestry. She called her brother in the next room and moved the embroidered picture out of the way to show him.

'That's got to be it,' he agreed. 'Have a go.'

They both knew that their uncle would not use a normal catch for his hidden door. He would have built something only a Myunan could open. Myunan flesh was unique; it could be shaped and reformed like modelling clay, allowing them to change their shape at will, an ability known as 'amorphing'.

Lorkrin watched as Taya pressed her right hand down on a side table, letting it go soft and kneading it out with the left until her wrist, palm and fingers tapered into a flat, knife-like shape. It was now thin enough to slip into the gap between the two blocks. In the cavity behind the wall, she felt a round handle and, keeping her wrist thin and flat, she let the rest of her hand go solid again and grasped the handle with her fingers. It turned smoothly and there was a click. The two children breathed out softly with excitement. They had found the entrance to their Uncle Emos's studio.

With a whirring sound, a section of wall swung inwards, and the two Myunans peered inside. A flight of steps led down into the darkness of a cellar. Taya slid her hand from the gap in the blocks and slunched, letting her arm return to its normal shape. Lorkrin found a lantern hanging just inside the door and fetched some matches from the kitchen to light it. Then the boy started down the steps, closely followed by his sister. The steps led further down than they would to a normal cellar. Taya counted fifty-two steps to the bottom, and what they saw there explained why it was so deep, so secret.

Here was the proof that their Uncle Emos practised the dark art of *trans*morphing – forcing other materials to become as pliable as his own flesh. The room was as big across as the whole farmhouse above it, with eight brick pillars supporting its roof and the walls lined with shelves and cupboards. One wall was given over entirely to a rack of deep, square pigeonholes to hold a huge collection of scrolls. Myunans did not use books; what little they did write down was in the form of pictograms on sheets of vellum.

Taya and Lorkrin had no interest in the scrolls, because all around them were several workbenches where Emos practised his craft. On each was at least one work in progress. Pieces of metal, wood, even some living plants, had been twisted and contorted into weird and unnatural shapes. There was a cactus that been sculpted into a winding centipede, a windblown tree crafted from dinner forks, and there was even a sheep's skeleton that had been transformed into an armchair. The plants were the most fascinating. Still living, they had been distorted beyond recognition as Emos honed his skills. All around, stumps of trees, shards of metal and other materials were in various stages of being twisted into human or animal figures. The half-finished pieces betrayed the unnatural way he could work any material as if it were clay, with fingerprints left in solid steel, and wood spread across bench-tops as if turned to liquid. So this was what transmorphing looked like. Emos Harprag was obviously a master at sculpting other objects as if they were extensions of his own malleable body. It went against everything Taya and Lorkrin had been taught, and it gave them the shivers. But the children walked around the room, spellbound.

'He's going to be really angry if he finds us here,' Taya whispered.

'He can't blame us for having a look around, can he?'

11

Lorkrin argued. 'It's not like he *told* us to stay out, is it?'

'No, he didn't tell us anything about this place,' Taya said back. 'That's the whole point. This is supposed to be a secret.'

'Well, think of it this way,' her brother persisted. 'If he had told us he had a secret room somewhere, but he didn't want us looking for it or going into it, then he could be mad at us. But seeing as he didn't mention it, and we've just happened to find it ... it's sort of like we've earned the chance to have a look around, yeah?'

Taya gave her brother a withering glance and he could tell that she was not convinced. But then, neither was he. Emos was away in Rutledge and would not be back for some time, so they decided to leave the worry about punishment for later. In the meantime, there was a fantastic new world to explore. Neither of them had seen transmorphing before; they had only ever heard stories about it. It was strictly forbidden for Myunans. Lorkrin picked up one of the curling hooks and admired the craftsmanship. He and Taya still only had novice tool sets, and, of course, they were only able to use the implements on themselves. Uncle Emos had the tools of a master.

'Ma and Pa said he'd stopped after Aunt Wyla died,' he said. 'Do you think they know about this?'

'Of course they know,' Taya grunted. 'Pa helped him build the house, didn't he? They just don't tell us anything, that's all.'

She came to a workbench near the centre of the room. On it were a few tools, some scrolls covered in sketches and a tray holding a clump of mushrooms that were on their way to becoming a crouching frog. She ran her fingers over one of the sheets of vellum and gasped. The notes on the calf skin were not made by ink; they seemed to have grown into the hide itself. The page was only half full, and there was a quill lying beside it. There was no bottle of ink in sight.

'Lorkrin, look at this! He can use the transmorphing to write.'

Lorkrin picked up the quill.

'He must save a fortune on ink,' he quipped.

Taya held up another sheet and studied the script. It was Sestinian, and she was not able to read some of it, but it was definitely describing some arcane techniques.

'Let me see!' Lorkrin snatched it from her to try to read it.

'Hey! I was looking at that!' his sister snapped and seized the page. Lorkrin pulled back automatically and the vellum stretched and tore. They froze, staring in horror at what they had done, and around them there was the sense of a breath being drawn. Then, from the very sheet in their hands, there came a sound like the shrieking of a cat. Staring down at it, they saw blood starting to ooze from the torn edges. They dropped the vellum to the floor and stepped back from it, covering their ears to block out the raucous crying.

'It's hexed!' Lorkrin moaned. 'Aw, bowels! What are we going to do?'

Taya didn't answer. She was already heading full tilt towards the stairs. Lorkrin darted after her, on her heels as she ran up the steps. At the top, they blew out the lantern, hung it back in its place and swung the heavy door shut. They leaned against it as if to hold it closed and tried to catch their breath. Lorkrin jumped as he realised he was still holding the quill. What should he do with it? He did not dare leave it out where their uncle might see it. He tucked the pen away in his tool roll and swore to himself to try to return it later.

'What are we going to do now?' Taya whimpered. 'He's going to kill us. He's going to go insane! What are we going to do?'

'I don't know,' her brother muttered. 'All I know is that I don't want to be here when he gets back. And we can't go home, because that would be just as bad as soon as he found us. We need to get out of here. I think we should run away.'

'What ... again?'

'Yeah, I think so. But not like the other times. I mean really far away, maybe Hortenz or even further. We went into a room we weren't supposed to be in, tore a page we weren't supposed to see and set off a hex. I think we need to get out of the country. We could go to Rutledge, hide on an esh-boat and maybe get a ride up the coast.'

Taya considered this. It was drastic, that was true, but they had seen Uncle Emos angry before and they had been trying his patience lately as it was. He would not take this well. Taya looked into her brother's frightened face. Deep beneath her feet, she could just hear the sobbing of the torn vellum. A lump rose in her throat and she gulped.

'Let's pack,' she said.

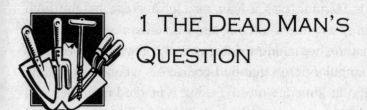

# 1 THE DEAD MAN'S QUESTION

Emos Harprag sat quietly in the passenger seat of the wagon as he was driven into the town of Rutledge-on-Coast to see a dead man. The oil-powered engine took up the entire front half of the vehicle and belched smoke into the air over his head, stamping its sooty mark on the sky. It was still early in the morning, and Peddar Murris drove the wagon at close to its top speed down the empty, winding streets. Emos was slightly amused and curious about his friend's urgency. Murris was normally eager to talk but today he was quiet and pensive.

He had said little about why he had come all the way out to Emos's farm, asking only that the Myunan come back with him to Rutledge, but it had something to do with a dead body they had discovered. Some poor soul who had been murdered, his corpse dumped where it should never have been found. Emos would not have considered himself an expert on the dead. He had trouble enough relating to the living, and there were constables in Rutledge whose job it was to deal with such crimes, but Murris seemed to think he was needed.

Emos Harprag was a lean man of average height, with long, grey hair and a solemn, almost sad expression. His face was mature, but had few lines, as was common in Myunans. The triangular tattoo that he bore on his face attracted little attention in Rutledge-on-Coast, but it marked him out as an exile to Myunans everywhere. Because of his past, he could never live among his own people again.

As they turned onto the road that led down to the docks, the esh came into view and Emos could smell the tang of sessium on the breeze. Rutledge was on the coast of Braskhia, and like most of the other coastal towns, had made its life from the esh – for there was no water off the coast of Braskhia, at least none that could be seen. Stretching from the docks to the horizon was an ocean of gas, white with a warm yellow tinge, which lay like a blanket of cloud over everything east of Rutledge. The gas was called sessium, and it was so heavy it sank through air to lie thickly on the ground. The sea of sessium that stretched out before Emos's eyes was called the esh and the people of Braskhia had made their living from it for as long as anyone could remember.

'The body's still aboard the *Lightfoot*,' Murris grunted, referring to his boat as he steered the wagon around the end of a warehouse and turned left along the docks. 'We didn't want to move him until you'd had a look at him. Bring a dead man down off a boat and soon every busybody in town will be hanging around wanting to know who he is. We figured it would be best to find out what we can about him first, before tongues start wagging. There are some odd things about this corpse ... and odd things do seem to be your speciality.'

Esh-boats lay at anchor in the harbour or moored to the docks. With three hulls and an array of masts, each one was lighter and more complex than any ship made for travelling on water. Murris drove past a number of different kinds of vessel before bringing the wagon to a skidding halt at a jetty that led out to a fishing trawler.

Peddar Murris was a stocky, jovial man with a bushy moustache that travelled down his cheeks and up to meet his sideburns. Despite the fact that as chief engineer on the *Lightfoot*, he was literally responsible for the lives of the crew by maintaining the hydrogen in its sealed hulls, Murris was a relaxed and mellow-natured man. But his face was troubled now, as he led Emos along the jetty and up the gangplank. The Myunan experienced the brief feeling of vertigo that he always got when stepping onto the deck of an esh-boat; he could feel the shifting swell of the gas beneath the hull. The captain waved his pipe at them from the bridge above and gestured at them to wait. The eshtran was on the deck in front of them, giving the Last Blessing to the dead man.

According to Braskhiam beliefs, a man had to meet his god with pure air in his lungs, and the eshtran, a Braskhiam priest, was administering that final breath with a small bellows. After he had muttered a few words, he slipped the bellows into a scabbard on his belt and made a sign with his hand from his chest to his mouth and back again. Murris walked over with Emos, both of them covering their noses and mouths against the smell.

'Don't mind the way the arms and legs are broken,' Murris told the Myunan. 'The healer says that was done after he was dead. It probably happened when his body got caught on the boat's anchor. This man suffocated.'

He held up a breathing mask and section of hose; the hose had been cut with a knife or other sharp tool. The man was also wearing a safety harness on his hips and the rope from this too had been cut.

'Definitely murdered,' Murris added, confirming Emos's unspoken thought. 'He'd been diving in the esh and some-one cut his air hose and safety line. He was left to die down there, out past Crofter's Point. He didn't have a hope of making it to land. The healer reckons by the extent of the rot that he's been down there nearly two weeks. Things rot slow in the esh. It was a chance in a million that he caught on our anchor. Someone killed him and left him where they thought he'd never be found. But it's what he was doing diving out there in the first place that has us puzzled. Apart from the fishing, there's nothing of interest out there, just weeds and rocks. Nobody who has any business bein' on the esh wastes their time diving off Crofter's Point.'

'Well, something down there must have been important to him.' Emos studied the bulging eyes and bluish skin. The man's tongue was protruding slightly and his lips were blue. Esh creatures had been taking nibbles out of him and there were open wounds, but no blood to speak of. His flesh was swelling as it decomposed and his clothes were tight on his body. The boots and harness were of a military style, but this man had been frail, and wore a long beard; he was no sol-dier. The rest of his clothes were simple garments. The knees of his trousers were dirty as if he had done a lot of kneeling and his jacket had pockets full of folded sheets of parchment. Emos unfolded a couple. They contained crumbs of soil. He checked the corpse's hands.

'He has earth under his fingernails – not the mark of a man who works out at esh,' Emos remarked.

'That's not all,' Murris added. 'He had a satchel around his neck when we pulled him in. Have a look at this.'

One of the men brought out the bag, handed it to Emos and stepped quickly back. Like others among the crew, he seemed uneasy around Myunans. Emos was not bothered; it was still better than the treatment he received from his own people. He unbuckled the satchel and opened the flap, emptying its contents onto the deck. He frowned. There was a trowel, an auger, a gardening fork, a small pair of shears and some more soil samples. There was also a sheaf of notes on parchment.

'None of us can read them,' Murris told him. 'They're in a language we've never seen before.'

'Actually, I think you have,' Emos replied. 'It's Sestinian, but he's used shorthand, a type their scientists use for making quick notes. These are measurements for things like fertiliser, moisture levels, temperature ... but what was this man doing walking around at the bottom of the esh?'

'That's what we'd like to know,' Murris said. 'And why did someone feel the need to kill him?'

'Well,' Emos shrugged. 'Judging by this, he was involved in nothing more mysterious than gardening, if in a slightly unusual location ...'

He stopped. One page in particular appeared to have been written in haste, as if the man was excited or upset. There was one last line scrawled across the bottom of the page. Murris looked over his shoulder.

'What does it say?' he asked.

'It says, "How many people will die?"'

Emos looked up at Murris.

'This might be something we need to know about.'

+ + +

Emos Harprag lived on his small farm in Braskhia, a day's walk from Rutledge-on-Coast, having given up the nomad life of a Myunan and settled down to make a living raising crops and livestock. The land was fertile and was also close enough to the esh to see the Harvest Tide every year. He had been exiled from his tribe years before, and his only contact now with the Myunans was the occasional, discreet visit from the Archisans: his sister, her husband and their two children. Sometimes they left his niece and nephew with him to stay for a few weeks. It was good for the children to experience a different way of life, and Emos was not the type to back down from a challenge.

It was late in the day when Murris left him back to his gate and waved him goodbye. They were both troubled by what they had seen and the ominous warning in the dead man's notes. With his mind mulling over the mystery, it took him some time to notice that there was no sign of his niece and nephew. From somewhere, he could hear the faint sound of a cat wailing.

The tapestry on the wall of his travel room was crooked. Breath hissing through gritted teeth, he opened the hidden door and hurried down the steps. Lorkrin and Taya had entered his studio. He should never have left them alone in the house for so long. A valuable sheet of ancient Parsinor curses shrieked from the floor at the bottom of the stairs. He silenced the hex by licking his finger and thumb and pinching the torn ends together. He soon discovered that the little maggots hadn't stopped at damaging the scroll. They'd made off with one of his transmorphing quills. He stormed back up the stairs and slammed the door shut behind him, his normally impassive face tensed in fury.

Emos packed his tools and some other essentials in a backpack, locked up his farmhouse and set out to track them down. He knew they would run, but he had tracked and killed more cunning prey than them and he would see them punished before the week was out.

They had left in such a hurry that they had not even bothered to try to hide their trail, so he followed at a fast pace, his eyes, ears and nose seeking out any sign of Taya and Lorkrin, but his mind occupied with what he had seen in Rutledge that day.

The mix of the dead man's military and peasant equipment, the notes made by someone with a scientific education, the way he had been murdered in cold blood – it was all very strange and, as Murris had said, Emos was fascinated by strange things. Whoever this man had been, he had carried some terrible knowledge, and it was probable that someone had killed him to ensure his silence.

He reached a fork in the road, one way leading east towards Rutledge-on-Coast, the right turn leading west to Hortenz. Emos followed the faint tracks in the dust up the left-hand fork, but they soon disappeared. He sighed, studying the hedges on either side, then backtracked and headed up the road to Hortenz where he soon came upon their trail again despite the fading evening light. They were going to have to do better than that.

+  +  +

Hortenz was big and loud on the morning of market day. The market was in full swing and the voices of traders competed with the sound of engined wagons and various animal noises. Taya and Lorkrin walked down a street past a woman selling bottled smells, and a tanner's stall, and through a rendacrid auction. The huge, hairless, slug-like creatures sat bloated and sleepy and ready for slaughter, and buyers wandered among them trying to decide which would give the best meat. Taya was leaning in to pet one when her brother grabbed her, pulled her down off the fence and in behind some crates. He put a finger to his lips and pointed. There, in the throng of people milling around the market, was their uncle.

'How did he find us so fast?' she gasped. They had walked late into the night to reach the town before they had slept; their uncle would have had to walk all night, tracking them in darkness to catch them up so quickly.

'He hasn't found us yet,' Lorkrin whispered. 'But what are we going to do?'

Taya spotted a grate in the ground not far from them and nodded towards it. They crept up to it, and between the pair of them they were able to lift it up. There were some iron rungs in the wall below it and they climbed down these, closing the grate above them. They found themselves in a sewer. Taya pinched her nose and grimaced.

'I thought the smell was from the rendacrids farting. If I'd known ...'

'Let's wait here for a bit, until we decide what to do. At least it's safe,' Lorkrin muttered, peering up through the grate. 'He can't stay up there forever. We'll hang around until it's dark, and then go.'

'All right then.' His sister searched around for a clean place to sit down. There wasn't any, so they walked down the tunnel a bit until they found a more open area with large pipes running across the floor and two support columns in the middle, Taya sat down on one of the pipes and rocked back and forth, thinking to herself. They were in awful trouble, and as usual it was Lorkrin's fault. Feelings of guilt about Uncle Emos's scroll gnawed at her conscience. She didn't say anything, because her brother would only laugh. He always said she only felt guilty when she knew she was going to get punished.

Lorkrin wandered down the length of tunnel to a junction where the path ended. A stream gurgled along a brick-walled gully in the middle of the tunnel, filled with things that Lorkrin did not want to think about. It emptied into a river that flowed through the junction. The only light in the sewer was from the grates spaced out in the arched roof, so he was careful where he put his feet. After a while, he got bored and went back to his sister. She was scraping her name on one of the support pillars with a stone.

Lorkrin was struck with a thought. Unrolling his tools, he pulled out the quill he had taken from their uncle's studio.

'Hey!' He held it up to his sister. 'I wonder if we can get this to work.'

Taya's eyes went wide:

'What are you doing with that? Weren't things bad enough without you going and stealing something as well?'

'I didn't steal it. I just took it by accident.'

'Oh, well that doesn't count then,' she sneered. 'I can't wait to see you explain that one. "I took it by *accident*, Uncle Emos." Maybe he'll only half kill you.'

'You can't half kill someone. Either you're dead or you're not. Anyway, do you want to see if this thing works, or not?' Lorkrin brandished the quill at her.

Taya's curiosity got the better of her.

'Okay,' she sniffed, trying to look bored by the idea.

Like all Myunan children, the pair had tried transmorphing on several occasions and had even got hold of a few chants. The fact that it was strictly banned by grown-ups was reason enough to attempt it, but the thought of changing the shape of anything the same way they could change themselves, to extend their powers beyond their own bodies, was irresistible. They had never had any success, but then they had never had a genuine transmorphing tool before either. They were hoping that it would not need a special trigger or chant, that it would just work, but they were disappointed. When Lorkrin drew the quill across one of the bricks in the pillar, no line appeared. He sighed and tried again. Still nothing.

'Try imagining that you're sculpting yourself,' Taya urged. 'As if you're using the pen like a normal amorphing tool; think of the pillar as an arm or a leg or something.'

Lorkrin pressed the nib lightly against the brickwork again, and concentrated. When he moved the quill this time, he felt a slight give in the brick's surface, as if he had cut it with a knife.

'I felt something! I think it's working!' He kept going, writing his name into the column, the pictograms appearing as if carved with a fine chisel. There was an unmistakable cutting sound, and yet it was as easy as writing with ink on vellum. Taya frowned and walked around the column to look at the other side.

'Lorkrin, stop! Stop writing!' she gasped.

He was about to scribble something else when the tone of her voice pulled him up short. Looking at her, he saw a frightened expression on her face. He came around to the other side and gazed at the opposite face of the pillar. His name was cut out of it in reverse. The writing had gone all the way through the brickwork, from one side to the other. The column groaned and there came a grating sound, the kind made by two hard surfaces grinding against each other.

'It's holding up the roof,' Taya breathed. 'And we've just cut through it.'

+ + +

In the garden directly above the newly decorated pillar, Shessil Groach stood soaking in the morning light before the high wall that separated himself and his colleagues from the outside world. There were times when he wondered what life would be like outside the project, where normal people did normal things ... whatever normal things were. It had been a long time since he had been able to walk down the streets of a town, to visit shops and stalls. He had been too young to visit storyhouses and taverns then, but he could do so now, if he were allowed outside, near normal people ... which he wasn't. He idly calculated the time it would take a tasherloc tree, one of the fastest-growing trees in the world, to grow high enough and strong enough for him to use it to climb over that wall. About two weeks, with regular watering, fertilisation and some violin music.

Other, more normal people might have considered using a ladder, but then as Groach would have been the first to admit, he was a little out of the ordinary. It was just as well then, that he was not really looking for a means of escape. He believed that he would one day be released from the project. He was not sure when, but surely not long now, now that he had solved a problem which the staff of the project had worked on for years.

It was only a pity that his friend, Haller Joculeb, would never see the successful completion of the project. Haller's death had been a shock to them all; a horrible accident had taken him only days before Groach had made his inspired discovery. Groach absent-mindedly patted the satchel that hung by his hip. He had not told anyone yet. Haller would have been so proud ... and excited. He had always been the most curious about the outside world and what went on beyond the walls. But now they were sure to be released; Groach would get to visit lots of different places and meet some normal people, folks who didn't talk about plants and earth and fertiliser all day.

In the meantime, there was work to do. He was about to turn away from the wall, when the ground shuddered beneath his feet. Groach looked down and was alarmed to discover cracks appearing in the ground at the base of the wall. There was a deep, hollow crack and then a rumble, and a section of the massive wall suddenly sank slightly, tearing more cracks in the stone and mortar structure. There were shouts and gasps from the garden behind him as some of his friends turned to see what was happening. Then the section collapsed altogether, crashing down through the ground in a cloud of mortar and dust and a bellowing cough. Groach just had time to realise he was in danger of following it when the ground beneath him gave way and the earth swallowed him whole.

# 2 A MEETING IN THE SEWER

Emos wandered through the marketplace, his senses alert for any sign of his niece and nephew. He came upon a tanner's stall, where leather wares were laid out neatly on display. Taking two small wooden sculptures from his bag, he caught the tanner's attention.

'I'm seeking two children, a boy and a girl. They look like this. They're brother and sister. Their names are Lorkrin and Taya Archisan. Have you seen them?'

Stopping work on the belt that he was cutting into shape, the tanner cast his eye over the two pieces of wood. Each was carved into a bust, the head and shoulders of a child. He did not know their faces.

'Sorry, sir. I haven't. Lost, are they?'

'I doubt it. Just missing ... and with a talent for mischief. Thanks, anyway.'

The sound of a crack made Emos spin around to look at the high, spiked wall that stood at the edge of the square, just across from the stall. A crack was creeping upwards, splitting the plaster. The tanner raised his head over the Myunan's shoulder to see. There was a rumble, and then part of the wall settled suddenly. Plaster burst off it, and the broken section of wall collapsed down through a hole in the ground. Shards of mortar and stone flew through the air – the tanner ducked down behind his counter, and Emos raised an arm to shield his face from the debris.

People were rushing about shouting, and many were coming over to have a look at what was going on. There was a large hole in the wall, and a cloud of dust was still floating like a thick fog, coating everything and everyone in a fine white powder. Through the gap, figures could be seen stepping over the debris and making their way into the marketplace.

They were men and women, all dressed in knee-length tunics and sandals. They were all of different ages and appearance, but most had soil or grass stains on their knees, and some held a trowel or shears in their hands. The men wore beards and they all had long hair. Wiping dust from their eyes, they peered around as if in some kind of new land. Several greeted the gathering crowd and one even shook hands with a bemused man standing near him. Emos watched as an old woman approached the tanner's stall and began examining the leatherwork with obvious delight. The simplest pieces of leatherwork fascinated her. The tanner, eager to seize the chance of a sale, offered some more of his wares for her perusal.

'Hello!' she chirped to Emos, as she examined a pair of sandals. 'Isn't this a splendid place? A veritable plethora of curiosities. Would ... pardon me, very forward of me, but ... would you happen to know where I might find some absinthe? It's been years since I've had a bit of tipple.'

'No,' Emos replied, politely gesturing towards the tanner.

'Sorry. Perhaps this man might know?'

'How do you like those sandals?' the trader enquired.

Emos turned to watch as the other newcomers wandered further into the market, scattering and finding objects of interest wherever they looked. They were all gentle-natured, polite and, the market traders noted, easy to please. The traders also noted that none of them seemed to have any money.

The Myunan was still trying to make sense of the strange group, when from the towers of the town walls, the horns sounded an alarm. The bass roar of engines and wheels was heard, and then catchwagons thundered into the square, manned by armed soldiers. Each wagon had an arm that swung from the top of its body, suspended from which was a man equipped with a net, a whip and a crossbow with restraining rope. They swung out above the crowd as the wagons circled the market and picked off the newcomers, snatching them where possible, shooting them down and dragging them back when they tried to run. The woman Emos had just spoken to went to hide behind the tanner's stall, but the trader wasn't about to tangle with soldiers. He pushed her away, causing her to stumble into Emos's arms.

'Sorry, missus, but I've my business to think about,' the trader grunted apologetically.

A pair of foot soldiers pushed through the crowd and grabbed hold of the woman, hauling her away out of Emos' grasp.

'Make yourself scarce, Myunan, if you know what's good for you,' one of them snarled. 'This is Noranian business.'

Resisting the temptation to get involved, Emos watched in contempt as they pulled the distressed woman away. He could do nothing for her, and he had his niece and nephew to think about. He watched as the captives were dropped into cages on the backs of the trucks. The drivers of the vehicles gunned their engines, forcing their way through the crowd, barging past people who were too slow getting out of their way. Many were hurt by the steel-reinforced wooden chassis or the iron rims of wheels. Screams mingled with the rumble of vehicles and the crack of the whips.

Then they were gone, the wagons disappeared back up the streets from which they came, and foot soldiers closed in around the square, checking for any that the catchwagons might have missed and questioning the traders and customers. With their carapace armour, and vicious-looking weapons, they were a threatening presence, offering trouble to anyone they thought was looking for it.

While the foot soldiers bullied the people of the market, two more wagons drew up at the hole in the wall carrying enormous stones. These were lifted off the flat-bed carts with a hoist and used to build a makeshift, but solid barrier between the square and whatever lay behind the wall. The tanner, having failed to sell anything to the mysterious people from behind the wall, turned to see if the tattooed man would be interested in a purchase, but the Myunan was gone.

+ + +

Groach spat dust out of his mouth and groaned. He ached all over and his head was spinning. He raised his head gingerly and squinted through the cloud of dust. There was a hole above and behind him in the ceiling (how was there a roof above him when he had been out in the garden?) and he was surrounded by rubble and debris from what looked like the garden wall and some other kind of brickwork. He was in a tunnel with curved walls that smelled suspiciously like a sewer. Sitting up, he discovered that he had landed on his backside, if the painful bruises were anything to go by. The contents of his satchel were scattered across the floor and someone was whispering nearby.

Peering through the settling dust, he could make out two figures, children by the size and shape, a boy and a girl.

'It wasn't our fault,' protested the boy.

'Well, it was ... sort of,' the girl piped up. 'But it was an accident.'

They both appeared to be frozen to the spot, as if they couldn't quite believe what had happened.

'I don't believe this,' the boy said to the girl, staring up at the hole in the roof. 'How much bad luck can we have?'

'What have you done?' Groach gasped. 'How did you do it? Are you telling me you destroyed this place all by yourselves? You'd better stay there until someone comes to sort this out. This is wrong, what you've done. Just stay right where you are.'

He got to his feet stiffly and winced as something in his back clicked. Behind the children, the wall had collapsed. He was standing between them and the only way out. Leaning forward, he got a better look at the two children. They were in their early teens. It was hard to tell who was older. The girl was a little taller, with brown hair in a long, braided ponytail. The boy had blond hair, cropped short. They both wore tunics bound with cloth belts; the girl had leggings and the boy trousers. Their clothes had a swirling pattern on them, the boy's more angular and coloured in greys, greens and blues; the girl's circular, in reds, oranges and browns.

They had similar patterns on their skin, and it was hard in places to tell where their clothes stopped and their skin started. The two looked enough alike to be brother and sister. Voices sounded above them. Some of the others from the project were standing around the hole in the ceiling.

'Shessil? Are you down there? Are you all right?'

'Fetch Hovem!' he called back. 'There are some children down here. They've broken something in the sewer!'

'I'll say they have ...,' came a voice from above. 'Broken the whole dratted sewer's more like. We can smell it from here.'

'You just hang on here for a bit,' Groach told the pair. 'There'll be someone along any time now.'

'I think you'd better let us go,' the girl said quietly.

Behind her in the darkness, the boy had knelt down and unrolled some tools. Groach tried to see what he was doing, but it was difficult in the bad light. While he waited for Hovem, the Groundsmaster, he bent down to pick up the sheets of vellum, the quills, the bottle of ink and the other odds and ends that had fallen from his bag.

'Look, we're trying to be reasonable here,' the girl continued. 'If you'll just let us go, we'll go away and you'll never see us again, we promise.'

Groach tried again to see past her. The boy seemed to be combing his ears back ... with a comb. The small figure twisted and dragged at his flesh, working quickly and skilfully with the tools from the roll of pouches on the floor. Then he stopped and lifted his head.

He moved out from the shadows, and Groach found himself facing a terrifying creature. It had the same colour and markings as the boy, but there the resemblance ended.

Narrowed triangular eyes sat above a short, wide snout. A ridge of hair flowed back past small, pointed ears and down a muscled back covered in spikes and armour-like scales. Its back legs were short and powerful, its fore-legs longer, ending in paws that held vicious, curving claws. It had the biggest, sharpest teeth he had ever seen.

Groach's breath caught in his throat, frozen in terror by the sight. The fiend let out a growl and launched itself at him. In a blind panic, Groach stumbled back, turned, sprinted down the tunnel and vaulted into the fast-moving river at the end of the path. The current caught him and swept him out of sight into the darkness. Lorkrin chuckled and slunched back into his natural shape.

'I think you went a bit far,' Taya said to her brother. 'We just wanted him to go away.'

'Well, he went away, didn't he?' Lorkrin said, shrugging.

'After the fright you've just given him, I'd say he'll keep on going. You always have to act the monster, don't you? You know how Uncle Emos is about us going around scaring people.'

'That was brilliant, though. Did you see him jump into that stuff? I couldn't even walk too close to it. This isn't turning out to be such a bad day after all.'

'Well, let's get out of here. Have you got the quill?' Taya asked.

Lorkrin knelt down by his tool roll, but then lifted his gaze to the pile of rubble under the hole in the ceiling.

'Aw, bowels!'

'Don't swear like that! What's wrong? Where is it?'

'I dropped it when the roof caved in.' He rolled up his tools and walked over to where Groach had been lying. 'It would have been about here. I can't see it.'

'He picked some things up ...' Taya started to say, then stopped.

They shared a look of horror.

'He's got the quill,' Lorkrin gulped. 'How far do you think we'll have to run away now?'

'How could you drop it, you idiot?'

'Sorry! I was busy trying not to be *killed*! How was I to know that ... that a man was going to fall through the roof and... and land right there and pick it up? How was I to know that?'

'We have to get it back; we have to find him,' his sister groaned.

'Well, we'd better do it fast, 'cos he's in that river and he's getting further away all the time.'

Whipping out their tool kits, they quickly fashioned their fingertips into claws and clambered up the wall where the path ended, then set off along it after the man they had just scared away.

+ + +

The water went up Groach's nostrils and burned a path down his throat. He flailed and threw his head back, snatching a breath before going under again. Sound roared in his ears, which gummed up more every time he submerged. The world numbed around him as the fight to catch gulps of the fetid air became the only thing that mattered. He knew he was moving; he did not know where, and he had never been a very good swimmer. The deep water was alien and overwhelming, trying so hard to fill his lungs and cover his head. He had never felt so out of control. Then strong light washed over him and he was able to breathe. It lasted only an instant; he was falling out into daylight. He splashed down into more water, but this time his hands and feet dug into mud, or something soft anyway. He pushed upwards and was rewarded with fresh, clear air.

Groach heaved in gulps of it – heaven compared to the stench he had been struggling not to inhale moments earlier. He studied his surroundings. He was in a river, a real one. The pipe that had dumped him in here was above and behind him, gushing sewage into the muddy water. He was standing in it, but it was bliss after the tunnel. His legs were knee-deep in the riverbed, his chin just above the waterline. The banks of the river were high and bare. Bushes and trees lined the top, but he could see no place to climb out. He waded out into cleaner water and found himself out of his depth. But he was too exhausted to care. He lay back and floated, drifting with the current.

+ + +

Rak Ek Namen regarded the garden wall with an impassive face. The ruler of Noran was a tall, handsome man with wise eyes and a warm smile. Despite his greying hair and the few lines on his face, he was the youngest ever to reach this position. He had got there through a combination of cunning and charm and was used to having things go his way. The jagged gap, now filled with large rocks, was an irritation.

Hovem, the Groundsmaster, was a somewhat less impressive figure, and stood nervously by as the Prime Ministrate surveyed the damage. He was struggling to come up with an explanation for how most of his staff had ended up wandering aimlessly around the marketplace.

'And you say that there is still one man unaccounted for?' Namen asked.

'Yes, Prime Ministrate. Shessil Groach. At first, we thought he might have been buried beneath the rubble. He was standing by the wall when it collapsed. He wasn't buried, but the wall crashed right down into the sewers and it's possible he was lost down there. We still don't know what caused the wall to collapse.'

'You will tell the Catchmaster everything he needs to know about this Shessil Groach. I want him found. Every person on the project is valuable, as is the knowledge they carry. We cannot afford any more lost time. The success of this experiment is vital.'

The Groundsmaster almost asked his leader why, if their work was so vital, six of his best people were lying in the infirmary with crossbow wounds, just for taking a walk around the market. But he bit his tongue. Crossbow wounds could be catching for those who questioned the Prime Ministrate's authority. He hoped Shessil was all right, and that he would find his way back before the soldiers had to seek him out. Ever since one of his team, Haller Joculeb, had been lost while diving under the esh, Hovem had been growing more and more uneasy about working for the Noranians. Rak Ek Namen was a charismatic leader, well respected by his people, but he had little patience for those who did not do what they were told. Shessil was a dreamer and a bit naïve – he might not realise how much trouble he was facing.

The Prime Ministrate strode out of the large garden and through the main building, once the home of a wealthy landowner, now the temporary quarters for over a hundred men and women who normally worked and studied in the fortified city garden of the Noranian capital. They had been brought to Hortenz to be near the coast, near the esh.

The soldiers snapped to attention as he came out the front door. He ignored them and nodded to Cossock, his body-guard. The huge creature, a towering figure of muscle and weapons, opened the door of the Prime Ministrate's carriage. Namen stepped up into the vehicle and was joined by his personal assistant, Mungret. The carriage was of Braskhiam design; its carved wooden sides, inlaid with precious metals, rested on an iron chassis in front of the enormous, bule-oil engine. An iron plough-shaped cattle shunt hung from the front and served as a very effective method for getting through crowds. The driver sat on the top, looking through the windscreen over the large, wooden steering wheel and the panel of gauges and valves. Bigger, more armoured versions of the machine squatted in front and behind it; soldiers peered out through the slits of these monsters, crossbows at the ready.

'Has he been found?' Namen asked, as he settled into the velvet upholstery.

'Not yet, Prime Ministrate,' Mungret answered. 'The gates have been closed since the alarm was given. It's unlikely that he could have made it out before that. Someone might be hiding him, or he may have taken to the sewers, in which case he could be hopelessly lost or could have got beyond the town walls.'

'Extend the search. Send out pigeons. Alert every town and village within two days' walk of here. Get men into those sewers. Block off every exit. I want this man back safe in the grounds by tomorrow.'

'Yes, Prime Ministrate.'

'What other business have I to cover today?'

Mungret consulted the agenda.

'The mayor of Wicklehoe has been keeping taxes from the treasury. You wanted to deal with that yourself, Prime Ministrate. There is the exhibition opening at the Ashglaft Gallery here in town, dinner with the High Priestess Malifluous ... and of course there're the negotiations with the Braskhiams.'

'Ah, yes. How go the negotiations?'

'The Braskhiams still refuse to build us any more warships, and the same goes for land-based weapons. They maintain that we are making plans for war and they want nothing to do with it.'

'Tell me something new, Mungret.'

'We have put it to them that we need stronger defences, especially in view of the Karthar build-up and their raids into the Braskhiam fishing territories. "If we can't defend ourselves, how can we help defend you", etc. but they won't have any of it. The council is afraid of upsetting the Karthars.'

'I think it is a bit late for that,' Namen grunted. 'If Braskhia were not so strong, it would have been part of Noran by now. But with their technology and their mastery of the esh ... If they were inclined to, they could build an empire for themselves. We must keep them on our side. The Karthars lie off our coast in readiness to invade and while they stay out on the esh, we can only watch and wait. Our fleet is no match for theirs.'

The Prime Ministrate fell silent, brooding. He had taken a failing empire and rebuilt it, making the Noranians one of the most powerful civilisations in history, but for all its might, the empire still relied on the ingenious technology from the nation of Braskhia.

'The Groundsmaster and his group are coming along well, but they still do not have results,' he continued. 'It could be some time yet before we're ready. We will have to tolerate the Karthars until we are ready to face them on my terms.'

He turned his attention to the street they were passing through. People were waving and cheering at him. The Prime Ministrate flashed them a beaming smile and raised his hand in salute. The carriages passed out the gate and left the town behind. Namen sighed. Taking his pipe from his pocket, he stoked it with tobacco and lit it with a match, blowing smoke rings at the ceiling. Mungret, who had a bad chest, muffled his coughs as best he could.

+  +  +

Shessil Groach felt himself carried gently with the flow of the river. He had tried swimming across the strong current and discovered that the more he thrashed around, the closer he came to drowning, so now he just relaxed and let the river take him wherever it wanted to go. It was quite pleasant.

As time wore on, however, he noticed that the light was fading. Evening was falling, and it would be getting cooler. It would not be wise to be floating down a strange river in the dark. Not having yet mastered swimming, he was not sure what he was going to do about getting out. A few minutes later, he caught sight of a tree in the middle of the river.

It was an eb-tree. There was no mistaking the way it floated in mid-stream like that, supported by a wide base of roots and rotting vegetation. Slumped on this base under the leafy shade was a man, a fishing rod jammed into the roots beside him. He was obviously asleep, and was not going to see Groach, who was floating right towards him.

'Hey!' Groach shouted. 'Hey you! Help me here, will you?'

The man awoke with a start and stared at the swimmer in surprise. He was standing up to get a better look when his fishing line started to jerk. Torn between reeling in the fish and helping the unknown man out of the water, the fisherman froze for a moment with indecision. His instincts took over and he seized the rod. Groach took the knotted roots of the tree full in the chest and hung there, stunned. The fisherman wound in the flapping carp with a practised motion and swiped its head against the trunk, before dropping it into a waiting basket. He reached down and grabbed Groach, who was beginning to slide under the base, and hauled him, and his satchel, out of the water in much the same way he had done the fish.

'Well you're a drownded rat and no mistake,' he grunted, as if he pulled people from the river on a regular basis. 'Uncommon for someone to be swimmin' with all their clothes on like that, but then I suppose it's another one of these new trends.'

'Thank you, sir. I'm very grateful,' Groach panted.

The fisherman was tall and wiry; his long, thin arms were brown, as was his face, with sleepy dark eyes surrounded by wrinkles. Pigtails hung down either side of his face, and he had a long nose and a narrow mouth that was short of teeth. He was in a blue shirt and ruddy trousers that were cut short at the knees. He had long legs and, judging by his boots, his feet were enormous.

'Brock Moffet's my name,' he said.

'Shessil Groach. Delighted to meet you.'

'Yes, well. Never seen you before. You must be from somewhere's else.'

'Yes, though to be honest, I'm not sure where I am now.'

'Crickenob, or just west of it anyhow,' Moffet replied. 'You were in the river Blales, heading towards Rutledge-on-Coast.'

'Ah, yes. Thank you,' Groach lay on the hard roots and enjoyed the soothing motion of the tree on the water. He would have been happy to stay there for some time.

'Would I be right in thinking you'll need a place to stay for the night?' Moffet enquired.

'I could quite happily sleep here all night. It shouldn't get that cold, I think.'

'Nonsense, man. The wife and I would be glad to have you as our guest,' exclaimed Moffet. 'I wouldn't have it said a person came through Crickenob and was not given a warm bed for the night. We're not a rich village but we know how to treat a tourist.'

'That's very kind of you. Thank you very much.' Groach shook his hand.

Brock Moffet had a boat moored on the other side of the tree. It was a small wooden dinghy, with just room enough for the two men and all of the fisherman's gear. Groach stepped in unsteadily and almost lost his balance, but Moffet caught his arm and sat him down. Then he climbed in and sat with his back against Groach's. He untied the line and cast off. With strong, smooth strokes, he propelled the dinghy towards the shore, and had soon pulled alongside the bank. He helped Groach out again and retrieved his fishing equipment.

The house was a short walk down the road, a white-washed cottage with a turf roof. There were flower pots arranged all around the house, from the gate all the way to the front door. But there was no garden, no grass, just brightly coloured flowers in earthenware pots sitting on a surface of gravel.

'The wife loves flowers, but she's scared of worms, see,' Moffet explained. 'I tell her they're harmless and all that, but it does no good. Still, she keeps the place lookin' nice, so I can't complain really.'

He unlatched the front door, and they were hit by the rich smell of tomato soup. Groach realised he not eaten all day. His mouth watered at the delicious aroma. A raucous shout greeted them:

'Moffet! What kind of cold sodden creature have you brought home this evening?' A squat, well-built woman stood on the far side of the warm kitchen. She looked Groach up and down and turned a questioning eye on her husband.

'He was in the river, wife, and he needs a place to stay for the night.'

'Well, put some hot tea in the man before he falls over. The soup will be a while yet.' With that she turned back to the selection of pots on the stove. The smells made Groach's stomach rumble.

'Do you smoke a pipe, Shessil?' Moffet asked, lifting a hot kettle from the big iron stove.

'No, I can't say that I do. Tobacco was forbidden where I come from. I've never tried it.'

'There's nothing to warm a man up like a good pipe. Have a seat there,' Moffet pronounced, waving to a battered arm-chair and eagerly stoking the two ends of his forked bone pipe. He lit it with a match and drew in a drag with relish.

'Aye, there's nothin' to make a man lazy like a good pipe

either, ya trog,' Mrs Moffet scoffed. 'You were making tea.'

'I'm getting to it, wife. A kettle should sit for a bit before making a brew,' her husband retorted.

'You mean a man must sit for a bit before making a brew,' she snapped back. 'Get this man some dry clothes and some hot water and soap to wash with ... and a towel. And take your boots off my clean floor.'

Moffet carried a tin bathtub into a cluttered back room and filled it with water from a large pot on the stove. Then he went to dig out some fresh clothes while Groach had a soak. As he sat there, Groach pulled his long hair under his nose and smelled sewer on it. Two washes later, he could still smell it. The stink was in his beard too. Moffet had left him a straight razor and a mirror, and there was a scissors on the shelf above him. After a long, thoughtful gaze into the mirror, he started cutting. He managed to make a half decent job of his hair by simply hacking it all off and cropping it close to his skull. Somehow it even made his thinning hair-line and growing bald patch a little less noticeable. His hair was darker near the roots, and he quite liked the look of it. He had not shaved in years, so that was a little bit trickier and he nicked the skin with the razor a few times before he had finished, but in the end, a younger, very different and definitely less smelly Shessil Groach looked back out of the mirror at him. He cleared up the mass of sandy-coloured hair, intent on throwing it away, but Moffet declared with delight that it would make wonderful flies for bait. And lots of them too, by the looks of things.

After Groach had dressed in a shirt and trousers that were too long but comfortable nonetheless, he thanked his hosts and flopped into his seat again. Neither of them mentioned the fact that he looked utterly unlike the man who had walked into their house, thinking this might be rude where he came from. Mrs Moffet was brewing a fresh pot of tea. She was a good deal shorter than her husband, with a long, wrinkled face topped by red cheeks and a flat nose. She wore her brown hair back in a massive bun. The little woman was wearing an old but carefully cleaned green and blue striped dress.

'Tea'll be a few minutes,' she said to her visitor. 'The lump here did not introduce you. What's your name and where are you from?'

'Shessil Groach. I'm from the Harvest Tide Project.'

'Are you really? Can't say I'm familiar with it. Is that near Ashglaft?'

'I'm not sure where it's near, to be honest. It's in a city, Noran, I think. We're staying at a big house at the moment, in another town, closer to here.' Groach shifted uncomfortably in his seat. He had an extensive knowledge of geography, but had little experience of it personally. In the project, the city had always been 'The City'. It was all they had needed to call it, as they were not allowed out to visit it anyway. He knew even less about the town the project staff were now staying in. 'I don't think it's Ashglaft, but then I'm not sure.'

'Odd, that,' she sniffed. 'Not knowing where you come from. Still, maybe that's normal in strange parts. Tea's ready. How do you take it?'

'Do you have any honey?' Groach asked timidly. He had a bit of a sweet tooth.

'Hah! Yes! I like a drop in my tea myself.' She reached up and pulled down a jar. Unplugging it, she put a couple of spoonfuls in Groach's mug with some milk and handed it to him. He nodded gratefully.

She then gave her husband his without adding anything and grasped her own cup. She started pouring the honey into the tea.

'He says I take too much of the stuff, that I should drink it black like him, that it's bad for my teeth,' she grunted, gesturing with her head in her husband's direction. 'And here's me with all my teeth still in my head and him quickly losin' the last of his.'

She finished pouring the honey and stirred the thick tea, slowly adding milk that took some time to sink in. Groach hugged his own mug, savouring its warmth. He had been colder than he realised and the comfort of the house was made all the more welcoming by his memories of the deep water. The episode in the sewers was already fading to the back of his mind.

'So, Shessil, tell us about yourself,' Moffet urged. 'It's not every day we get such a mysterious type floating down the river to us. Have you travelled far?'

He offered the pipe and Shessil, thinking it might be rude to refuse, took it.

'Not all that far, I suppose,' he mused. 'But a long way for a person like me. I have lived in the same place since I was a boy and have not left it, except for a few trips to the coast, which were made in a curtained wagon so we could not see out during the journey. So, even though I may not be all that far from home, this is something of a strange land to me.'

He paused to take a pull on the pipe as he had seen Moffet do, only to feel the back of his throat burning down to his lungs. He gagged and started coughing uncontrollably. Mrs

Moffet threw her hands up in disgust and the fisherman seized the pipe from his hands and slapped him hard on the back, which made him cough harder.

'It would be easier for the man to breathe if you would stop *hitting* him, Moffet,' the woman said. 'Drink some tea, Shessil. That will help a bit. My husband sometimes forgets that not everyone's lungs are immune to poisonous fumes.'

Shessil's coughing died down enough to allow him to drink a bit and wash the acrid taste from his throat, but his eyes continued to water. He swilled some tea around his mouth and sank deeper into his chair. Moffet sat back down in his own chair and dragged smoke from the pipe once more.

The meal started with the tomato soup Groach had smelled on first entering the house. It was as good as the aroma had promised, but was outdone by the main course of fresh trout. He could not remember a meal that had tasted so good, but then he had never had a day as exhausting as this one. His full stomach made him groggy and he sat back in his armchair with a sigh. Mrs Moffet, who was one of those cooks who ate very little and insisted everyone else had mountainous second helpings, nodded in satisfaction at a job well done. Moffet himself re-lit his pipe (Mrs Moffet would not have it at the table) and settled down opposite Shessil, in a posture that said he would be staying there for the evening.

Mrs Moffet washed up, rejecting Groach's offers of help, and then perched on a tall stool with another syrupy cup of tea. At Moffet's urging, Groach told the story of how he had ended up in the river, though he was wary that the couple might accuse him of lying about the boy who had become a beast. But as they listened with a keen interest to his description of the events in the sewer, they just nodded at each other and muttered that this kind of thing was known to happen in foreign parts. Moffet then told his wife how his day had been, during which time Shessil, already drowsy, dozed off.

Moffet tapped the remains of his double-barrelled pipe out on the hearth and stood up. With little effort, he lifted Groach out of the seat and carried him into the back room, where his wife was preparing a bed. He laid the sleeping man on the sheet and covered him with some blankets. Then the pair retreated from the room and closed the door.

+ + +

Taya was the same grey-green as the bush she was hiding in. Her skin was even mottled to match the shadows of the leaves around her. She crouched, watching the stone cottage, and thought about how much trouble she and her brother were in. Uncle Emos was after them, their folks would probably hit the roof when they found out, and now there were *more* strangers involved. She was going to give Lorkrin a good bashing when all this was over. And where was he? He should have been here by now. They had followed the current of the stream in the sewer and found the opening to the river. But not knowing which side the man was going to get out on, they had split up and each taken a bank to search. She had found their quarry's trail leading from the river, and followed it to this house. They were to meet on this side, and Lorkrin was to track her if he did not see her. She had expected him before sunset and he was still nowhere in sight. There was a soft whistle nearby, and she gave the bush a gentle shake.

Her brother crept in beside her and studied the stone cottage.

'What kept you?' she whispered.

'There's some soldiers camped down the road. I was having a look around.'

'We're not interested in soldiers, Lorkrin.'

'Aw, I could have got a great chase off them, Taya. Besides, I think they're searching for somebody. It could be our sewer rat. We need to get that quill off him before they catch him.'

Taya sighed and turned her gaze back towards the house.

'I think they've settled down for the night. He won't be coming out of there before dawn,' she murmured. 'This is all going so wrong. Uncle Emos is going to find out what we did and Ma and Pa will keep us in peeling potatoes and turnips for the whole summer.'

'If we're lucky,' Lorkrin snorted. 'All over a pen.'

'Do you think this is why transmorphing's banned?' Taya wondered aloud.

'Probably. If we can collapse a sewer by accident, think about what somebody like Uncle Emos could do on purpose.'

That thought silenced them both. After a while, they pulled blankets from their bags and covered themselves up; the night was becoming colder. They would have to take turns to stay awake if they were to catch the man when he came out of the house, but neither of them wanted to offer to take first watch. In the end, they both fell asleep.

# 3 THE SOLDIERS AND THE SCENT-SELLER

It was dark in the laboratory, and Groundsmaster Hovem was glad that he had made this discovery after all the others had finished for the night. The glass tank before him was the width of a man's outstretched arms on all four sides, but reached up to the ceiling, hidden in the shadows high above him. It was one of thirty in the building. The tanks were the centre of the project; its success would be decided in one of these glass columns. No, Hovem thought, its success had been decided. What he saw before him in the glass vessel was the end of the project. And it would be the end of more than that. He had known it would happen eventually. The people here may have been ignorant of the ways of the world, but where the ways of plants were concerned, they were geniuses.

'This is the tank that Shessil was working on?' he asked, already knowing the answer.

'Yes, Mr Hovem,' the young lab assistant replied. 'Isn't it fantastic?'

'Yes, lad it is. It is fantastic.' Hovem gazed into the misty contents of the vessel.

With Shessil gone, this tank contained the only key to the completion of the project. He had delayed making a decision about this for some time. A message should have been sent to Rak Ek Namen immediately. He drew in a deep breath and grimaced.

'Lad?'

'Yes, Mr Hovem?'

'I think you'd best fetch me an axe.'

When the axe had been brought, Hovem muttered a brief, but sincere prayer to Everness, the god of greenery, and hefted the heavy handle over his shoulder. Waving the young man away, he swung the axe back and slammed it into the side of the tank. The glass exploded outwards and sluiced down in razor-sharp sheets and splinters. Hovem dived for cover, almost making it clear. A long triangular shard plunged into his back and pinned him to the floor. By the time the distraught lab assistant had gathered his wits enough to rush forward and help, the Groundsmaster was dead. Lanterns were being lit all over the building and the guards were on the scene, standing over the debris, unsure of what to do. They stayed there and kept everyone else back. They had no thoughts on what had happened; they would simply stop anything else unusual happening until somebody in authority arrived.

+ + +

The land known as Sestina, one of the union of countries ruled by the city-state of Noran, was the home of the mollusc called the ornacrid. This large creature, a close relation to the snail, could weigh as much as a small pony. It had a shell not unlike an armadillo's armour, but thicker and invulnerable, with joints to allow its huge, soft body to move about. The head that protruded from the front of its shell was frog-like but with eight light-sensitive stalks instead of eyes. Ornacrids were harmless and docile; they fed on grass and leaves, and their slow movement meant they were feared by no one.

It was unfortunate, then, that an empty ornacrid carapace was the perfect shape for the bulky form of a Noranian soldier. These shells were the favoured armour of the professional warrior, which meant that the ornacrid was farmed in great quantities in order to remove them from their shells – a process that was fatal to the mollusc.

The creature that had given its life to provide the foot soldier named Grulk with her body armour had been a particularly handsome specimen. The shell was a deep green with grey streaks that glistened in the morning sun. Grulk, however, did not gleam in the morning sun. Grulk was not a morning person. And she was enjoying being a soldier less and less. There were the constant early mornings for a start. The fact that they had to walk wherever they went. And the fact that they went *everywhere* – whenever they were told to. And it looked as if she would never be promoted, so she would never be able to tell anybody else when and where to walk. The fighting was getting her down as well. It was pretty certain that one day she was going to go into battle and not come out again. Old Noranian soldiers did not retire or fade away; they got killed. Thoughts like these kept Left-Speartrooper Grulk in a bad mood for most of the time that she spent awake. Lately, even her comrades tried to avoid her; they felt she took the job too personally.

Today was another house-to-house search. Grulk followed

Forward-Batterer Wulms with their battlegroup away from the campsite and on into Crickenob. One more dump full of farmers and fishermen. She was so sick of these places. Every house had clean, white-limed walls and turf roofs; the roads were cobbled and children ran around, shouting and screaming like little animals and playing games as if that was all that mattered in the world. Not one of them would have lasted a day in an army training camp.

One child, not four years old, trotted towards them. She was chasing a ponyip. The colourful bird tweeted and scampered from side to side. Unable to fly with its feathers clipped, it played the little girl's game, leading her a merry chase down the street. It had a red ribbon tied round its neck, and was obviously a favourite pet. The girl giggled and snorted at the little drop of snot that hung from her nose as a result of all the excitement. She stopped giggling when a big hand swooped down and seized the ponyip by the neck. Grulk held the bird up for closer inspection, and then deposited it in her leather satchel. Lunch.

The girl stood frozen at the unfairness of this and put a fingertip in her mouth as she decided whether or not she should ask for her pet back. The huge creature with the hard, shiny clothes and the long knives on her belt stared down at her as if she might well be the next into the bag. The little girl turned and scurried back up the road, wailing. Grulk rolled her eyes back and shrugged at the soldiers beside her who were shaking their heads in disdain. There were some depths to which even a Noranian soldier did not sink. Grulk did not care. They would not object to a wing or drumstick come lunchtime.

+ + +

A stray mongrel watched the soldier confiscate the ponyip, grimacing in an expression of disgust that had no place on a dog's face. It was a slightly outlandish-looking dog, with a spiky mane, protruding teeth, and big claws, because Lorkrin liked turning himself into weird things. He had awoken before dawn and, after a short row with Taya over who should have taken first watch, decided to do some scouting around. Strange children were the kind of thing people noticed in a village, but stray dogs could wander relatively unnoticed. He pitied the little girl's folks, helpless to stop their daughter from being bullied by soldiers. The young Myunan knew his ma and pa would never have stood for that kind of thing, but humans were such a brittle lot.

Lorkrin was sure that Taya blamed him for this mess they were in. She always did that. She'd go along with his ideas until they got into trouble, and then she would say it was his fault. Well, it was she who had grabbed the page from him; it was she who tore it. And he'd tell, if it was the only way to save his own neck. Not that it would work. They were in so deep now. It didn't matter who had started it.

People were peering out windows at the soldiers now, some coming to their doors, or even out onto the street. They were all careful to stay out of the path of the battle-group, but they got in Lorkrin's way as he tried to follow the soldiers. He pushed impatiently through the forest of legs, struggling to see what was going on.

The Forward-Batterer directed his troops to start the search with the houses at the edge of the village and work their way in. Doors that were not open by the time the soldiers reached them were kicked in.

They obviously had a description of the man they were

looking for. Anyone fitting that description was dragged out into the village square and made to kneel under armed guard. The villagers did not put up a great struggle. There were shouts and plaintive crying, even women trying to hold onto their men as they were dragged out into the street. But no weapons were raised against the soldiers; no one struck out or stood up to them. Lorkrin looked on with morbid fascination. Myunans were nomads, and had little contact with the army. But for the villagers of Crickenob, raids were like storms or floods, freak events that they bore with dignity if they could, each villager keeping up a dignified front and hoping they would not fall victim. Raids were just another part of life. There was nothing the villagers could do about them. So the people assembled in the square to find out what would happen next. Frightened and worried, they were nonetheless fascinated to know what had taken place beyond their small world to bring the soldiers here.

+ + +

Shessil Groach and his hosts were enjoying a breakfast of milk, plums and butter on a tomato-flavoured bread, when they heard the shouting and screaming. Moffet, who had just opened the shutters to let in the morning sun, grunted to himself and stuck his pipe in his mouth.

'Soldiers're coming,' he rasped to his wife. She tutted and started taking the more fragile pieces of crockery from the shelves and putting them in cupboards. She moved the furniture well clear of the door and unlatched it, leaving it closed over. She would not have her door knocked off its hinges, but she was not going to open the door of her home in welcome to any Noranians either. There were principles to be observed after all.

She put a pot of tea on the table and the couple sat back down with their guest to finish their breakfast. Groach was pouring the tea when the door was kicked in. It bounced against the wall before swinging back on its hinges, nearly hitting the burly soldier who had kicked it. The trooper stopped it with his hand and stepped into the kitchen, followed by two others. Groach, his eyes wide at this violent intrusion, froze, the teapot poised in mid-air. Moffet blew a smoke ring.

'What is it this time?' he asked. 'Kartharic spies, I suppose, or bush demons maybe. I liked the last one. What was it?'

'Witches,' his wife supplied.

'Ah yes, witches. I remember you cornered quite a few of them that time. Damned clever test you had. If they didn't burn when you put them on a bonfire, they were witches. Damned clever. 'Course, they all burned as I remember.'

'There is a fugitive loose in the area,' the soldier growled. 'There's a reward for his capture. You two I have seen before. Who is he?'

His finger pointed like a weapon at Groach, who was still holding the teapot up in the air. The teapot started trembling. Could he be the fugitive they were searching for? Surely not. Why would they send so many soldiers just to find him? Suddenly he was afraid. He tried to think of something to say, but all he could do was squeak quietly. Moffet's eyes flicked towards Groach momentarily, but the rest of him stayed slouched in the chair.

'He's my cousin from Rimstock, come to bring news of my aunt,' he said around the stem of his pipe. 'Pay no mind to him. He's a bit simple, if you know what I mean.'

The soldier smirked, and took one more look at the man holding up the teapot. The little wretch did not match the description anyway, but it was good to check out new faces. He waved to the other two men and they left the house. Moffet followed them out to watch them leave his property. Groach peeked round the door at them, clutching the teapot like a good-luck charm. The soldiers were gathered in a group at the gate, talking. They were waiting for the rest of their group to finish the houses along the road.

The clink and jingle of bottles drew everyone's attention towards the corner of the cobbled road, the space beyond hidden by a copse of trees. The clinking grew steadily louder until a figure appeared, pushing a cart the size of a wheelbarrow. It had shelves running up both sides to a point at the top; the shelves had holes in neat rows, and in each hole there was a vial or bottle. The tall barrow hid most of the figure behind it, but a head topped with a thick mop of curly red hair could be clearly seen over its peak.

The troops went quiet. There was a space between the shelves down the middle of the cart for the person pushing to be able to see ahead of them, and one or two of the soldiers hunched to try to see through this gap and get a glimpse at the figure.

The cart rolled right up to them and halted. The soldiers scattered around it and assumed aggressive stances, weapons drawn, battle cries rising in their throats. But it was a small, albeit slightly plump, young woman who unhitched the barrow from the belt around her waist and arched her back with a great stretch. She ignored the heavily armed ogres around her, and flicked her thick red hair over her shoulders. Pale blue eyes stared out of a round, brown, freckly face at the soldier who stood in her way. She wore an ankle-length, green cotton dress, belted at the waist, a dark green cloak and soft leather boots. She also had a long suede waistcoat on, lined with dozens of little pockets. The girl cocked her head to one side and addressed the soldier:

'Good morning. Can I help you at all?'

'What's your name?' the soldier demanded (and Groach realised for the first time that the soldier, too, was a woman).

'You can call me Hilspeth. Would you mind moving aside?'

'I can *call* you anything I *like*,' the armour-clad woman retorted. 'We're here on an official manhunt. State your full name and your business here in Crickenob.'

'Hilspeth Naratemus; and my business is the same here as anywhere else,' she gestured towards her cart. 'Would you care for a sample? I have several preparations that can help ease an unpleasant temperament.'

'Don't give me any of your snotty talk ...'

'Yes, I imagine you have more than enough snot of your own. I have a tonic here that can cure that, too.'

'You are getting right up my nose, little girl,' the soldier hissed.

'Not yet, I'm not.' The girl's voice carried a note of warning that rattled the warrior even further.

'What are all these bottles? Are you a medicine woman?' the soldier asked, voice tinged with superstition.

'No, a scentonomist. I mix aromas for people's pleasure and wellbeing.'

'You sell smells?'

'Yes, that's a crude, but accurate, way of putting it. I could prepare one for you if you like.'

'Why would I want to pay for a smell?'

'To hide the ones you seem to have collected for free.'

There was a moment of grim silence as this sunk in. Then a fist the size and weight of a turnip hit Hilspeth across the side of the head. She crumpled to the ground. The soldier raised her spear over her head, intent on impaling the girl, but she did not notice the small man who had run from the house behind her. Without warning, an arm swung over her shoulder, smashing a teapot against the side of her face. Hot tea sprayed in her eyes and she shrieked. Her elbow caught Groach under the chin, lifting him off his feet and sending him sprawling across the road. Two soldiers rushed him and, several kicks later, he was unconscious.

+ + +

Taya could not see what was going on. She was squatting inside a henhouse, watching the cottage where the man named Shessil was staying, but there were a couple of soldiers right outside, so she couldn't stick her head up without being spotted. There had just been some kind of struggle and she was desperate to find out what had happened. She took out her tools, including a small mirror, and slunched the muscles that acted as a skull in Myunans, letting them relax so the flesh of her head became soft and pliable. She hurriedly sculpted some crude feathers over her scalp and worked a rough chicken's head up out of her forehead, which she then crefted, tensing it so that it kept its shape. With a moment of concentration, she changed the colours of the disguise to match the plumage of the hens around her.

The soldiers standing next to the henhouse paid no attention when a scruffy hen appeared at the raised door. Taya peered out and her heart sank as she saw two armoured figures lifting Shessil's inert form into the back of a gaol wagon. Some red-headed girl, who was barely conscious herself, was hauled to her feet and pushed in after him. The troops then rounded up the other men they had taken captive and they, too, were locked in the confinement of the wood and iron cage. Soon they were getting ready to leave.

Lorkrin appeared around the wall of the henhouse, trying to look nonchalant in that stupid mad dog disguise. Ducking behind the fence, he slunched back into his normal shape, then crept in beside her. He regarded her chicken-shaped head with a straight face.

'I preferred your hair the way it was,' he breathed. 'What's going on out there? I couldn't get a good look.'

'That Shessil fellow has just been chucked into a gaol wagon. They're taking him away.'

'Aw, bowels,' whispered Lorkrin.

'Shh!' Taya was trying to listen to the talk of the soldiers. A few moments later, she put her hands to her face and slumped back against a shelf of nests. 'They're taking them to Hortenz. Wonder why he cut off his beard and hair like that ...'

Shape-shifters were not easily fooled by a change in appearance.

'Well isn't that just the icing on the cake,' her brother hissed. 'Arrested by soldiers ... we'll never get that bloody quill back now.' He paused. 'Here, you don't think they arrested him for wrecking the sewer, do you?'

'You mean, you think this is our fault too?' Taya's eyes widened beneath their camouflage of fake feathers.

'No. No chance.'

'We'll have to go after them.'

'Have you popped your cork? What do we do then? Let's go back to Uncle Emos and tell him what happened. He'll be annoyed all right ... well, he'll probably be out of his mind ... but he's not about to actually *kill* us. Those are Noranian soldiers. Getting a chase off them is one thing, walking right up to one of their wagons under their very noses and messing with one of their prisoners is another thing altogether.'

'Are you saying you're scared?'

'No.'

'Sounds like you're scared to me.'

'I'm not scared. But I'm not stupid either.'

Taya regarded the departing troops thoughtfully. She wondered when she and her brother would ever be able to go home. They certainly couldn't go back without returning their uncle's quill, but their tribe would be moving into the forest in the autumn, and all the girls would change their body colours for the new season. She couldn't bear to miss that. Turning to her brother, she sat down and let her head slunch out of its chicken shape.

'Ma made me promise not to tell you this, but I think you need to know now.'

'Know what?' Lorkrin's eyes narrowed.

'You remember those two lads who were causing all that grief around the area last year, the ones who dumped the dead cow in Uncle Emos's well?'

'Yeah.'

'Well, what you don't know is that when he pulled that cow out of the well, he went and found them. And he shoved both of them into it.'

'He threw them in the well?' Lorkrin grinned.

'No, he shoved them into the *cow*,' Taya hissed. 'He buried them up to their necks in its belly and used the transmorphing to seal that rotting meat up around them. They were stuck like that until the constable came and dug them out. And that cow had been dead for *days*. That's what happened last time Uncle Emos got really angry with someone.'

Lorkrin's face turned green. They locked eyes for a minute, weighing the risks as the chickens clucked quietly around them. The limitless array of possible punishments open to their uncle played through their minds.

'Let's get out of here,' Lorkrin muttered. 'I need to pee.'

+ + +

Mungret stood before the Prime Ministrate, in the plush wood-panelled study, waiting for his master's reaction to the news. It was an expansive, square room, with a large fireplace. To the right side of the fire was the desk of the mayor of Hortenz, which was, for the time being, the Prime Ministrate's desk. The fire was always lit; with the result that anyone standing in front of the desk was always a little too warm.

'Can anything be saved from the remains of the tank?' Namen enquired.

'There are four botanists examining it now, Prime Ministrate, but they are not optimistic,' his secretary replied. 'They believe that any samples will have been ruined.'

'But we can be sure that Hovem took the action that he did, because he had realised the true nature of the project, and believed the tank contained a successful conclusion. A well-meaning man, but misguided. We shall have to pick a new Groundsmaster. And make sure he fully understands just how important this project is.'

'Yes, Prime Ministrate.'

'What about Shessil Groach's research materials?' the Noranian leader continued.

'We cannot find any of his recent notes. It is suspected that he took them with him, Prime Ministrate.' Mungret was ready with his answers. It was important to pay attention to details if one was to keep working for Rak Ek Namen. Namen paid close attention to details.

'He does not know anyone,' his leader observed aloud. 'Apart from these little trips to the coast, he has not been out of the compound in Noran alone for fifteen years. There cannot be many places for him to hide. And he has lived hidden away from the outside world for so long that he will find it hard to fit in.

'Put more troops on search duty. This man must be found. And raise the reward. He is out there. Someone must know where he is.'

# 4 'THEY CHANGE INTO MONSTERS'

Something stabbed its way up Shessil Groach's nostrils and burned his sinuses until he woke up. A soft hand was patting his face, but it was out of rhythm with the throbbing in the side of his head and around his jaw, so he clasped the hand and pushed it away. As his vision cleared, it filled with the round, expectant face of a young woman.

'What did you stick up my nose?' he mumbled.

'Just gave you a whiff of some smelling salts, to bring you back to your senses,' she reassured him.

'Wanna go back to sleep.'

'All right, but let me just check you over while you're awake. You might have hurt your head.'

''kay.'

She splayed the fingers of both hands and placed them on his head. Then she prodded his scalp in various places.

'Aaagh!'

'Where did it hurt?' she asked, frowning.

'Everywhere you poked. Leave me alone, madam. I'll be quite all right once you keep your fingers and chemicals to yourself!'

'I was only trying to help,' she sniffed.

'I have no doubt.' He clutched his throbbing head.

The woman moved away from him and sat back against the wooden wall separating them from the driver. Her face was a careful mask, hiding all emotion. From what little he knew of women, Groach knew this was a sure sign that she was ready to burst, either with rage or hurt feelings. Embarrassed and ashamed at his behaviour, he knelt up and leaned towards her;

'Madam, I must apologise. My head was sore and I was disoriented. I did not mean what I said. I would be grateful for any help you could give me.'

She ignored him for a moment, to be sure he understood how hurt she had been. Then she reached into her leather waistcoat and withdrew a small vial.

'For people with sore heads,' she said. 'And thin skins.'

He blushed and took the vial.

'Take two drops under the tongue, three times a day. No more,' she added. 'It will ease the pain. Whether or not it will fix your head is a different matter.'

'Thank you.' He nodded. As he looked around the cage that made up the back of the wagon, he could not help noticing that the other occupants had a number of features in common. They were all men about his age, with long beards. Each had thinning, sandy-coloured hair or was completely bald, and they were all frightened. A realisation dawned on Groach. He had looked the very same up until the previous night.

'My name is Hilspeth,' said the woman. 'And it is I who should be doing the thanking. You saved my life. That soldier would have killed me. I'm sure of it.'

'Yes ...' Groach was barely listening. He was thinking back to the gardens, back to his safe life, working as a botanist on the project – before two little monsters had destroyed the ground beneath his feet and thrown him out into the wider world. He was obviously being sought by the Noranians. They were arresting anyone who even resembled him. It was hard to believe his work on eshweed could be so important to them. Most people just did not take plants that seriously. He had every intention of returning to work; but now that he had seen the world outside the project, he was reluctant to go back immediately. Obviously his appearance had changed enough to fool the soldiers. But they still had him securely locked up. He decided to keep his secret for a while yet.

'And your name is ...?' Hilspeth prompted.

'Eh?'

'Your name? Most people have one. You're generally given one at birth.'

'Oh ...' he thought for a moment. 'Eh ... Panch, Panch Gessum.'

'Pleased to meet you, Panch Gessum.' She held out her hand.

'Delighted, Miss ...' He had forgotten her name already.

'Hilspeth, Hilspeth Naratemus,' she chirped.

'Delighted, Hilspeth.' He took her hand and shook it, but his attention was still on the other prisoners. He wondered if they suspected. Probably not – why would they? They had no idea why they were here. They did not know they were here because of him. Perhaps he should give up and admit to the soldiers who he was, save these men the trouble and go back to the project. He did feel some guilt for their plight, but he found it hard to care much about people, who for the most part were merely a distraction from his work. He peered between the reinforced wooden bars of the cage.

In a cloud of steam and smoke, with chugging engines and tramping boots, the convoy was making its way along the course of a dried-up river. Above them on both sides, grass hung from the edges of the banks, giving way to clay and gravel where the water had cut a swathe through the landscape. A fisherman's hut broke the skyline here and there along the ridges, bringing to mind the hospitality of the Moffets and the pleasure of the evening before. Above the front wall of the cage, the arm of a catchwagon could be seen, holding aloft a manhunter who used the position to act as lookout for the convoy. Groach gazed past the elevated soldier to the sky beyond. The sun was high and was burning away the clouds that clogged the blue expanse above. In the distance, the sharp peaks of a mountain range were just visible above the riverbank.

He remembered his friend Haller's comment, a few weeks before his death, that they were captives in the project, the walls around the gardens like a prison. Groach had laughed at the idea. Prisoners did not get to spend their days in some of the finest gardens in the world, or work on such important research. They were just being kept safe. That was all. But Haller had been unhappy in his last days, frustrated with the project and its masters. Now, Groach could see why. There was a lot to be experienced in this outside world.

'Where do you think we're going?' he asked Hilspeth.

'I heard them say they were taking us to Hortenz,' she answered.

'Is it far?'

'A bit more than a day's travel, if that's where we're going.'

Groach thought about this for a minute. Then, speaking quietly, asked, 'Is it a big town? Beside a river that runs through the hills?'

'That sounds like Hortenz. A walled town. With a fortified barracks on the square.'

'That's the one – do you know it well?'

'Well enough; I do some business there. Is that where you're from?'

'Let's just say it is a place I don't want to return to just yet.'

'All right.' Hilspeth lowered her voice. 'Is that why you're whispering?' She had a sharp, amused glint in her eye that held his gaze.

'Yes. I would appreciate you not mentioning it to anyone.'

'Done. It's the least I can do.' She patted his shoulder. 'But I would watch out for that soldier you hit with the teapot. She has been walking behind the wagon for the last few minutes ... and she hasn't taken her eyes off us. I don't think she's even blinked.'

As the convoy travelled along the dusty road, a sharp eye would have spotted a pair of young deer that appeared from time to time, keeping pace with the group by travelling cross-country, but none of the guards were on the lookout for deer. Later in the afternoon, they pulled into a village and stopped for a while to rest the infantry who were marching alongside. Left-Speartrooper Grulk came up closer and squinted between the bars of the gaol-wagon. She hissed at Groach: 'This will be short trip for you, little man. It'll all be over for you as soon as it gets dark. Bad things happen in the dark. Accidents. People can fall over and get their heads chopped off. You'll die slow and messy, I promise you that.

Slow and messy. Might cook ya and eat ya if I'm hungry enough.'

'Grulk! Stand down!' Forward-Batterer Wulms shouted. He put up with Grulk because she was stubborn and cruel, good qualities in a Noranian foot soldier, but she tended to take things personally and forget that you were not supposed to act without orders. Wulms never did anything without orders.

'These prisoners are to be taken to the capital. You will not harm them without the proper authority. Is that understood, Left-Speartrooper?'

'He's only here because he attacked me. Why not just deal with him now?' Grulk argued. 'Do we have laws or not? It's only just that he be put to death. I know my rights.'

'He shall be put to death only after a trial. That is the law, Left-Speartrooper Grulk. Now stand down. I will not say it again.'

Grulk aimed one last venomous stare at Groach. She had broken the rules enough times before to know she would be punished for killing a prisoner. And she knew it would be worth every moment of it.

Their destination was the stronghold of Hortenz. It lay on the far side of some treacherous hills and they would not reach it that night, so the Whipholder commanding the convoy decided to camp in a field in the lee of a small forest. The wagons were circled into a protective formation and the first watch posted outside as the cooks set the barbecues inside for the evening meal. The prisoners in each gaol wagon were given a bucket of water and a loaf of bread among them. Fights broke out in some cages over the paltry bit of food.

In their temporary prison, Hilspeth and Groach sat silently. Hilspeth had commandeered the bread when it had been handed in, and the rest of the prisoners, all men who knew when not to argue with a woman, waited for their portion in civilised silence. From one of the array of pockets in her jacket, she produced a sachet of powder.

'This is a spice. It has a flavour that will take away your hunger. I will add it to the portion of anyone who wants it. This bread will not be enough and we all know it. I can put herbs in the water to help keep up our strength.'

The fighting in the next wagon nearly drowned out her voice. She looked in the eyes of each man. They all nodded in turn. She was known in their villages as a sage of sorts. Though most of her customers were women from wealthy families, her reputation was that of an honest, if slightly dubious, medicine woman. Her remedies were unlikely to harm them and might even do some good. The men kept this opinion to themselves. She had a large number of other potions that might not be good for their health.

Groach took his piece of bread and scoffed it down. It tasted hot and he knew he had eaten it too fast. He had a burning sensation in his mouth, but Hilspeth was as good as her word. He was no longer hungry. Now he needed some water to cool his mouth. He crouched by the bucket and scooped water into his mouth with his hand. As he did so, he caught sight of Hilspeth slipping something up her sleeve. She was peering out into the gloom that filled the view beyond the circle of vehicles. Groach followed her line of sight and saw only the sentries, standing like short, stout trees out on the perimeter. He was turning back when he heard a sound that did not fit with the scrapping of the nearby prisoners or the slurping and tearing of the soldiers tucking into their food.

It was a soft sound, one that did not want to be heard. At first, he could not place where it was coming from. He strained to track it in the surrounding racket. Then he lifted his head to search the darkness above the heavy wooden grid that formed the roof of the cage. Fingernails on wood. Someone was climbing up the side of the driver's cab onto its roof, still out of sight of the back of the vehicle. Someone who did not wish to be seen.

He looked down to see Hilspeth's upturned face following the same scratching, clutching hint of movement. They came to the realisation at the same moment. The soldier woman, the one who had sworn he would not survive the night. She was coming to make good her threat.

The silhouette of a head popped into view.

'Hey ...' it began.

Some of the other prisoners in the wagon stood up. But faster than any of them, Hilspeth sprang to her feet, launched herself off the studded front wall of the cage and up towards the shadowy face. With a flick of her wrist, she caught the figure full in the face with a small bag of powder which burst on contact.

The figure on the roof began sneezing. By the tone of the sneezes, Groach knew this was no soldier. It was a child, probably a young girl. Something was wrong here. Hilspeth, too had realised her mistake. She had her hand to her mouth as she tried to catch sight of her victim. Up there somewhere, a child was having a merciless sneezing attack.

'Oh my gosh, I'm sorry,' Hilspeth whimpered in genuine concern. 'I'm sorry. I thought you were someone else.'

The camp was starting to turn its attention to the noise. Behind them, another child appeared at the door. He was probing at the padlock with his finger, which looked vaguely key-shaped. Groach knew this boy.

'Don't let him near me!' he shouted. 'That must be his sister up there. Keep them away – they're insane ... and they change into monsters!'

'Shut up, you idiot!' Lorkrin hissed, struggling with the bulky lock. 'We're rescuing you!'

For their rescue operation, he and his sister had taken steps to blend in the shadows. His skin was a dull grey-green colour and had a mottled pattern, both of which helped to break up his shape in the darkness.

'Keep them away!' Groach moaned.

'Oh, that poor little girl.' Hilspeth was still begging the forgiveness of Lorkrin's sister.

'They're coming to get me!' Groach cried.

'Well, yeah. We are ...' Lorkrin grimaced as he managed to turn his finger in the stiff lock. The padlock clicked open. He let out a grunt of satisfaction and then another, more painful one as he was lifted up by his hair from behind.

'A little pup, trying to break the dogs free,' said Wulms, raising the boy up to get a look at his face. Lorkrin thrashed and kicked, but was held fast. Other soldiers ran towards the wagon, some of them climbing onto the driver's cab to get hold of the girl. Seeing the boy held up like a hen for the slaughter, Groach knew that whatever else this young whelp was, he was just a boy. He would be severely punished for defying the soldiers and no child deserved that. From the front of the cage, he charged towards the back, hitting the unlocked door with one foot and slamming it into the shoulder of the Noranian. It struck with enough force to knock the big man over, causing him to let go of the boy.

Lorkrin was free, but surrounded on all sides by Noranians many times his size. He would not get far by trying to break out of the circle. He dived under the gaol wagon and scampered along its length, bursting out from under the front to go straight under the next one in the circle. Soldiers struggled to reach under and catch hold of him, but he was quick and their bulky armour prevented them from getting too far in.

Above him, Taya was still sneezing, tears pouring from her eyes. She knew she had to get away. It had all gone wrong. Wiping her eyes, she saw a shape climbing onto the top of the wagon. She turned the other way and ran across the wooden grid, over the heads of the prisoners. She was not going to make the jump to the next vehicle, but a helmet-clad head appeared over the edge at the last second and she stepped onto it and over the gap. She was unaware that beneath the circle of carriages, her brother was going in the opposite direction. This next roof was flat boards. Under these, something loud and savage shrieked up at her, infected by the excitement. Feral voices turned her blood cold. Whatever creatures were in this wagon, she hoped they stayed there. Hate and violence screamed from inside.

Her sneezing was easing off. The cool night air cleared her eyes, and she was getting her breath back. She ran across the roof and dropped onto the engine cowling of the next vehicle, this one a steam-powered catapult. The bonnet was steel, barrel-shaped with four small chimneys along the top. She felt heat under her feet; the fires were still smouldering in the furnace. Guards had caught up with her on the ground on both sides: She stepped onto the first chimney and out of reach of two who had followed her onto the roof. The girl hopped to the second one, head swivelling from side to side to find an escape route. But she was surrounded. There was only the roof of the driver's cab ahead of her. She skipped across the last two pipes and climbed up onto the arching roof. The soldiers had anticipated her and were climbing onto the roof ahead of her. Taya was cut off.

Lorkrin ducked under an axle, pushed past a flailing hand on one side and dodged a spear thrust at him from the other. He could see large booted feet on both sides, but the soldiers were having trouble seeing him. They were holding lanterns under the vehicles to try to light the blackness. With the soldiers getting in each others' way, he had managed to stay out of their grasp. But as long as he stayed under the wagons, he was going to keep going round in circles. He could not escape the guards for long.

In the gaol wagon, Groach was trying to get the other prisoners to join him in an escape. The turmoil caused by the two children had resulted in the door being left unlocked. Wulms had run off after the boy he had dropped and everyone seemed to have forgotten their captives. Surprisingly, Groach was having some difficulty in persuading anyone else to come along.

'... but we can escape! The door's open! Come on – what are you waiting for?'

'You go. I'm staying right here,' one man replied.

'Me too. I'm fine where I am,' said another.

'Safer in here than out there,' muttered a third.

'I don't understand,' Groach whined, perplexed. 'You've all been taken from your homes against your will. These people mean you nothing but harm. We can break out of here and make a run for it. Why won't you try?'

He did not want to admit that he was afraid to try it alone, but he found their attitude bewildering.

Lorkrin came to a space between two of the vehicles. There were sacks and a couple of metal barrels on the ground in front of him. The guards had lost sight of him for the moment. He crouched in the shadows, glad of the rest. He poked at the sacks by his side, grain or corn or something. The barrels were about half his height, but wider than the wooden ones he was used to. He wondered what was in them. Unscrewing a cap, he put his nose to it and took a sniff. Bule oil – the refined stuff used for fuelling engines. In a moment of mischievous glee, he tipped it over on its side. It gurgled out and under the sacks and around them to the carriage.

A guard saw it fall and rushed over, holding a lantern. He stuck it in through the gap and Lorkrin shouted and kicked out, knocking the lamp against the metal grill of the wagon, smashing the glass. The burning fuel spewed out and fell upon the oil-soaked grass. Lorkrin yelped. The flames were creeping under him. They reached out for the still gushing barrel. Lorkrin and the soldier bolted in different directions in time to escape the explosion. The boy was thrown to the ground by the force of it. He lifted his head and could hear a fast, popping sound in his ears. At first he thought he had damaged his hearing, but then he saw white fluffy tufts springing from the flames.

That's popcorn, he observed, dizzily.

The soldiers were rushing about, trying to put out the fire. He was lying outside the circle, a short run from the nearby trees. He got up and started running towards them.

Taya was trapped. There were guards on all sides. While her body froze, her mind raced. She had to think of something, fast. Nothing came to her, so she charged at the three soldiers on the roof, diving between the legs of the first, rolling away from the second and finding her feet in time to leap to the neighbouring wagon before the third could snatch at her. A quick sprint across that roof and she was launching herself over the next gap when it exploded.

A wave of heat lifted her up and caused her to miss the edge of the wagon's roof, but dropped her neatly into the arms of a soldier. Though grateful for the soft landing, she poked him in the eye and he let go. She slipped away into the darkness as chaos took hold of the camp.

'Hilspeth? What about you?' Groach did not know what was going on out there, but it seemed a perfect diversion for an escape.

'I won't, thanks. You don't understand, Panch. These men have all been taken from their homes, so the soldiers know just where to find them again if they escape, but it's not just that ...'

'That's enough games!' the Convoy Commander bellowed. 'Release the skacks and be done with it!'

Hilspeth leaned past Groach, closed the door to the cage and snapped the padlock shut. He gaped at her and tried the door as if he could not believe what she had done. She took his hand in hers:

'Believe me, Panch. It's for the best.'

Forward-Batterer Wulms gave the soldiers some time to apply skack-repellent ointment to the bare areas of their skin, before taking a short, stout oak staff in one hand and unlocking the door of their van. The pure hate Taya had sensed, only minutes before, hissed and growled from within. Creatures, the like of which should only appear in nightmares, struggled with each other to get out. Wulms beat them back with the stick, screaming hysterically at them in a beast-like tongue.

Skacks were predators about the size and weight of an adult man, but there the resemblance ended. Native to Guthoque, an area of Noran infamous for its dry, rocky, almost lifeless landscape, they had evolved to survive by being more savage than any other form of life. The area's only feature of interest was its range of volcanoes, which regularly wiped out most of the animal life in their vicinity. From this unforgiving environment was born the skack. They were as quick and agile as cats, more intelligent than dogs and hardier than mountain goats. Their skin was purple and grey to camouflage them against the volcanic rock. Instead of eyes, useless in the poisonous gases of Guthoque, they had deeply ridged foreheads that could sense vibrations in the air, enabling them to find and identify their prey in daylight, fog or absolute darkness with equal ease. Short, blunt snouts carried heavy jaws, poisonous fangs and nostrils that could track better than a bloodhound.

A skack's legs were short, and had the extended shins of an animal born to run at speed. It had big, ropey arms at the ends of each of which hung a single, serrated claw, nearly the length of its shin. This would be tucked up while running, but could be unfolded for digging, climbing, or tearing its victims limb from limb.

The Noranian nobles had captured and bred these creatures for hunting, only to find that even the best-trained skacks ate everything they caught, leaving little to hang on a wall as a trophy. The breeding of the animals had been handed onto the army.

Wulms loved his skacks. He loved their savagery; he loved the way the soldiers were scared of them (and therefore, of him) and he loved their simple language, having only about sixty words, most of which referred to prey, and how to catch and kill it. He batted them back, slamming his staff down on any head that poked though the doorway, and threw in a tuft of hair that he had pulled from the Myunan boy's head. There was a moment's silence as the skacks sniffed this. Then Wulms stepped out of their way. The vehicle bounced on its suspension as each creature leapt from it, bounded over the grass and disappeared off into the night towards the forest.

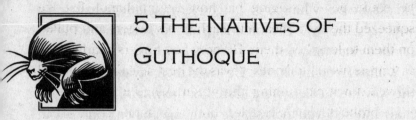

# 5 THE NATIVES OF GUTHOQUE

Lorkrin ran as he had never run before, weaving between tree trunks and springing over brambles and ferns. He knew that this time, he and Taya had got themselves into a predicament that might well be the end of them. For the first time in his life, Lorkrin wondered if he was going to die. He did not know where his sister was, and he was terrified that she might already have been caught. His legs pumped hard and his heart pumped harder. His breath was coming in gasps, and he could just hear sounds of pursuit over the beat of his pulse in his ears. There were high screeches coming from the things that were chasing him, things he knew were not soldiers. At least, not normal ones. He had heard of skacks, but had never seen one. They were the kind of thing that boys talked excitedly about – like any other monster. The thought of them did not excite him now.

He had some idea where he was going. He and Taya had come this way when they had sneaked up on the camp. The young shape-shifter began slunching to soften up his arms, kneading flesh down towards his hands. There was no time for proper amorphing, but he would need every advantage he could get. Massaging his now plump hands flat, he squeezed the extra meat into each of his fingers and pulled on them to lengthen them. He now had fingers nearly twice as long as his natural ones; it was the best he could do. It had slowed down his running and was making him tire faster.

He broke out into a clearing, lit by a bright moon in a suddenly cloudless sky. Off to his right, a powerful, hunchbacked animal emerged from the tree-line. It scanned the clearing, picked him out, and bolted after him. Lorkrin whimpered despite himself. The thing was unbelievably fast. It would be on him in no time.

Ahead of him, he could see where the ground came to an end and, beyond it, the tops of trees. With his short legs lifting high to clear the long grass, he made for the cliff edge. He was breathing in sobs, and his heart felt like it was going to burst from his chest. Behind him, he could hear the pounding feet closing in on him. He was not going to make it. It was right at his heels. He was not going to make it ...

Lorkrin hurled himself off the edge, his arms and legs flailing in empty space. He fell, grabbed at a tree branch, missed it, grabbed at another, caught it, slipped and then held on to the very end of it with his long, strong fingers. His weight swung him in and the thin trunk curved but did not break. Above him, the skack launched itself off the brink, but its cruel claws were badly suited to clinging to the light limbs of treetops. It scrabbled at the foliage of a neighbouring tree, grasped nothing and tumbled down through the branches, hitting the ground below with a crunch. Lorkrin worked his way in to the trunk of his tree and clung to it, trembling.

+ + +

Taya knew her brother had escaped. She could hear him somewhere ahead of her. She could also hear the commotion in the woods behind her. There was no chance she would outrun them. These were not soldiers giving chase; they were something else and they were very, very fast. Inhuman screeches pierced the night air, and snarls and panting were growing louder all the time. If she could have caught her own breath, she would have been crying. They were in terrible trouble. She risked a glance behind, but could see nothing in the darkness cast under the trees in the moonlight. This frightened her even more. Whatever was back there was not having any difficulty tracking her in this gloom. If she was going to escape, she needed a faster form than that of a little girl.

Up ahead, she saw the bright glow of a clearing and she turned away from it. She would never make it across that open space. Her only chance was to keep dodging through the shadows of the trees. She took another look back and tripped, falling headlong into the undergrowth. Instinctively, she squinted back to see what she had fallen over. It was a large burrow. A badger or something even bigger lived down there. She was getting to her feet when she changed her mind and dived down it. Whatever was down here could not be worse than those things that were closing in on her. The tunnel was a tight fit, but she was in no position to complain.

The three skacks slowed their pace when their quarry suddenly disappeared. With their noses to the ground, they followed the scent. It was a slightly different smell from the one they had been given by their master, but it was close enough. They found a hole where the spoor was still strong.

None of them could fit down it, but that would not be a problem for long. They started digging, tearing up chunks of earth with their claws. They could sense the prey beneath. They would have it soon, very soon.

Taya dragged herself further down the burrow and found it widened out as she got deeper. Soon, she was able to sit up. There was even soft grass on the floor. This was a mole-bear's tunnel. The smell was unmistakable. She knew a bit about these animals. Their burrows were labyrinths. Gardeners hated them because they could dig out one part of the tunnel system, and find that it stretched for hundreds of strides in any direction. If you had a mole-bear beneath your garden, you would find it hard to get rid of and they could eat huge amounts of vegetables. Above and behind her, she could hear the sound of digging. Beyond where she sat, the tunnel grew too narrow for her. She could dig at it, make it wider, but not fast enough. She snuffled, feeling panic rise. With a determined sniff, she wiped her nose with her sleeve and smoothed her hair back. Taya Archisan was not the panicking type. She tried to ignore the way the burrow seemed to be crushing in on her, robbing her of air. Opening her backpack by feel, she took out her tools and began to reshape her legs, fingers working nimbly even without light to see by. When she had done her legs, she started her head and shoulders. The digging drew closer.

The skacks were getting feverish in their excitement. They were almost upon their prey. They had uncovered a long length of tunnel and had discovered a wider section. The tree roots were slowing them down, but they could sense their prey moving under them, and their mouths were watering at the prospect.

When they had dug further and still had not found her, they began to get agitated. The tunnel had narrowed again and its roof was thick with roots. The quarry had gone further in, even though they knew she was too big for this part of the burrow. They stopped digging and argued in a crude, guttural language. One stayed by the mouth of the hole. The other two split up and searched the ground for the spoor. Few animals were capable of tracking a creature once it went underground, but the skack was one of those exceptions.

If Taya had been standing up, she would have been taller than any adult she knew. Her arms were much shorter than usual and her legs had become a flexible part of her snake-like body, with her feet doing all the work at the back. Her neck was now holding her head up from the back of her skull so that she did not have to keep lifting it up to see where she was going. Thin strands of muscle crefted into whiskers told her what her eyes did not. In this long, thin, short-legged shape, she was able to move quite fast through the tunnels. She had left the digging sounds behind and was, she thought, putting as much distance between herself and her hunters as possible. It was hard to tell in the absolute darkness underground and in the cave-like hollows that twisted and turned with no obvious direction. She still had not met the creature that had dug this maze. She was not sure what she would do if she ran into it.

Footsteps overhead caused her to freeze. Could that be the Noranian creatures (she was still not sure she believed in skacks)? Surely they could not still be following her? How could they track her? Taya stayed quite still. This part of the burrow might be shallow enough for someone to hear her moving about, if they were close enough. The footsteps were very close. She could feel the vibrations through her feet and in her side where she was pressed against the wall. Suddenly she felt trapped again. The walls were too close; she was being smothered in this blackness. The footsteps were moving away. Shutting her eyes, Taya imagined herself in a wide open field. She pretended she could feel the breeze on her face and grass underfoot. Wondering where Lorkrin had got to, if he had made it away, she felt tears welling up in her eyes. Her whiskers twitched. Air moved in the tunnel; something was coming towards her. It was the burrow's owner. But her thoughts of that were quickly quashed as the footsteps came thumping back. The skacks too had heard the animal moving. There was an impact, then another and blue moonlight broke through the earth between her and the mole-bear. She backed off, but the mole-bear did not. Taya saw it in the shower of light, a stocky, silk-furred animal with powerful forepaws lined with thick curled claws. The skack – she was sure now what it was – drove both claws into the ground and pulled a sod of earth away. It dug in again, tearing open a hole big enough to get its head and shoulders in. And there it made a mistake.

As soon as it stuck its head in, the mole-bear took hold with its large forepaws and pulled hard. It was on its own territory down here; it knew how to take advantage of it. The skack, unable to get its head out, was being dragged into a space with no room to fight. The smaller creature was not nearly as strong, but it was firmly wedged in and had a tight grip. The skack screeched at a pitch high enough to hurt Taya's ears. She crouched, transfixed by the struggle. The mole-bear growled, backed further in, and the skack was now halfway into the burrow. The light was almost completely blocked out. From what she could hear, the tunnelling creature had started using its teeth and claws on the bigger beast. She worked her way backwards until she came to a junction and took another route.

Some time later, she saw a patch of light ahead and made carefully for it. It was a hole that came out under a slab of rock; a shallow stream ran nearby. Taya looked carefully around, then slid slowly out and into the stream. She waded down through the cold water until she thought she had hidden her scent enough, then grabbed an overhanging branch and hauled herself up into the foliage. There, she slunched back to her normal shape, and climbed as high as she could while still hidden from view. By jamming herself into a fork in the trunk, she made herself secure. Drained by her ordeal, she shivered, wishing she and Lorkrin could be safe at home in their warm lodge with their folks. The thought that Lorkrin might have been caught by those beasts was unbearable and she turned her face into the tree trunk and closed her eyes, trying not to think of what could have befallen her brother. Uncle Emos would still be hunting them, and she fell asleep hoping he would find them.

+ + +

Groach woke to the noise of the soldiers breaking camp. They were packing equipment and weapons away, and falling into marching formation. Everything smelled of smoke and soot and oil from the fire of the night before. The driver had cranked up his engine and was waiting for his turn to pull into the column of vehicles. Groach yawned and stretched, shifting uncomfortably on the hard board floor of the cage. He was cold and damp from dew. They had not been given blankets for the night. He shivered in the chill morning air. Hilspeth, still drowsy, rolled against his side and snuggled up for warmth. He was about to point out that he wanted to stand up and move around, but he did not. Let her get a bit warmer first, he decided.

The day was dry and fresh. He felt awake and ready for whatever was going to happen. They were headed for Hortenz, he knew. There, he would be put back to work on the project. He would regret not spending more time out in this outside world. He might even resent being locked away having seen it for himself. But the other men in this gaol wagon did not deserve to be here. He was certain they had been captured because of their resemblance to him. They would be released at the town – he would see to it.

It would be good to get back to work again, in the peace and quiet. No mad children or skacks or cages on wheels. Having slept on it, he decided he missed his research; it was time to return to it. He realised he had left his notes back at the Moffets', but it did not matter. He had an excellent memory, and he knew his tank back at the manor house contained all he needed to finish the project. That was what he had kept from everyone else – that he knew how to trigger the blossoming of the esh-bound bubule. He had finally cracked the oily esh-plant's secrets. Groach had little idea what the future would be now that their years of work had come to fruition. What was going to be done with the knowledge? It was exciting to contemplate; it could affect the whole world.

The gaol wagon shuddered and rolled into its position in the convoy. Hilspeth sat up, brushed the hair out of her face and stared through puffy eyes at the forest as it passed beyond the bars of their prison.

'What's going to happen to us, Panch?' she wondered aloud.

Groach was about to admit who he really was, when it occurred to him that it would not help her. They were both under arrest for a different reason. One he might die for. The other men would surely be released when they were not identified as him. He might still be held, especially if they found out he had defied them twice. And he could not answer her question. He did not know what was going to happen to either of them. Suddenly, the morning seemed much colder.

'What happened last night?' he asked in order to hide his despair. 'I fell asleep in the end, I think.'

'They all climbed into the wagons after they put out the fire, and waited for the skacks to come back. No one wanted to be outside when those things came into camp.' Her voice was dull and flat, drained after a sleepless night of worrying about the two young shape-changers. 'You should have seen them all, crammed into vans and even the cages. The skacks did come back, eventually. I don't know if they caught the children. They were dragging the remains of ... a mole-bear, I think. It was hard to tell. One of them had wounds on its face and neck; one was being carried by the other two. It had a broken leg.'

'Perhaps they didn't catch them.' Groach put his hand on her shoulder. 'What little I know of them is that they are not normal. I don't think they'd be easy prey.'

'They're Myunans,' murmured Hilspeth. 'Shape-changers – you can tell by the skin markings. But they're just children and skacks are savages that know nothing but hunting.'

It hurt him to see her upset. He didn't often think of other people and their feelings, but this argumentative, opinionated woman was not like the women on the project. She had aroused a strange, disturbing emotion in him, stronger than he had ever felt for plants, and seeing her despairing for those little rogues reminded him that they were only children after all. He found himself suddenly anxious for the two Myunans.

'They might have escaped,' he tried again.

'Even the soldiers are scared of these things.' She regarded him with an expression of grief. 'What chance did two children have?'

+ + +

Part of the way up a crumbly moss and shale slope, a lichen-covered stone stuck out an arm and brushed off some of its feathery growth. Lorkrin had hidden since late the night before, having worked his way clear of the injured skack by creeping through the treetops. He stirred now, because he had heard his sister calling his name. Shedding the last of the covering and letting his back take its natural shape again, he put his backpack on. He yelled out an answer. She shouted again, and he turned to peer into the tree-line at the bottom of the steep slope.

'Where are you?' she cried.

'Here, out past the trees. I'm coming down. Hang on.'

He worked his way down the loose hillside. Taya appeared at the bottom. She was covered in clay from head to foot. Under normal circumstances he would have laughed, but he was too happy to see her to tease her with any conviction. They each wanted to hug the other when he reached her, but neither wanted to be the first one to do it. They looked each other up and down instead.

'You all right?' he asked.

'Yeah,' she answered. 'They were horrible, those things. Absolutely horrible. They were like something you'd turn into, but real ... and ten times nastier.'

Lorkrin grinned sheepishly in agreement. He knew that some day soon, he'd try amorphing into a skack. Just to see if he could do it. Not to scare anyone, or anything like that.

It took a while for them to tell their stories. They had started a fire and were making nettle soup by the time they had finished. Taya had seen the convoy leave. They were going north, continuing towards Hortenz. Pondering on this, the two children sipped the hot soup in silence, savouring the much needed warmth and strength it gave their weary bodies.

'What do you want to do?' Lorkrin enquired of his sister, when he had finished.

'I don't know. What do you want to do?' she said in return.

'Well, I don't think making Uncle Emos mad would be as bad as getting torn up by skacks, do you?'

'Do you want to go back? I don't mind if you want to. It's okay to be scared. Everyone's scared of skacks. And soldiers.'

'I didn't say I was scared.' Lorkrin drew himself up. 'When did I say I was scared? Are you?'

'No, but if you want to go home, it's fine. I don't mind.' Taya sighed graciously.

'I don't want to go home. Do you?'

'Not if you don't want to. Don't you want to? Uncle Emos will understand. He must have done stuff when he was our age. We could go back if you want. I think it'd be all right.' She eyed her brother.

He eyed her back, a noncommittal expression on his face.

'It would be a shame to let that man get locked up by the army. It's sort of our fault he's in this mess. He'd still be in

Hortenz if we'd left him alone.'

Taya had not thought of this. She doubted Lorkrin would have thought of it either if he was not in danger of looking more frightened than her.

'You're right. It would be wrong to leave him there. We could rescue him and get the quill back. Uncle Emos would probably forgive us if we made up for stealing the quill by helping someone.'

'Yeah,' Lorkrin agreed. 'That would make him proud. He might even not tell Ma and Pa about us stealing the quill at all.'

'So we'd only get punished once ...'

'Yeah.'

'So anyway, we'll try again,' Taya said slowly. 'See if we can help him escape.'

'...Yeah,' her brother agreed, after some hesitation.

'Right.'

The two Myunans sat opposite each other across the fire and wondered what they had just argued themselves into.

# 6 JUSTICE AND GRAMMAR

Emos Harprag sat slumped at a table in a storyhouse tavern in Hortenz, a half-finished plate of food pushed aside, his head buried in his arms. After spending the last two days and nights searching for his niece and nephew, he had lost their trail and was considering going back to the farm to see if they turned up there. Deep in exhausted slumber, he dreamed – old memories replaying in his troubled mind:

> He took in the scene around him as his friend Murris and two others prepared the diving gear. The esh-boat's deck rose and fell gently beneath his feet with the motion of the sea of gas. The boat was a trawvette, a Braskhiam fishing boat made up of the usual three wooden hulls full of compressed hydrogen, each with two masts and six sails, which were now lowered to allow the craft to sit still at anchor. Emos had joined the crew of the *Lightfoot* that day at the request of Peddar Murris, the boat's chief engineer, to help with a salvage operation. The captain of the fishing vessel sometimes used quiet periods during the fishing season to bring up valuables from boats lying wrecked beneath the surface of the gas. Murris had convinced the captain that it could be useful to have a man along on dives who could take all sorts of shapes,

and fit through impossibly small gaps. For the Myunan it was a bit of extra money to put into the farm.

Emos could see from the looks he was getting that not all of the crew was comfortable having him around. Eshers were a superstitious lot, and anything out of the ordinary was grounds for suspicion ... and that included shape-shifters. But there were many places where Emos was not welcome. He had become accustomed to staying out of the way of people and he did so now, standing by the rail, his faded grey eyes staring down at the balloon buoy that marked the place where they would dive, the place where a Karthar frigatch carrying a small, but valuable cargo of gold had hit rocks after being caught in a ferocious storm.

Murris stood up straight and bowed when he saw the eshtran step onto the deck. No dive could take place without the blessing of the Braskhiam boat's holy man. As the eshtran chanted the Diving Prayer, the engineer assisted Emos in putting on his equipment. There was the harness girdle attaching him to the safety rope, flotation bags that could be inflated with hydrogen from canisters in an emergency, and the breathing apparatus made up of a mask and goggles that strapped to his head, from which a hose led to an air pump on the deck of the boat. There was also a glowjar full of fluorescent green fungus to help light his way; lanterns did not burn underesh. Murris wore all of this and more, with a tool belt and large pouches for holding various bits and pieces of his trade.

The eshtran passed Murris a small canister with a breathing mask on it and Murris inhaled some of the purified air, holding his breath and closing his eyes for a moment before handing the cylinder over to Emos, who did the same and then gave it back to the eshtran. Every diver had to have one last breath of pure air before the dive in case he died. Braskhiams had to meet their god with clean lungs. Murris let his breath out and made a motion with his hand from mouth to chest and back again and then pulled on his own breathing mask. He took several breaths to make sure air was feeding through. Emos pulled down his mask, checked his own air flow and then they waited as a deckhand pulled up a section of the boat's rail to clear the way over the side.

Emos went first; being the less experienced diver, he could be helped more easily from above if he ran into problems and would be less of a danger to his partner. He climbed down the side of the esh-boat using the foot and handholds that ran down the hull. As he reached the surface of the sessium, the gas of the esh, he looked up to see Murris following him down, both of them linked by the rope that trailed up the side to the deck. When Murris got down to the Myunan's side, he pulled up his mask:

'Right, you know how it goes – there's only one speed underesh: nice and slow. Take your time, whatever you're doing. That wreck's not going anywhere. It's pretty shallow here, so we'll be going straight to the bottom, no stages. Breathe slow and easy. Don't hold your breath. Keep me in sight at all times, and watch for my signals. Let's go.'

The one thing that Emos always missed most about diving in the esh was sound. Everything was muffled down there, as if his ears were stuffed with cotton wool. As he dropped beneath the surface of the sessium, the sounds of the men moving up on deck became dull thuds through the wooden hull. His air hissed in along the hose from the pump and he exhaled out of the mask's valves. As the side of the esh-boat curved down away from him, he tested the rope by settling his whole weight into the harness, and then let go of the hull. There was a moment of butterflies in his stomach as he swung back and forth slightly, and then he was lowered further, swinging again as Murris let go above him. The winch on the deck dropped them down through the yellow-tinted white of the esh, light filtering down in a haze from the sky above them.

Emos could see esh floaters around them and hear their calls. The bass boom of flocks of round dunds, the crackling clicks from swarms of paper-thin interts, and the lazy, buzzing drone of a sleek spatch as it glided by with the fluid grace of a predator. The esh grew darker and thicker as they went down and, by the time his feet touched the ground, Emos could see only a few strides in any direction. He held up his glowjar and that helped. He stepped to the side in time to get out of Murris's way as he landed, and the engineer led him to the point where the buoy was anchored.

They were surrounded by an eshweed called the bubule, a plant that grew to the Myunan's shoulder height. They had to push it out of their path and keep their air hoses clear of it as they trudged through the gas. The plant's fronds left greasy marks on their clothes as they brushed past.

The frigatch came into sight. It had been a streamlined and handsome vessel in its day, heavily armed with harpoon guns, but now it was furry with fungus and moss, and hundreds of different esh creatures had made it their home. Murris led the way towards it, watching for hazards and studying the position of the wreck carefully. It lay at the base of the huge rock that had torn open its hulls. The gaping holes were clearly visible and Emos could imagine the terror of the crew as the ship had sunk below the surface. The holes were huge; the Kartharic ship would have sunk quickly, upending and plunging down through the sessium. Most of the men would have died instantly; some would have survived their injuries only to suffocate.

Emos arched his neck, gazing upwards through the foggy depths, but the dull yellow glow was all that could be seen of daylight, and the air that was keeping him alive. Even as he looked up, a faint but distinct smell of paraffin filled his mask. Smells were used as signals to divers, garlic for bad weather, wood polish for a time check ... paraffin was danger. The hiss of his breathing through the valves grew faster as his heart began pounding and he looked instinctively up through the gas, feeling suddenly hampered by all his equipment. He and Murris turned as one and hurried back through the tangle of the bubules to the point below the *Lightfoot* where they had landed. Murris wound in the slack of the safety rope and jerked hard on it three times. Moments later, the rope started disappearing up into the gas, pulling taut and lifting first Murris, then Emos, up towards the trawvette.

Frantic hands pulled them on board and Murris stripped off his mask to ask:

'What is it? What's wrong?'

Sitting off the bow was a Karthar war frigatch, a more fearsome version of the vessel that lay beneath the esh, and its harpoons were trained on the *Lightfoot*. The fishing boat's captain looked down from his bridge at Murris and shook his head. They would not be diving again today. They were in disputed territory here, and their little trawvette was no match for a battleship. Murris cursed and shrugged out of his harness.

'That cargo was ours for the taking. Salvage is fair game and they know it,' he growled to Emos. 'But there's no messing with those war frigatches.'

Emos's thoughts went to the wreck beneath their feet.

'Not unless you have the esh on your side,' he murmured.

+ + +

Emos woke with a start as someone slammed a tankard of mead down on the table before him. He was taken aback to find himself staring into the face of a Karthar, but then relaxed when he realised he was in the tavern and he recognised the crooked-toothed grin.

'Emos Harprag! Haven't seen you in an age, get some of that drink down your neck, man – you look half dead!' The Karthar flopped into the seat beside him and thumped his shoulder.

Emos managed a tired smile, and raised the tankard in salute, before taking a sip. The Karthar who had just sat down at the table was a merchant eshsailor named Neblisk, whom Emos had not seen in several seasons.

'So, what brings you to Hortenz?' Neblisk asked, taking a swig of his own drink.

'I'm after two errant children. I could ask you the same question. I haven't seen you around here in a while.'

'Business with the Noranians,' the Karthar replied. 'Had to moor the ship just off the coast not far from here. They don't want us coming near Noran. It's all a bit hush-hush, you know.'

Emos raised an eyebrow. Neblisk specialised in hush-hush. He could get anything for anyone who would pay, and he could do it quietly. Unlike most Karthars, he was not a religious man, preferring to devote himself to the making of money.

'What use would the Noranians have for you?' the Myunan

asked. 'I would have thought they could look after them-selves.'

'You might think that,' Neblisk replied. 'But sooner or later, everyone comes to Neblisk. It seems that the Braskhiams have not been too friendly of late, and the Nora-nians needed some special ... esh-related items. Not a word, mind you. I know I can count on your discretion, Emos. Par-ticularly since you don't normally talk to anyone anyway.'

Neblisk, on the other hand, seemed unusually eager to talk, so Emos took another drink of his mead and let the Kar-thar fill the silence. With three short, downward-pointing horns over a long goateed face, and thick grey hair over most of his body, the Karthar was like no other man in the room. He had four thumbs, one on each side of each hand and he had the long arms and short legs of a climber. He shifted in his seat and turned his tankard between his hands.

'These Noranians I'm dealing with think the Braskhiams are set to declare war on the Kartharic Peaks. They want it stopped, so they're preparing something that will teach the Braskhiams a lesson. Don't ask me what. It all went over my head.'

'What did they ask you to get for them?' Emos asked casually.

'Odd stuff, really. Eshweed seeds, diving gear, underesh charts of the coast. Things they could normally only get from the Braskhiams. All very mysterious, if you ask me.'

Emos looked up sharply at this. He was remembering the scene he had witnessed in the square, the strange people who had come through the broken wall. He stared out the window into the square as he ran the events through his mind. The people had smelled of something that he had recognised, but could not put his finger on. Neblisk, he suddenly realised, had the same smell, but he had just got off a boat. Those people had smelled of the esh, and yet they had all the appearance of having been working in a garden. But why had the Noranians sent in catchwagons and foot soldiers when the wall came down? No garden could be that valuable.

Now that he thought about it, the men had worn long beards, and had been dressed like peasants ... like the dead man in the esh. That man had carried soil samples and gardening tools.

Neblisk glanced around the crowded room, squinting through the smoke to ensure no one was listening. 'I was hoping to find Draegar, to see if he'd made any new coastal charts lately.'

Emos nodded, distracted from his thoughts.

'I was hoping to bump into him myself. I could do with his help finding the children. This lesson that the Braskhiams are going to learn – is it going to hurt anyone?'

'All the hardest lessons hurt, Emos. They want a war. They need to be persuaded otherwise.'

'They say it's the Karthars who want the war.'

'And who do you believe?' Neblisk leaned towards the Myunan.

'I think if you both keep accusing each other, then soon it won't matter.' Emos returned the Karthar's gaze. 'And you say the Noranians don't want it to happen?'

'Nobody in their right minds wants it to happen,' Neblisk grunted. 'Have you ever been to war, Emos?'

'I was never a soldier, if that's what you mean.'

'I was a cabin boy on my father's ship during the war

against Noran all those years ago. My father was wounded, a small wound in the arm, but it got infected with the rot. We were near the Braskhiam coast, but they wouldn't let us land as they were allied to Noran. We set out for the Peaks but we were too far from home to get him to a healer in time. I watched the ship's carpenter saw off my father's arm to stop the rot reaching his body and killing him. Father had nothing to kill the pain, just a piece of rope to bite on, and some men to hold him still.

'Only a fool looks for war, Emos, but if the Braskhiams start something, then the Karthars have the will to finish it.'

'And you're sure they are starting something?' Emos urged. 'It's not just rumours and back-biting?'

'My boat was attacked out in the Gulf of Braskhia not long ago. Attacked by a Braskhiam vessel. We escaped with our lives, but not before they put some crossbow bolts through our sails.'

'It's fortunate you lived to tell about it,' the Myunan said, almost to himself.

He was troubled – the Braskhiams had high-powered harpoons fired with compressed gas. Braskhiam vessels did not carry crossbows. Nor, for that matter, did Karthar ships.

'Two children, did you say?' Neblisk sat up suddenly. 'Didn't two Myunan cubs try to break a man out of a Noranian convoy last night? I heard they set the skacks on them.'

+ + +

As it approached the forbidding gates of Hortenz, the convoy of gaol wagons and armoured vehicles slowed, waiting as the Whipholder's lead vehicle drove ahead to show his papers and gain entry. Once the guard had waved them through, the convoy rolled under the stone arch and into the town.

In the shaking and shifting gaol wagon, Groach considered his options. To keep quiet and go unrecognised, which might mean more misery for the other men. Or, to announce who he was in the hope that he would be put back on the project and the men released, which might not happen. He decided to wait and see what the Noranians did next.

The six gaol wagons split off from the other vehicles at the town square and turned into the barracks' compound, where the gates closed behind them. The barracks was a menacing rectangle of grey plastered stone buildings with towers at two corners. The walls had no windows looking out on the town; they were high and solid, with walkways to allow guards to patrol around the top and see through the triangular battlements that looked like the teeth of a trap. The towers had slits to allow light in on each floor and crossbows to be aimed out. Altogether, it was a place that was built to be easy to defend ... and hard to escape. Shessil Groach looked about him with a sinking heart.

Guards unlocked the cages, and the men were made jump down and stand in line before a small, slight man in a grey waistcoat and shirt, green trousers and jacket, and a string tie held in place with a silver clasp. He had wispy blond hair that was so thin on his scalp as to be almost invisible, and his skin was like taut tissue paper, barely hiding the blue veins beneath. He regarded the prisoners without emotion. It was obvious that they were a task to be completed and nothing more.

Groach moved to get out of the wagon and was pushed back inside by a guard. He was not a part of these proceedings. The small man inspected a notebook in one hand and then brought his gaze back to rest on the men.

'My name is Rulp Mungret. I am the aide of His Most Political Wonder, the Prime Ministrate, Rak Ek Namen. I have one question to ask of you men. If I receive a satisfactory answer, you can all return to your homes. If not, you will all remain in the cells beneath this barracks until such time as I receive that answer. The question is this: I am looking for a man named Shessil Groach. Is he here among you?'

There was complete silence. The men scanned each others' faces for a reaction. Then there was a clamour of protests as each man shouted out who they were and where they were from. Groach watched and listened, and decided he must come clean. These men did not belong here.

'I'm Shessil Groach!' he yelled.

Some of the men heard him, but Mungret was at the other end of the yard. Groach opened his mouth to call out again, and was quickly silenced by a punch in the face. He fell back, clutching his bloody nose, his eyes watering and blurring his sight. A hand pulled him to the bars and a rough voice hissed in his ear:

'You'll be staying with me, little maggot. Not another word from you or I'll kill you and your woman friend right here. You'll be staying with me.'

Left-Speartrooper Grulk thumped him in the ribs for good measure, knocking the wind out of him, and stood back. The other men were being herded into the barracks. Mungret had decided to hold them for a few days, just to be on the safe side. Groach and Hilspeth were taken from their cage and dragged in opposite directions, to different parts of the barracks.

Through half-closed eyes, Groach saw to his dismay that Grulk was one of the guards gripping his arms. She was a demon, he decided. Come to haunt and perhaps even kill him. He wished he had never broken out of the project; he wished he had never seen those two warped children or Hilspeth, or the teapot that had got him into this mess. He was pushed and kicked down a flight of metal steps into a dark, cramped room with a corridor leading off it. A scaly, stumpy creature without armour, but otherwise dressed in the same style of clothing as the soldiers, greeted them. He stood up from behind his battered desk and came around to inspect the prisoner.

'What's he in for?' he asked, ignoring Groach and directing the question at the guards.

'Attacking a member of the Noranian Armed Forces,' Grulk answered.

'What? This thing attacked a soldier? Did he have a weapon?'

'A teapot.'

The creature let rip an hysterical laugh. Groach could not help but give a little smile.

'A *teapot*?' the stunted figure roared. 'And I suppose he mercilessly struck the trooper down with a buttered scone while the noble warrior lay mortally wounded on the ground! Lying in a pool of their own tea! Ha ha ha!'

'This is not a joke, Gaoler,' Grulk snarled.

'And why did he commit this most terrible of crimes?'

'You're trying my patience, Gaoler ...' Grulk could see the other two guards grinning and it was getting her temper up.

'... No, wait. Don't tell me. He was defending his secret stash of cucumber sandwiches! Ha ha ha ha! Got to watch out for those cucumber-sandwich smugglers, they're a desperate lot ... *fanatics* you might say ... ha ha ha ... lethal with a teapot ... and you should see the damage they can do with an apple crumble ... ha ha ha ...'

His laughing stopped abruptly when Grulk, who stood head and shoulders above him, slammed him against the wall hard enough to dent the grey plaster.

'Lock him up!' she bellowed. 'And not another word out of you or I'll feed you your innards!'

Suppressing a scared giggle, the gaoler took a bunch of keys from a hook on the wall and gestured to them to follow.

'Give him your worst cell,' Grulk urged as she shoved Groach ahead of her.

They followed the gaoler, Grulk glaring at the small man as they walked down between the rows of cells. The stunted man's keys jingled as he walked.

They walked past a number of heavy, iron-banded wooden doors. The gaoler stopped at one and inserted a large key into its lock. It opened with a creak.

'This is our worst,' he sighed. 'The walls are damp, the bench has woodworm and the grate in the ceiling is beneath the outhouse.'

'It's perfect,' said Grulk. 'We'll take it.'

+ + +

Left-Speartrooper Grulk was bunking in the soldiers' quarters in the barracks. As the other men and women drank cheap mead and played knucklebones, she lay in her bunk and fumed, tormented by the memory of Shessil Groach's attack. She also thought about how the gaoler had laughed at her, and how the others had joined in. She knew that there would be a trial tomorrow of the little man and his woman friend, and that the story would come out at the trial. And she knew that she would be made a laughing stock.

The story must not be told. Her fellow soldiers already knew, but they had seen the attack and had witnessed how she had been dishonoured. They understood. But the trial would be public. Everyone in the town would know afterwards. And they would laugh at her behind her back. She couldn't have that. Life for a woman in the Noranian Armed Forces was gruelling enough, without little snots coming along and attacking you with teapots. So, the trial must not take place. Groach would have to have an accident in his cell. And the girl too; she must not be tried either. But Groach first. Left-Speartrooper Grulk climbed out of her bunk and put on her boots.

+ + +

The cell smelt. Shessil Groach crouched up on the bench with his knees supporting his chin, his arms wrapped around his legs. There was a draught from the tiny grate in the ceiling over one wall that brought relief from the musky stink, but chilled his tired flesh. His face was still puffy from the soldier's blow, and his nose was itchy and very sore, which meant that scratching just hurt it more. He had a headache right behind his forehead, and was thoroughly miserable. He knew he would not sleep. Eventually, he remembered the tonic Hilspeth had given him; she had said it would ease pain.

Taking the blue glass vial from his pocket, he held it up in the dim light from the corridor. He could not remember how much she had told him to take, but he was in quite a lot of pain. He drew out the cork and, holding his head back, let six or seven drops fall onto his tongue. Moments later, the world went bright orange and turned inside out. He collapsed off the bench onto the damp floor.

When his vision cleared, he was gazing along the floor at the bottom of the door to his cell. Something in Groach's head dragged a memory from a dark corner of his skull. *Two drops under his tongue, three times a day.* No more. It was true that he did not feel any pain in his head any more. He could not feel his head at all – nor any other part of his body for that matter. He was completely unable to move. He became worried that he would wet himself if he stayed here too long. But there was nothing he could do, so he continued to watch the bottom of the door. When the door opened with a sound one would expect it to make if it were being dragged through syrup, he was grateful for the change in scenery. A pair of feet stepped into view, and the world swung around him until his face ended up pressed against somebody's back. He was unable to see who was carrying him, but he knew the sweaty, smoky body odour. It was Left-Speartrooper Grulk, and she was alone. Fear flooded the numbness of his body as he realised she was taking him up out of the gaol.

She was talking to him in a hoarse whisper, but it might as well have been a pig snorting at him for all the sense he could make of it. They were carrying on up the steps, beyond the courtyard, up further. They must be ascending one of the towers. He tried counting the steps, but the jolting of her body as she climbed was making him feel disorientated and sick. He felt like he was going to throw up.

They came out into fresh air, and his head started to clear a little. She dropped him to the floorboards like a sack, and he knew that as soon as he could feel his ribs, they would start to hurt. Deep down in his belly, a knot was forming. It was only a small cramp, but it promised big things. At the top of the tower an oil lamp burned in one corner, hanging from a nail in a roof-post. The triangular battlements were sharply defined in the orange lamplight against the navy blue of the night sky. The space beyond seemed like an abyss.

'... Can you hear me, you little weed?' He could just hear Grulk's voice saying, 'This is it. This is your end, little man. You have escaped the cells and made your way up here, where you will try to get away by climbing down from this tower. You will, of course, die in the attempt. It's not such a long fall to the bottom, but you will be leading with your head. No one will suspect, and no one will ask questions. You are a nobody, and not a soul will care when you are gone.'

Groach thought the idea of his trying to climb down from the tower to escape an absurd idea, but she obviously knew what she was talking about. He was a bit hurt by the bit about him being a 'nobody', but she had a point. After all, who would care when he was gone? Mostly though, he was concerned about the growing cramp in his stomach. Grulk did a quick circuit of the top of the tower to check that no one was watching, then bent down to pick up Groach.

The bellyache signalled a gradual return of feeling to his body and limbs, and as he was hoisted aloft, the full realisation of what she was doing dawned on him. He struggled weakly, but he was no match for her. Instead, the thrashing made his stomach convulse, and he threw up. Grulk gagged in disgust, letting go of him with one hand to cover her face. His weight crumpled onto her shoulder and knocked her sideways. As she tried to wipe the mess from her armour, she dropped him, slipped on a patch of vomit, and fell against the battlements. Her armour-encased torso rolled between two of the teeth, stranding her there, kicking and twisting like a tortoise turned on its back. Groach choked and coughed for breath, on his knees at the base of the battlements. Trying to give room to his lungs, he shifted his weight onto his feet and stood up. His shoulder caught one of Grulk's kicking feet, and she pitched backwards over the wall, disappearing into the empty space with a desperate scream. A thump followed some moments later.

Gasping in shock at what he had done, Groach staggered to the edge of the wall and gaped down at the body below. She was dead. There was no doubt about that. He threw up again, and when he was finished, he slumped down with his back to the mottled plaster. People were starting to come out of their houses around the square; lamps were being lit. In a daze, Groach stumbled down the six flights of stairs and out into the compound. People were milling around him, but in the commotion, nobody noticed the small man in the dirty clothes who walked out the now-open gate, and into the crowd. With everyone else trying to get a look at the dead soldier, Groach passed unhindered across the square towards the only familiar place in town. The guards, drawn away to help deal with the crowds, did not notice him slip past in the shadows and into the huge house from which he had originally escaped – the building that housed the Harvest Tide Project.

+ + +

Hilspeth was woken from a fitful sleep by a shouting match between the female occupant of the next cell and the stout woman who yelled from down the hallway, where she sat at her desk. The prisoner bellowing from the adjacent cell had been arrested the night before for being drunk and disorderly, and was demanding to be released on the grounds that she was now sober. It was the law, and she knew her rights, she shrieked. Over and over again. The guard replied, in an equally vocal manner, that the woman would not be released until she shut up. This match of wills went on for some time. It ended with the female guard walking past Hilspeth's cell, in the process of rolling up her sleeves, and then opening the door to the next room. There followed a loud smack and a brief silence. Hilspeth guessed that the guard was in a hurry to get the prisoner released. Sure enough, the guard then walked past the other way, leading a woman who was holding a hand to her left cheek.

The episode served to take Hilspeth's mind off her plight. They had told her that she was to face trial today, first thing in the morning. It was still a gloomy grey outside, but there could not be much time left. From inside her jacket, she pulled out a packet of powder and unfolded it. It was Ground Clublick Root, for Strength and Forbearance in Adversity. She sprinkled some on the inside of her left wrist and rubbed it against her right. Then she folded the packet carefully and placed it back in one of the dozens of small pockets she had in her waistcoat. The vapours soothed her and helped her focus her mind.

Down the corridor came the tramp of big feet carrying

heavy bodies. Two soldiers stopped outside her cell door, and, peering through the barred window, waved at her to stand up. The door was unlocked by the guard, who then retreated to her desk. Hilspeth was taken out of the women's gaol block, upstairs and out across the courtyard. The barracks was even more forbidding in the bleak yellow dawn and Hilspeth shivered. But this was not the time to be intimidated. She squared her shoulders, and in order to take the initiative, strode faster than the two soldiers who marched either side, an effort that resulted in the three competing in a less-than-dignified run past the guardhouse to the courtroom.

Watching out the window of his chambers, Judge Rile Pliskett observed the three figures trotting past, and finished buttoning his wide cuffs. Pulling on his thick fur robe, he laid his weighty gold chains of office over his chest, and donned the expressionless white wooden mask that covered his face from his hairline to his top lip. This, according to tradition, was the face of justice, unemotional and just and fair. Judge Rile Pliskett took tradition very seriously.

Hilspeth was seated on a bench in a rectangular pit that put the floor at her shoulder level. Steps led out of one end, and a low railing ran around the top of the pit. The position meant that the accused, that was to say, Hilspeth, could be looked down upon by everyone else in the large room. The rest of the room was filled with rows of benches, with a raised platform where the judge would sit with the Town Accuser standing in front of him. The Accuser passed up papers to the judge's assistant, who gave them a cursory glance and agreed to point out the important bits to the judge. The Accuser was notorious for producing huge amounts of paperwork, and the judge had eventually given up trying to read it, much to the Accuser's annoyance.

The courtroom was nearly empty. The regular crowd, who regarded the court as one of the best sources of entertainment in town, was not up and about yet, and no one was very interested in Hilspeth's case. She waited for Panch to appear, or Shessil, or whatever his real name was, but there was no sign of him. She began to feel very lonely. She had no friends here; no one knew her and no one would take her side. There were more soldiers here than anyone else, some from the convoy that had brought her here, and some from the barracks. The two groups kept apart from each other, and eyed one another in suspicious rivalry. The barracks soldiers were standing watch over her; the others were witnesses against her. The chief witness, Left-Speartrooper Grulk, had not appeared either. That worried Hilspeth. She hoped Panch was all right. Her concern for him outweighed her fears for herself, and she had to snap back to the courtroom as the judge was announced. Judge Rile Pliskett entered, his fur robe following for some distance after him. He sat up behind the podium and gathered his furs around him. Perched above the gold and fur, the white mask swivelled and gazed down, short-sighted eyes squinting out through the dark holes to study Hilspeth.

Hilspeth readied herself for the fight of her life. The Accuser stood and read the charges:

'Let it be known to the court, that this woman, a Miss Hilspeth Naratemus, is charged with wilfully obstructing a soldier in the execution of her duties, and participation in the assault on said soldier during said obstruction ...'

'I object!' yelled Hilspeth.

'Young lady,' said the judge peering down at her. 'You cannot object to the charges. The whole point of the trial is that you are accused of these things and you argue against them. You may object to the Accuser's *method* of accusing you if you wish. But you have to let the man begin.'

Hilspeth bit her lip. She had never taken part in a trial before and did not know the rules. She could hold her own in any argument and had started quite a few in her time, but they had not been hampered by rules. This was going to be tough.

'I will produce evidence, as listed and described in the papers provided for your Judgeship ...' The Accuser indicated the pile on the podium. '... that the accused and her co-defendant, whom we will be trying in his absence, as he is not here, did on the day concerned commit the afore-mentioned act.'

Hilspeth noticed the man had a way of speaking that bored and annoyed her at the same time and wondered if this was one of the things she could object to. Probably not, she decided. It did make what he was saying difficult to follow, though, and as he continued, it took all her effort to keep her attention from wandering off.

'... whereupon, the aforementioned soldier, whom we shall henceforth refer to as the third party, did in the course of this event, suffer a blow to the head with a porcelain vessel, specifically ...' The Accuser checked his notes. '... a teapot. Subsequently ...'

'Did you say a teapot?' the judge asked.

'I did, your Judgeship.'

The judge lifted his mask slightly to see the paper where he made a note of the information.

'I see. Continue.'

'Subsequently, the third party did turn and defend herself ...'

'I'm sorry. You've lost me. Who is the third party?'

'The soldier who was attacked, your Judgeship.'

'Ah yes, of course. Continue.'

'The third party did turn and defend herself in a manner in keeping with her training as a member of the Noranian Armed Forces.' The Accuser straightened and lifted his chin.

'I call the first witness for the accusation. Right-Speartrooper Flivel.'

The soldier, a wiry individual with a jutting jaw, wide, round eyes and bad skin, stepped up to the stand. The judge's mask pivoted to take in the new participant. The judge's assistant stepped up.

'What is your name?'

'Right-Speartrooper Boxxus Flivel.'

'Do you promise not to lie, to tell the story, the whole story, and nothing but the story, on pain of death by hanging?'

'Aye.'

'Good. You are now under oath.' The assistant sat back down in his chair.

'Right-Speartrooper Flivel,' the Accuser began. 'Did you, on the day before yesterday, witness the assault on Left-Speartrooper Grulk by the aforementioned parties?'

The trooper, still trying to digest the question, stared back at the Accuser, who carefully nodded once.

'Aye,' replied Flivel, relieved.

'Tell us what you saw, Right-Speartrooper.'

'Aye, well. We was on a manhunt ...'

'"We *were* on a manhunt", Right-Speartrooper,' Pliskett corrected as he made another note. The soldiers from the barracks sniggered.

'Aye, sir, we wa ... were on a manhunt, see, and while we was ...'

'Were ...'

'... While we were searching this village, see, this cart came up the road. Full of bottles and jars it was, see,' Flivel narrated. 'And it sort of made this jinglin' sound, so we all turned to look at it, see ...'

'Right-Speartrooper,' Judge Pliskett interrupted. 'Let us assume that I see now, and will continue to do so for the foreseeable future, negating any need for you to keep checking.'

'Sorry, your Judgeship?'

'Stop saying "see" all the time, Right-Speartrooper.' The mask's eyeholes held him in their gaze.

'Aye, sir. Anyway, we was ...'

'Were ...'

'...Were watchin' this cart, and we were thinkin' how there wasn't no instructions for no carts ...'

'Mr Flivel,' the judge snapped, slamming his fist on the podium. 'I do not know from which barracks you come, but here in Hortenz, we insist that our soldiers exercise a proper use of grammar. And I find yours lacking, sir. Already you have, on a number of occasions, evinced the incorrect use of a verb and now you blatantly, *blatantly*, sir, employ a double negative. For which I am fining you the sum of fifty drokes. You will continue your narration in a manner befitting our beautiful language, or you will not continue at all. Carry on with your testimony.'

Hilspeth kept her silence through all of this, struggling to keep up with the lawyer, and patiently waiting for the soldier to finish his story. Now she wondered if she would ever get to tell her side of it. At this rate, it was going to take all day. Flivel gave the impression that he had not understood the bulk of what the judge had said to him. He had understood the bit about being fined, however. Fifty drokes was a lot of money by any standards, but especially if you were on a foot soldier's pay. His face scrunched up as he tried to recall his early schooling. His money was at stake now.

'We had ... no instructions about ... carts. It were ... was a woman with bottles and ... objects. On the cart. She were ... was alone. The cart jingled and therefore, we did ... pay it our full attention. Left-Speartrooper Grulk did stand firm ... before it. Wherefore the cart's owner did stop.'

A glance at Judge Pliskett did nothing for Flivel's confidence. He continued, 'Grulk did proceed to question the owner, whereupon the owner did give Left-Speartrooper lip about her smell. Grulk did then proceed to thump her head in.'

'I have been more than patient with you, Right-Speartrooper Flivel. But I will not stand by while you end a sentence with a preposition. I am hereby imposing a further fifty-droke fine, payable at the end of session. Have you more to say, Right-Speartrooper Flivel?'

Flivel stood in shock at the unfairness of this. Good grammar was not of great use to a soldier. Good grammar did not keep you alive in the chaos of a battlefield. He had not asked to come to this courtroom; he had been ordered to, and now he was losing half a moon's pay over it. Giving testimony was proving expensive. When it came right down to it, he had never really liked Grulk anyway. And besides, she was dead.

'That was all I saw,' he concluded. The Accuser's face clouded over.

'Thank the gods for that,' Judge Pliskett muttered. 'Mr Accuser, call your next witness.'

'Yes, your Judgeship, I call Forward-Batterer Wulms.'

'Didn't see nothin',' Wulms grunted from the group at the back of the courtroom. He had seen what had happened to Flivel, and had no intention of putting his money on the line. The Accuser twisted around to glare at this betrayal.

'Did I hear another double negative, Forward-Batterer?' Pliskett asked.

'No, your Judgeship.' Wulms' answer was quite final.

'I see. Next witness, Mr Accuser.'

'I call Crossbow Carrier Rects.'

'Wasn't there,' came the reply. The Accuser hissed through his teeth. He called four more soldiers as witnesses, only to meet with refusals each time. He had no one else to call.

'Finished, Mr Accuser?' the judge asked.

'It would seem so, your Judgeship.' The Accuser sat down, his face purple with rage.

'Miss Naratemus, you may begin your argument,' Pliskett told Hilspeth.

'Your Judgeship,' Hilspeth stood up to speak. 'As the Accuser has not even managed to present a complete accusation, other than describing how a heavily armed woman, twice my size, thumped me on the side of the head, I put it to you that there is no charge to answer. I have been imprisoned for two days and nights, and have lost my cart and all my stock. Punishment enough, I think, for standing up to a bully, if that can be called a crime. I think I should go home, your Judgeship.'

There was a silence in the court as the white wooden mask aimed its expressionless gaze at her.

'Agreed,' said Pliskett. 'Case dismissed. Miss Naratemus, you are free to go.'

The Accuser sourly gathered up his papers and prepared for his next case. The soldiers filed out of the room, and Hilspeth stood uncertainly in the pit, surprised and slightly wary that there might be more to come.

'You may go, Miss Naratemus,' the judge urged her gently.

Without further hesitation, Hilspeth left.

A soldier escorted her as far as the gate, where she stood for a moment, looking back into the barracks and thinking of Panch. Where had he gone? Was he alive? Had he escaped or had Grulk got him? She knew she would have to find out before she could take up her normal life again. She spun on her heel and strode out of the gateway, walking right into a tall, thin figure in a navy, hooded cloak. A grunt sounded from somewhere near the figure's waist, and it toppled over. Hilspeth gasped an apology, and bent over to help the person up. As she recognised the face of the girl under the hood, she also realised that the girl's elongated body had broken at the waist – broken completely in half. The girl gave her a pleading look. Hilspeth thought for a second, and then nodded. Gathering as much as she could of the top half's weight in her arms, with the girl holding her shoulders, she lifted it up, keeping the robes of the cloak draped over the bottom half. The legs and hips got up by themselves, a fact that was hidden by the cloak.

'You come with me now, or I rip off the cloak,' said Hilspeth.

'Okay,' replied Taya.

# 7 GETTING ANSWERS IN THE STORYHOUSE

Hilspeth had heard of Myunans, but she had never met any before. As she led them away from the town square, she attempted to find out more about these two. The girl's name was Taya Archisan. She was the face Hilspeth could see inside the hood of the cloak. A muffled voice at waist-level introduced itself as Taya's brother, Lorkrin. Hilspeth could not help but admire the two shape-changers for their ingenuity. There was no way the guards would allow children into the barracks, but adults could walk in unchallenged if they appeared to know where they were going.

Standing one child on top of another does not make the shape of an adult, however, and the two Myunans knew this. Taya had increased the size of her head and even coloured her skin as if she were wearing make-up. She had lengthened her arms, at the same time making her legs much smaller and thinner, leaving them just strong enough to allow her to keep her balance on Lorkrin's shoulders. Lorkrin had flattened his head to conceal it under the cloak, shortened his body and lengthened his legs so that he could stride like someone twice his height. His shorter arms helped Taya keep her balance. The effect was very convincing, and would probably have worked if Hilspeth had not bumped into them.

'We were trying to help your friend, Shessil,' Taya explained once they reached a small alleyway where the children could regain their shapes. Watching Taya's head shrink was something Hilspeth would remember for the rest of her life.

'You mean Panch?'

'We heard him called Shessil,' Lorkrin grunted as his body expanded back down into his legs. 'We ... eh, met him here, well, under here, in the sewers. A couple of days ago.'

'Then he is the one they're all looking for,' Hilspeth mused. 'They had him and they didn't even know it. But where is he now?'

'Isn't he in the barracks?' Taya asked.

'He was, but not any more. He seems to have disappeared, along with this guard who was out to get him.'

'We know her. She was found dead last night,' said Lorkrin. 'She'd fallen from one of the towers. Wow, you mean Shessil did that? He's tougher than I thought.'

'Why were you trying to help him?' Hilspeth asked. 'What has all this got to do with you?'

'Well,' Taya said, making a very close study of her feet. 'He has something of ours, something we need to get back. And we sort of owe him. We made him fall into the sewer. And then we gave him a bit of a fright ...'

'A lot of a fright, actually ...' Lorkrin put in with a hint of pride.

'... And he jumped into the river in the sewer and got washed down the drain. The army seem to have been looking for him ever since,' Taya finished.

'I see,' said Hilspeth, in a cold voice. 'And would it be too much to hope for that there is a grown-up that I can deliver you to nearby? Parents? Relatives? Anybody with a sense of responsibility?'

The two Myunans exchanged looks, and Taya answered, 'We're not going anywhere until we find Shessil and make sure he's all right. And we get our quill back.'

'Is that so?' Hilspeth raised her eyebrows at them.

'And you can't make us and you know it,' Taya finished, in a resolute tone.

'Now why would I want you to miss out on all this trouble?' Hilspeth replied. 'It would be a shame if you didn't get your fair share of it. Now, we might have a better chance of finding him if we knew where he came from. He said he had been staying somewhere here in Hortenz. We can bet wherever it was, it will be guarded by soldiers. Whatever he was doing, he was doing it for the government.'

'We met him near here,' Lorkrin offered. 'It was close to the square.'

'That sounds like a good start,' Hilspeth nodded.

It was a short walk, and when they got there, the children showed her the freshly repaired section of wall where Groach had fallen through the ground into the sewer. She went to the end of the wall to see what there was to see. There was the barracks, but she had been in there and was sure that whatever Shessil did, he did not do it there. The damaged wall itself was very high, too high to see over, and ran the length of the square to the side of a large building, surrounding wide, spacious grounds. The building was a manor house of some sort, with three floors and dozens of windows, most with window boxes full of plants. This was a wall made to keep people out ... or perhaps to hold people in. She moved out into the square, followed by the Myunans, to get a better view, and saw soldiers standing to attention by the heavy double doors under the verandah.

'I want to know what they are doing in that house,' she told the two children.

+ + +

Brock Moffet was having a short nap before bedtime. His two-barrelled pipe lay on the hearth, ashes spilled on the slate in front of the fire-grate. Mrs Moffet finished oiling her frying pan and washed her hands with water heated in the kettle. She turned and looked at her man, his head tilted back, mouth open in mid-snore, and shoeless feet propped up on a short stool. On his lap lay a sheaf of vellum pages that Mrs Moffet recognised as having belonged to Shessil, their visitor from up-river. She picked some of them up, straightened them out, and slapped her husband across the head with them.

'Huh! Wha—? Who's there? What?' Moffet struggled his way free of slumber and scowled at his wife. 'What was that for? Can't a man take a nap in his own home in peace, without some biddy taking a shot at him with some gardening documents?'

'These are Shessil's. They are no business of yours, we agreed to keep his things in case he came back. That does not mean we nose through them as if he left them to us.'

'I'm not hurting the man. I was trying to find out who he is.'

'You know who he is. Now put these away and show some respect. What are they about anyway?'

'I told you. Gardening,' he replied huffily.

'Oh aye?' She raised her eyebrows in sudden interest, casting her eyes over the pages. 'What kind then?'

'Gardening under the esh.'

'Now you're being ridiculous as well!' She slapped him with the pages again.

'I'm only telling you what I've *read*, woman!' he protested. 'And what little I understood. It's madness, some of the things he says. The man is some kind of magician with plants I tell you.'

'Well, all the same. You shouldn't be reading his writings. They might be private. Give the rest here.'

Moffet handed the remainder of the notes to his wife, and she put them back in the leather folder that lay on the floor. Shuffling them into place, the rotund woman noticed that one of the quills in the folder was of a different style, and had no cut down the center to channel ink. It was a different shape too, quite the strangest pen she had ever seen. She shrugged and replaced the folder in Shessil's satchel, which they kept now in a drawer in the kitchen dresser. Shessil would return for it, and they would keep it until he did.

+  +  +

Hilspeth watched the guards on the door to the manor house for a while. They would know something about what went on within, but she decided they would get suspicious if she simply walked up and started asking questions. She was wondering what to do next, when another bunch of soldiers came along and relieved them. The first team of guards, now apparently off-duty, made their way across the street to a storyhouse. Hilspeth nodded to herself. Now they would be a bit more relaxed. The storyhouse was a two-storey, brick-and-plaster building with round, latticed windows and a rickety veranda. Vines hung off it, and attracted flies and other insects, as did the man sleeping in its shadows, his head concealed by a large floppy hat, the brim of which fluttered when he snored. The front wall was adorned in animal parts, trophies from a dozen hunts, skins, heads, paws and hooves hung from cords dangling from the veranda posts. Hilspeth wrinkled her nose in disgust at the place as she walked closer. She was about to go in when Lorkrin stopped her.

'You can't, he said. 'Look.'

On a sign by the door were the words 'Men Only'. And then, in case that was not clear enough, beneath it was: 'No Women. No Children.'

'Well, isn't that just typical.' Hilspeth rolled her eyes back. She thought for a moment, and then turned to the others. 'Give me that cloak.'

Lorkrin, who had it rolled up under his arm, handed it to her. She took it and put it on. It had holes in it, a badly worn hem, and it was damp with something – she wasn't sure what.

'Where did you find this?' she asked.

'In a pile of rubbish behind a shop,' Lorkrin replied. 'I don't think anyone in a place like this will notice how bad it looks.'

'Well, let's hope not.' Hilspeth shrugged the cloak into a more comfortable position on her shoulders. Its loose shape hid her figure and her skirt. This way she might pass for a young man.

'Wait, the rest of you looks too clean,' Taya said. She took some dust from the road and rubbed it on Hilspeth's hands and face, and into her hair. The scentonomist growled at having her hair mussed up but she said nothing. The two Myunans studied her for a minute or two.

'Hair still looks too girlie.' Lorkrin said.

'I can't hide it with the hood,' Hilspeth gasped in frustration. Taya took in their surroundings before settling her gaze on the man sitting on the ground against the wall.

'Oh, you must be kidding ...' Hilspeth began, but Taya gently lifted the man's wide-brimmed hat from his head and handed it to her. 'We'll give it back,' she reassured Hilspeth.

Hilspeth exhaled sharply as she bundled her hair up into the hat and pulled it down on her head.

'Forget talking to them, I'll be lucky to get close to them smelling like this.'

'You'll fit right in,' Lorkrin assured her.

'Yeah. Well, whatever. I'm not coming out of there without some answers.'

Hilspeth shifted the hat again slightly and walked through the door and into a large, dark, smoky room filled with rough, mean-looking men sitting on stools around round wooden tables. Not seeing the guards she wanted to talk to, she decided to go up to the bar and order a drink while she took a look around. Excusing herself politely did not get her anywhere, so she kept her arms folded and shouldered her way past, noting that everyone had bigger harder shoulders than her. She got to the bar, and reminded herself that she had to act manly. Sticking out her chin, she called to the landlord in her deepest, gruffest voice:

'By the gods, I've a mouth like a Reisenick's armpit! A flagon of ale, there, sir. Your strongest stuff!'

'Eh?' The man squinted as if it would help him hear better, genuinely puzzled by the request.

'A flagon of ale, please?' Hilspeth's voice faltered. She wasn't sure what men drank in storyhouses. This wasn't her type of place.

'We don't have any flagons, sir. Would a mug do?'

The proprietor was a medium-sized, wiry man, obviously from Traxea, where they had a green tinge to their skin, and six fingers to each hand. He had a very large head with blue-black hair that formed a near-perfect circle round his face, from brow to chin.

'A mug'd be just damned fine.' she replied, only just remembering to keep her tone as gruff as possible.

Afraid that she wasn't expressing enough masculinity, she spat on the floor for good measure. The landlord frowned at the feeble attempt.

'Mind if I ask what age you are, sir?'

Thinking quickly, Hilspeth leaned over and sniffed his breath.

'Older than that whiskey you keep for yourself,' she retorted. 'That's not the cheap, watered-down rubbish I'm smelling off your customers.'

'All right, all right, keep your voice down,' the Traxean muttered.

'A mug of ale, please.'

'Right you are.' With a charming smile, he took a clay mug from line of similar cups hanging from hooks above the bar, and poured some ale into it from a jug beneath the counter.

She thanked him and paid for the drink. She tasted it tentatively and was surprised to find it quite palatable.

A storyhouse was a place where travellers could come and earn a meal, and sometimes even a bed for the night by telling a story. Locals would buy them drinks and tobacco in return for being entertained. The more entertaining the story, the more hospitality the traveller would enjoy. At the tables in the room, men from all over the land were telling tales of adventure, and pranks, and war, and exotic places. Those who kept the customers happy would be offered a place to stay for a few nights by the owners of the house. The room was noisy, and everyone had to talk at the top of their voice to be heard.

'I must say, sir,' the landlord commented, 'you have the cleanest fingernails I've ever seen. They're cleaner than my wife's. How do you keep them so?'

Hilspeth smiled and self-consciously drew her hands back into the cloak. She could see the guards now, quite near her, listening to a Parsinor who was gesturing excitedly with his huge hands to illustrate his account of being chased by a maddened raspidam. A stocky, muscled figure with natural, hinged armour, and webbing holding an assortment of tools and weapons, he commanded a large gathering. She decided to wait for him to finish. She wouldn't get a word in edgeways with him going on like this anyway.

'... so it cornered me in this gully. I had no way out, my axe lost, my sword broken and this thing bearing down on me, drooling, so close now I could smell the stink on its breath from the last man who had crossed it. All six claws reaching out to tear me limb from limb, and I stared it in the eye and screamed my curses at it, and picked up a rock to put up a last fight when ...'

He paused, dramatically to stare around the table at his audience, then lifted his left hand (the right was poised as if holding the aforementioned rock), and whispered hoarsely:

'... it turned its head, just for a heartbeat exposing its ear ...'

At this, some of the men at the table nodded and smiled knowingly, for the ears were the only weak points in a raspidam's thick, hairy hide. The Parsinor roared:

'... and I flung that rock with all my might, hitting it just where the jawbone meets the earlobe! It fell and blocked up the gully, barring my way, weak but still alive. Strong enough still to lunge forward and get its jawblades around me. It bit down, but couldn't break through my armour. We were held together, and it was only stunned. I was dead as soon as it came back to its senses. I thrashed around, but it had no effect. Then, as it started to growl, I tried one last thing in desperation. I took a big bite of its tongue!'

Some men laughed at this; others recoiled in disgust. Hilspeth was beginning to feel mildly sick.

'... That woke it up, but it made it open its mouth as well. It dropped me and let out a roar like this ...' He held his own tongue and bellowed at the top of his voice. 'I could taste its blood and spit in my mouth, bitter and poisonous, but I was free, and I finished it off with another rock to the ear. The thing toppled over like a tree and died noisily. I ate some of the meat, sold the skin and made tools from its bones.'

He finished by smacking his big hand down on the table, and there were cheers and some clapping. In the brief, relative silence that followed while the Parsinor took a gulp of his drink, one voice chipped in:

'Rubbish.'

With that, the entire room fell silent. The Parsinor slammed his mug on the table, and, kicking his stool back, stood up to his full height, which was head and shoulders above anyone else in the room. Hilspeth noticed the four stout legs that ended in only two feet (two legs, one in front of the other, for each foot) and the wide, heavy body that made Parsinors such a formidable race. He glared at the speaker and growled in a voice low with menace;

'Are you calling me a liar?'

It was one of the guards that Hilspeth was hoping to talk to. Her heart sank.

'Only a very poor, desperate liar could come up with such an outlandish tale,' the soldier said. 'You should make yourself scarce, rather than wasting our time with rubbish like that.'

'Sir, I think you should perhaps get behind the bar,' the landlord muttered to her.

'Sorry?'

'I think you might like to get behind the bar,' he urged her again.

'What are you talking about?'

'I'll give you one chance to take that back,' snarled the Parsinor to his accuser.

'Liar,' came the reply.

The landlord seized Hilspeth's cloak and dragged her over the counter just as havoc broke loose. He smiled at her as she landed on the floor beside him, and he motioned at her to keep her head down.

'It's for the best,' he shouted over the crash of bodies and furniture being tossed about the room. 'It'll quieten down soon enough.'

Hilspeth risked a glance over the top of the counter, and saw every man in the room involved in a free-for-all. Men were punching men, who were falling back and bumping into others, whom they hit for being there to bump into. Stools and tables were picked up and used as clubs, as well as anything else that came to hand. Nobody seemed to be taking any sides; they just hit anyone who came along.

Ducking back down again, she found the landlord whittling the broken leg of a stool that had landed beside him. He was making some kind of fish.

'Does this happen a lot?' she asked.

'On occasion.' He shrugged, without looking up from his wood carving.

Holding her hat tight to her head, Hilspeth raised her head to watch the mayhem.

Outside, Taya and Lorkrin listened in amazement to the sounds of the fight.

'She's really serious about getting answers,' Lorkrin gaped.

'I didn't think she had it in her,' his sister added.

The Parsinor aimed the beaten, bruised soldier at a window, intent on throwing him out into the street, but he was knocked into, and the unfortunate man hit the wall instead.

Another came at the storyteller, who side-stepped and brought up his arm, the guard running into it as if it were the low-hanging branch of a tree. His feet swung forward and he dropped square on his back.

A third piled towards the Parsinor, but fared no better. His head clamped in one huge hand, he was lifted off his feet and thrown across the room.

The fourth soldier took no chances. He drew a double-headed axe, and, pushing other brawlers out of his way, he advanced on the bigger man.

The Parsinor was wearing weapons, but he did not pick any. Instead he waited, shoving back the fighters around him and standing his ground. The soldier charged, swinging the weapon with all his strength, but the Parsinor stepped to the side, snatched the axe and spun in a circle, taking his opponent with him. Then he dropped to his knee, flipping the soldier over onto his back and slamming him to the floor. He had his fist raised to deliver the finishing blow, when Hilspeth cried out for him to stop.

The group of brawlers fell into some confusion, and the Parsinor hesitated as he looked around for the source of the female cry.

'There's a woman in here,' someone said.

Suddenly the mood changed to one of annoyed embarrassment, and the men pulled apart and started brushing themselves down. There was the sound of one or two men getting a last thump in, but most were righting tables and straightening stools.

Hilspeth stood up and took off her hat with an apologetic smile. The men mumbled under their breath, and threw sour glances at her. The landlord was very upset.

'Now really, madam. This is most improper. Really, the rules are very specific. This is a men-only house. I'm sure you saw the signs. This is very bad for business, you being here. Really.'

'I'm sorry.' She gave him a tight smile, then said to the Parsinor, 'I really do need to talk to that man before you pulverize him. Seeing as you have already put his three friends beyond reach. Would you mind?'

The Parsinor groaned, but turned the soldier's head to face Hilspeth, asking:

'What do you want to know?'

'Just what kind of work is going on in that house he's guarding?' she said.

'Well?' the Parsinor asked the guard, who considered

refusing, then thought the better of it.

'Just gardening,' he wheezed. 'Loads of people who can grow any kind of plant, they're all doing something to do with bules and the esh ... I don't know what. Don't know what all the fuss is about, to be honest.'

'Is Shessil Groach in there?'

'He's the only one in there, now,' the guard moaned. 'He had escaped, and then he showed up out of nowhere last night. But they shipped all the other freaks back to Noran yesterday, so now he's the only one there. He's being guarded as if he's the Prime Ministrate himself. Don't ask me why. They don't tell us anything. Look, if you don't mind, you're really hurting my head ...'

The Parsinor let him go. He passed out and flopped to the floor.

'Thanks very much,' beamed Hilspeth. 'You've been a great help.'

The Parsinor took a firm but gentle hold on her hand and led her towards the door.

'You shouldn't be here,' he said. 'Let me show you out.'

She could feel everyone's eyes on her back as she walked out, and the Parsinor's grip left her under no illusions that it might be possible to stay around and chat. She was almost hauled to the door. When they stepped outside, Hilspeth tenderly placed the sleeping man's hat back on his head, and turned about to find the two Myunans dumbstruck, gazing up at the Parsinor.

'Aw, bowels!' gasped Lorkrin.

'Young man, where did you pick up language like that?' said the Parsinor in a stern voice. 'And I thought you two were staying at your uncle's this summer?'

# 8 DRAEGAR DOESN'T HELP

The Parsinor's name was Draegar. He was apparently a friend of the Myunans' Uncle Emos and their parents. Hilspeth could not help but notice his lack of surprise at the fact that these two children were wandering around without adult supervision, a couple of days' walk from where they were supposed to be. The two shape-changers had made excuses and pretended to be coy and innocent but he was having none of it. Draegar obviously knew them quite well. He was suspicious of Hilspeth, and did not try to hide it.

'Their uncle will be beside himself with worry,' he rumbled. 'He knows what they're capable of.'

'Do they wander off a lot, then?' Hilpeth asked.

'Stop talking about us as if we're not here,' Taya snapped. 'We're not babies.'

'Normally after they have done something they are likely to be severely punished for,' Draegar supplied.

'Sometimes we wander off just because we want to,' Taya interrupted again. 'What's wrong with that?'

The Myunans were trudging ahead of the other two along the street. Draegar had suggested they start back towards Uncle Emos's farm. The shape-changers had tried to object, but his tone had left scant room for argument. Hilspeth was walking with them as far as the outskirts of town, hoping she might convince the Parsinor to help her get to Shessil.

As they made their way along the street, she had time to get a closer look at him. His shell and the other armoured parts of his body were knobbly and sand-coloured, well suited to the desert where the Parsinor tribes made their home. His skin was a redder shade of the same colour. His eyes were lined with long, curving lashes that she supposed were for keeping out the dust and sand; his nose was quite flat and he could close his nostrils when he needed to. His ears were tiny and they too could close up. His wide skull was covered with thick tendrils of braided hair. His feet, with their two sets of ankles, were long and wide and encased in the same hard shell; his hands and arms were huge, even in proportion to the rest of his body, and you were left in no doubt about his strength. He carried a battle-axe and a broadsword in sheaths on his back.

'Have you any idea what they've done this time?' she pressed. 'I think they've been messing around down in the sewers. There's a chance that Shessil Groach was tangled up in all of this because of them. Couldn't you help? Just help me get inside that building.'

'We didn't do anything!' Lorkrin protested. 'She doesn't know what she's talking about.'

'It gets worse every time.' Draegar shook his head. 'And interfering strangers don't help. You would do well to steer clear of them in the future. They are a mischievous pair of rascals, but Emos is a close friend and I would not have any family of his put in danger by letting them mess with soldiers. The Noranians rule this land, and they are a hard race. They are not people you want to cross. Noranians have no honour; they act out of greed and self-interest, but they have power. You do not. Whatever it is you want from them, these children are not going to be involved. And for your own safety, I suggest you let it go.'

Lorkrin had stopped to look at a stall displaying monstrous animal puppets. Draegar prodded him and he started walking again.

'I can't do that. Shessil is a friend of mine,' Hilspeth continued. 'And they're holding him prisoner. I think he has been a prisoner for years and he doesn't even realise it.'

'Then maybe it would be better if he never did,' Draegar commented.

'I know how he bloody feels,' Lorkrin muttered.

+ + +

Groach sank deep into the suds of the bath and groaned as all the bruises and stiffness faded from his body. He lathered up his face and took a straight razor from the wooden cup on the side, starting at his right sideburn and shaving down his face. He missed the thick beard he had worn before his escape, but it felt good and cool and neat to be clean-shaven. He considered for a moment the possibility of growing a moustache, but decided against it and shaved the stubble off his upper lip with a few short strokes. Botanists wore beards; it was a kind of unspoken rule. Except for the women, of course, unless they were very unfortunate. But he felt he had grown since his escape, that he was something more than just a botanist now.

He thought about Hilspeth, still being held in the barracks. Picturing her lively, brown, freckled face, he wished he could see her again, and hear her voice, and he realised he was frightened for her, locked up in those cells. At least that Grulk was dead. He should have felt sorry for the woman soldier, but he didn't. He wasn't sorry at all.

The other men who had been arrested for looking like him had been released; that only left Hilspeth. But he was sure he could get her let off – she hadn't done anything wrong anyway, and he was quite an important man now. He had made the esh-bound bubule bloom, and now he was being taken home to the project, in the city-state of Noran. This house was conveniently close to the part of the esh where the esh-bound bubule grew, but the main workshops, greenhouses and tanks were in Noran itself.

Apparently, all his friends had already left for the city, and, this evening, he was to be taken to join them. He looked forward to the reunion. He wondered how that stubborn old dog Hovem was doing, and Rufred, and Carston, the lunatic. The stories he had to tell them! They would never believe him. But they would believe him about the Harvest Tide. He would make them believe. Picking up the scrubbing brush and the nailbrush, he played boats in the soapy water.

There were four guards standing around him as he waited in the hallway later in the afternoon for the wagon that would take him to Noran. Six more stood to attention outside. He wondered what all the security was for – surely not for him? It did not make sense.

Mungret walked down the corridor towards him.

'Have you got everything, Shessil? Are there any notes or samples you might need to bring? It's a long drive to Noran.'

'No, I don't think so....' He shifted the rucksack of clothes and the few personal things that he owned on his shoulder. 'We're driving all the way? Isn't it quicker by esh? Oh, I left my notes at the Moffets' house in Crickenob, but I don't need them. I can do without.'

'We'll have them picked up anyway,' Mungret assured him. 'The Moffets did you say? In Crickenob? And to answer your question, the esh is not the safest place to be right now.' He indicated to one of the guards to take Groach's bag. Groach obediently handed the soldier his luggage and found he now had nothing to do with his hands, so he stuck his thumbs in his belt and stared at his feet.

A soldier who was keeping watch at the door gave a signal. Mungret straightened Groach's tunic collar and brushed down his shoulders.

'Now, just act yourself. Don't try and impress him. He doesn't like that. Address him as 'Prime Ministrate', and do not speak when he is speaking. Answer him promptly, and keep your answers short and to the point. Don't make any sudden hand movements – his bodyguard will be watching, and he is very protective. Too protective sometimes. Be polite at all times, and do not raise your voice above a civil speaking tone. Now, go.'

'What are you talking about?' Groach protested. 'Are you telling me I'm meeting the Prime Ministrate? I thought I was going back to Noran.'

'You are going back to Noran with the Prime Ministrate,' Mungret said in his ear as he pushed him out the door. He was led by a soldier out to a waiting carriage. Its door was held open by a huge creature with a mane of orange hair tied back in a ponytail, and three pairs of nostrils, one above the other. It had yellow skin and stark, ice-blue eyes with no pupils. Groach regarded the creature with fear as he clambered inside the vehicle.

'He is a bit of a monster, isn't he?' said a warm voice from the interior of the carriage. 'Don't let Cossock bother you, Shessil. He's a Barian, a frightening-looking brute, but an honourable one. He's a good man to have on our side.'

At the back of the lush, purple, velvet-lined cabin sat a handsome, athletic-looking man in the black and gold robes of government. He shook Groach's hand with a firm grip and motioned him to sit opposite him. The door closed, and through the back window, Groach could see Cossock jump aboard the vehicle. And Cossock could see him. Noticing the smaller man's nervousness, the Noranian leader reached back and closed the curtains on the window, blocking the bodyguard out.

'Do you know who I am, Shessil?'

'Em ... the Prime Ministrate?'

'That's right. I am Rak Ek Namen. I have a lot of titles. If Mungret were here, he would no doubt list them all, but Prime Ministrate is the only one that matters. At least to me.' Namen folded his hands across his lap, and Groach found himself in the full glare of those intelligent eyes.

'You solved the esh-bound bubule problem, didn't you, Shessil?'

'Yes.'

'Did you know Groundsmaster Hovem was dead?'

'What? ... No! What happened? How did he die?'

'A terrible accident. When the bubule in the tank you had been working on bloomed, he tried to lower himself in to take samples. He slipped, smashing the tank in his fall. The whole thing came down on top of him. It was a horrible sight.'

Groach felt a lump rise in his throat. To hide the tears welling in his eyes, he turned to take in the passing buildings that led to the outskirts and walls of Hortenz. He was not sure how to feel. He was shocked; it did not seem real. And it had been his tank. If he had not run away, Hovem might still be alive.

'You mustn't feel responsible,' Namen reassured him. 'It was an accident.'

'I suppose,' Groach whispered.

'He was devoted to the project. He would have wanted you to continue your work.'

'Yes, I suppose he would. Of course, we have to go on.'

'So I can count on you to continue? I can tell we're almost there – it's almost within reach.'

'Yes, it is,' breathed Groach. 'Prime Ministrate, can I ask you a question?'

'Of course, Shessil.'

'What is almost within reach? What is all the work for? What will you do with it?'

'I'm glad you asked,' Namen sat forward and unfolded his hands. 'Let me tell you how it's going to be. Let's talk about the future. I'm sure a man of your intellect will appreciate it.'

+ + +

Taya and Lorkrin were walking ahead of Draegar and Hilspeth. They were both feeling thoroughly miserable. Taya's colour had even turned slightly bluer than normal. Their uncle would be absolutely furious with them when they got back to his house. They were sure to be punished, probably by being made to weed the garden and paint fences and things like that. There always seemed to be loads of work that needed doing whenever they had been up to anything. On top of this, they were beginning to feel ashamed of what they had done to Shessil back in the sewers. Then there was the fact that Shessil still had the quill from Uncle Emos's studio, and that there was a large hole in the town of Hortenz that somebody would have to fix. The more they thought about it, the worse the whole affair seemed, and the worse it seemed, the more they each wished they could do something to make things better.

The sound of heavy engines behind them made the group look back, in time to step off the road into a doorway to get out of the way of a convoy of military vehicles. Two armoured battlewagons passed, followed by a luxurious wooden-panelled coach with a liveried soldier driving, and a huge yellow-skinned warrior sitting on the back, staring at them as he rode past. They were charging out the gate in the town wall ahead, at high speed.

'There's Shessil!' exclaimed Taya over the noise of the wagons. Lorkrin and the others followed her pointing finger and sure enough, there he was, visible through the window of the coach.

'That's the Prime Ministrate's vehicle,' Draegar told them. 'This is the main road to Noran. They'll be taking him back to the city.'

'We have to help him,' Hilspeth urged him, her voice tinged with desperation.

She was surprised at the passion she was feeling. Shessil was little more than a stranger to her, and she wasn't sure she even liked him that much, and he was definitely a bit odd for her taste. But he was interesting too, and she couldn't deny that seeing him stand up to that soldier with nothing but a pot of tea had made an impression.

'You do what you like,' Draegar answered. 'The children are going back to Emos. If you're smart, you'll leave well enough alone, get on with your life and let your friend get on with his. You are not cut out for crossing the Noranians.'

'How noble of you,' Hilspeth smiled bitterly. 'I'm touched by your concern.'

Draegar said nothing. His face was impassive as he watched the last of the convoy roar past.

The two children carried on walking. Taya caught a look on her brother's face as his eyes followed the dust cloud of the vehicles.

'Are you thinking what I'm thinking?' she asked, careful that the two grown-ups behind them did not hear.

'We wouldn't have a hope of getting him out,' Lorkrin mumbled as if trying to convince himself of something. 'I wonder why he's so important. Didn't look very important to me.'

'We might be able to help him escape with Draegar's help,' his sister pondered aloud.

'Except that Draegar just wants to take us home.'

'We'd go home afterwards. It's just this thing we have to do first.'

'Right, but *he* won't see it that way.' Lorkrin shook his head. 'Although, we would be sort of doing it for our honour, wouldn't we? He's always talking about honour. Especially when it's about him getting into fights. Maybe he'd understand.'

'Yeah, he's always getting into fights over honour. Why not this time?'

'Aww ... he'll never go for it, Taya.'

'No. But if we tried it anyway, he'd help, wouldn't he?'

Lorkrin regarded his sister with narrowed eyes.

'You mean, if we were rescuing Shessil and Draegar just happened to be there, he'd have to help us to rescue Shessil?'

'Right.'

'But we'd have to get him there first. He'd never just let us follow the wagons.'

'No,' Taya continued. 'But if we catch up with the wagons, he'll have to catch up with us.'

'And this road winds about a lot. If we go across country, we should be able to get ahead of them.'

'Right.'

'Right.' They walked on in silence for a bit.

'So,' Taya clucked her tongue, 'how do we get away from Draegar?'

Now that she knew where Shessil was heading, Hilspeth carried on out of the town with the others. She would walk as far with them as possible. Despite not wanting to involve the two young Myunans, she still hoped she could persuade Draegar to help her. They were now passing through a corn-field, the corn on either side of the road almost as high as her head, and the wind rustled gently among the stalks with a whispering noise. Ahead of them, a large flock of sheep was coming down the road, guided by a stout shepherdess and her three dogs. Draegar and Hilspeth moved to the side to let them pass, but the two children, walking a good way out in front, stayed in the middle of the road. Draegar called out to them to move aside for the animals, annoyed that they should be so rude, but just as he did, they ducked down into the flurry of bleating wool that filled the road from one side to the other.

The Parsinor stopped when he saw this, and waited for the two shape-changers to reappear. When they did not, he strode towards the sheep. Wading into the flock, he searched ever more frantically for the children. But he found nothing, and let out a bellow of frustration. The sheep panicked and scattered in all directions, dashing into the tall cover of the corn. Draegar tried to catch sight of the Myunans, defying the shepherdess who was hurling abuse at him.

'You stinking pig's bladder!' she shouted at him while whistling directions to her dogs. 'Raised on a vegetable patch, were you? Sand in the skull – it's the same with all you bleedin' Parsinors!'

'Madam ...'

'Don't you madam me, slug-breath. It's market day today, and thanks to you I may have nothing to sell,' – a pause to give a whistle – 'you drizzle of ditch-water...'

'Madam,' Draegar was struggling to get a word in, while still searching for the two escapees.

'... like something that was dragged from the bottom of a bog, if you ask me,' – whistle and a yodel – '... stupid and pig-ugly to boot, cost me my stock, will you? You great lump of dried manure.'

'Shut up, you old bat!' Hilspeth barked. 'The man is trying to apologise.'

The shepherdess, her greying hair askew, and wrinkled face like a crumpled paper bag, stopped in mid-insult as if she were only noticing Hilspeth for the first time. Draegar, who had given up trying to find the shape-changers, took advantage of the relative silence.

'Madam, I am very sorry for the trouble I have caused. I

will, of course, help you get your sheep back. Though I must say that you have a mouth like a sewer, I am not a man who shirks responsibility for his actions. Please forgive me my mistake.'

The woman uttered some crude grunt, then, avoiding his earnest expression, she stiffly nodded her head. Draegar gazed helplessly out across the cornfields at the lines of movement that marked dozens of straying sheep and, somewhere, a couple of straying young scamps, and he sighed. Turning to Hilspeth, he told her:

'Just so you know. I blame you for this.'

Hilspeth rolled her eyes and snorted.

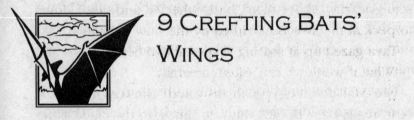

# 9 CREFTING BATS' WINGS

Lorkrin and Taya lay on their stomachs and watched the convoy driving away from them down the valley below. They had been giving chase all afternoon, and it was proving more difficult than they had expected to get ahead of the Noranians. Although the vehicles were not especially fast – they could be outstripped by a fast horse – they did not tire, and the same could not be said for the two Myunans. The two would-be rescuers had thought they could catch up on the wagons by going cross-country, but they were still far behind.

'We're not going to make it if this goes on,' Lorkrin grunted. He was fiddling with his hand, sculpting his fingers into octopus tentacles.

'I'm not just going to give up,' said his sister.

'I didn't *say* I was giving up. It just doesn't look good, that's all.'

They lapsed into silence once more, alone with their thoughts. Taya turned over onto her back and stared at the sky. They were lying in the low undergrowth at the top of a hill, a herd of ornacrids chewing weaving trails through the scrub nearby. Above them, birds wheeled and dived down to peck at the insects disturbed by the slow animals.

Taya gazed up at soaring shapes above her.

'What if we flew?' she asked, dreamily.

'We'd fall and die,' Lorkrin answered. 'Limstom tried it last year, remember? He got way up, almost to the clouds, and then lost it. I still hear the sound when I think of it. He hit the ground so hard they had to roll him up to carry him back to the village. And he was two years older than us.'

'We're better than he was. I talked to his sister after. She said he never could get the hang of crefting properly.'

'Well, he'll never get the hang of it now, and I for one can wait to learn flying properly. I have no intention of dying as a Lorkrin-shaped carpet.'

'Can you think of a better way?' Taya pressed.

There were many stages of study for a shape-changer. The ultimate aim was to be able to mimic any creature, and mastering amorphing was considered an art. Myunans had unique flesh that could take almost any shape, but sculpting that flesh into different forms was a skill that took years of hard training to attain. Their parents and their Uncle Emos were considered artists among their peers. Flying was one of the more advanced accomplishments, as a person needed first to achieve a suitable form, and then to grasp the principles of flying itself. Neither Taya nor Lorkrin had ever been taught it, and their few attempts had been only as part of simple gliding games with their friends. To catch the convoy they would have to fly high and fast, assuming they could get up at all. Lorkrin contemplated this as the dust cloud marking the passage of the wagons drew further and further away.

'Okay,' he said. 'Let's try it.'

They unwrapped their bundles of tools and picked out the ones they would need. Then they let their bodies go soft, making them into living modelling clay. Gravity did the first bit of the shaping for them, their torsos sinking down to mix with their legs. They allowed their legs to shorten, then tooled and tensed them into shape. Then they crefted, holding the form once they had achieved it. With their legs done, that left a loose slab of flesh from their hips to their shoulders. They gathered bulk around their chests and stomachs, moulding the strong, broad chests they would need to take the strain of flight on their bodies. Then they started on the wings.

They did not even consider trying to mimic birds. Even the best Myunans in the world found feathers difficult. They were too big to use insects' wings, and could not generate enough hot air to glide like balloon fish or esh floaters, so they settled on bats' wings. They had to help each other, as it was hard to sculpt your own arms and shoulders. But eventually they had their new forms finished. The final touch was added, each of them smoothing their head back into a long, sleek shape, before they made their way to the edge of the hill for take-off.

'Want to go first?' Lorkrin prompted.

'No, you can go first if you like.'

'This was your idea.'

'Yes. I came up with the idea, so now it's your turn. You have to try it out,' Taya said primly, pleased with her logic.

'Okay, I'll do it. But only because you're scared,' retorted Lorkrin.

'I am not. I just don't see why I should do all the work.'

'Scaredy-cat!' her brother taunted, spreading his wings

and wiggling the little claws at the bend in the joints.

'I am not!'

Lorkrin clucked like a chicken and Taya charged at him. He giggled and set off down the hill, both of them flapping their wings to keep their ungainly bodies balanced as they ran. Then, without meaning to, Lorkrin took off. He let out a yelp and pushed down with his wings in reflex. The push lifted him further into the air and his heart slammed up into his throat. Taya wobbled into the air behind him with a squeal. Lorkrin struck out strongly for a few moments and then lost his rhythm, thrashing in a panic instead of flapping smoothly. He lost control, and felt himself slip down through air. Screaming, he fell.

He hit the slope and rolled, folding his delicate wings to protect them, and bouncing down the grassy hill. He skidded to a halt and lay there on his back, panting. Taya sailed over him:

'Are you all right?' she called, gliding into a turn to get a closer look at him.

'I'm fine,' he snapped, more embarrassed than hurt.

'This is easy!' she shouted. 'We should have tried this ages ago!'

Lorkrin snorted and picked himself up.

'You need to keep calm. Don't rush things,' she cried down to him. With that, she went into a steep turn too slowly and dived straight into the ground. Lorkrin burst out laughing, but then stopped when his sister did not get up.

'Taya!' He sprinted over to her as fast as his short legs could carry him.

Taya had landed head-first in a patch of deep mud. She was stuck in up to her chest. Stunned and unable to breath, she was struggling weakly. She could not push herself free because of her wings, which scrabbled uselessly on either side of her. Lorkrin grabbed her feet and yanked her out. Taya coughed a few times and dragged air into her lungs.

'How's your head?' he asked.

Taya wiped mud from her eyes and nose, and spat mud out of her mouth. Her long, sharp face was coated in the stuff. She wiped it clean clumsily with her wing and sat down, tears welling in her eyes.

'This was a stupid idea,' she grumbled miserably. 'This is all just stupid. How are we going to rescue Shessil anyway? He's got soldiers and all those people around him. We should go home.'

Lorkrin sat in front of her and said nothing. He was very close to thinking the same thing, except that he had seen his sister flying. If they could fly, he thought, they could do anything.

'My head's sore,' she continued at last. 'But I don't think I really hurt anything.'

Because Myunans could turn their bodies to something near jelly at will, it took more than a bit of a fall to injure them. But even Myunans bruised. Lorkrin could see that Taya was going to have a fabulous black eye. At least she could hide it a bit by changing the colour of her skin. It was something Lorkrin was not so good at. He was better at mimicking dangerous or disgusting creatures – a gift his mother despaired over.

'I want to try again,' he urged her. 'You had it there for a bit. I think we can do it.'

Taya shuffled her wings and looked away.

'One more go each. We'll keep really low,' he said. 'If you

still want to stop then, we'll catch up on the wagons some other way. We can't just give up, Taya. Draegar says the Noranians torture their prisoners, and we know they kill people all the time. I don't even want to think about what they're doing to Shessil ... and it's our fault he ran into those soldiers.'

Taya did not move at first, but then she lifted her head up and clambered to her feet.

'You're right. Let's try again. I'll go first.'

Without another word, she jogged down the slope, wings striking out and down, lifting off and touching back down again until she had gathered speed, and then she was off. Flying a hundred paces, she dipped to the left, turning in a half circle and landed again, stumbling to a halt in front of him.

'Stay low, keep your feet back and your head up,' she told him. 'Mind the updraft off the hill – it catches you as you turn in to land.'

Lorkrin sighed to himself. His sister was back to her old self again; two flights and she was an expert. Bracing himself for the effort, he trotted down the hill and pushed down with hard beats of his wings. Then he was airborne again, more relaxed and careful this time. He felt his rhythm go for a moment, a sharp drop that flipped his stomach and made him flail with his feet, but he caught the updraft and glided on the rising air. The lift gave him a chance to get his timing back. With the wind rushing in his ears, Lorkrin swooped low across the grass and howled with delight. Taya cheered him on, then took off herself and gave chase around the top of the hill. The two Myunans played in the fading evening light, forgetting everything else in the giddy joy of flight.

+ + +

Groach rocked with the movement of the cabin, the engine revving loudly as it tackled a hill. He was still trying to come to terms with all that the Prime Ministrate was telling him. The Noranian leader had been talking for so long, Groach had hardly noticed the sun setting. Now it was dark and they were passing through a town, he could hear dogs barking and saw the silhouettes of people at lit windows as they peered out to see the noisy vehicles that passed their houses. He numbly watched it all roll by.

Rak Ek Namen had described a different world to him. The Prime Ministrate had big plans for Noran and the lands around it. He had said the war with the Kartharic Peaks would soon be fought and won, and that with that victory would come a time of peace. Science would take its rightful place over the traditions of old. Used wisely, it would put an end to hunger; farms would produce more food than the world could eat. Machines would change life forever, speeding up work and carrying loads no animal could bear.

The Prime Ministrate's face had a fervent expression as he spoke of his dreams. He had laboratories and workshops all over Noran, where scientists and inventors were at work, creating things that would change the world, devices that would allow people to talk over vast distances, and flames that burned ice cold to keep food fresh. Rumours came from across the world of wood that was stronger than steel, steel that was lighter than silk, even seashells that could capture music and play it again and again. He envisioned crops that grew in any season, fields that could be rolled up and turned over instead of having to plough them and weather birds that could carry bags of chemicals into the clouds to make it rain, or make it stop raining.

All of this spun through Groach's thoughts, dazzling him as he tried to remember what it was he had meant to ask the Prime Ministrate. It did not matter. He sank back into the deep-red cushions and let the dreams of the future wash over him. Noran would be a wonderful, enlightened, exciting place, and he was going to be part of it.

The rocking of the coach had been lulling him into a sleep, sleep that he welcomed as it weighed him down with its covers. Rak Ek Namen had opened a hamper while he had talked, and they had eaten crusty sandwiches, crisp salads and an assortment of pies, all of which were followed by honey and almond cake with fresh cream and sugared wafers. The food had been accompanied by a bottle of wine, and the whole lot had left him feeling like a very round stomach with some small limbs and a heavy head attached.

He was just on the point of falling asleep when the coach made a tight turn and rumbled to a halt. The engine cut out, and he was startled by the sudden silence. The chill night air flooded in when the door was opened, and the Prime Ministrate climbed down and beckoned him out, standing aside as he clambered sleepily down the steps. It was cold out, and he was sorry to leave the warmth of the cabin, longing now for the sleep that had just been taken from him. He saw a massive gate being swung shut behind them. They were within the walls of some kind of fortress. A small party of servants stood waiting.

Namen waved to one of the aides, a smartly uniformed man with bright eyes and a warm smile.

'This is Shessil Groach. He is a very special young man. I

want him shown every hospitality.'

Namen turned to Groach:

'I have to leave you now. Bertley here will show you to your room and make sure you have everything you need. Good night, Shessil. Sleep well. We have a long journey ahead of us tomorrow.'

With that, he strode away, pursued by a small crowd of advisors and officials. Left suddenly among complete strangers, Groach sank into dismay. Bertley took his bag and gestured towards a nearby building that illuminated the night's gloom with the warm yellow light from its windows and open doorway.

'Welcome to Tabanark, Mr Groach.'

They were in the grounds of a keep, the yard around him encircled by high walls. The keep itself loomed over them, five floors high not including the battlements. But it was warm inside and he was led up a flight of stairs along a luxuriously carpeted corridor to a door where Bertley stopped. He opened it and ushered Groach inside.

To someone who had spent all his life in humble, simple, living quarters, the room was a place fit for the gods. A polished, hardwood floor was almost completely covered by a thick rug, paintings hung from the stone walls, and the narrow latticed windows had panes of coloured glass in patterns of dancing figures. The furniture was dark, varnished and exquisitely carved. The bed was a huge four-poster affair, with curtains and richly woven blankets. He pulled the covers back to reveal silk sheets. It was all slightly overwhelming. He took off his shoes and stood wiggling his toes in the deep rug.

'Is there anything you need, sir?' Bertley enquired.

Groach shook his head.

'Then I'll wish you good night.' Bertley laid his bag on one of the chairs and retreated from the room with a bow.

Groach twirled slowly, his hands by his sides, taking in all the details in a daze. He had never been in a room like it. With heavy eyelids, he undressed, pulled on his nightshirt and flopped onto the enormous bed, burying himself under the covers. He felt half-dead with tiredness, but found he could not settle. The strangeness of the room was part of it, he supposed, as he lay awake, staring up at the drapes above him. But it was also his thoughts – things he could not work out in his head.

He gave a start when he felt the bed shudder, and a rumble sounded deep below him. As he leapt out of bed, the floor continued to tremble beneath his feet. He ran to the door and looked out. A servant boy was passing, carrying a pile of laundry that he could barely see over.

'You there!' Groach called. 'Do you hear that?'

The boy stopped, and regarded him with a look of scorn.

'Of course I do,' he snorted and carried on his way with his washing.

Taking this as a sign that tremors and rumbling were a part of life in this keep, Groach peered up and down the corridor to see if anyone else was panicking, and turned to go inside. He paused, then crept tentatively out into the hallway to a table at the end. On it stood a rubber plant. Picking it up, he walked back to his room and shut the door. He set the rubber plant on his bedside table and got back into bed.

'You're not going to believe what's happened to me over the last few days,' he murmured to it. Then he began telling the plant all about it. Before long, he was fast asleep.

# 10 THE MARK OF THE SCURG

Hilspeth awoke to the chirping of birds in the tree above her. She was lying on a bed of moss, under her cloak. Rolling onto her back, she gazed up at the shelter of thin branches, woven with twigs and broad leaves, that stood over her. Draegar had made her this lean-to last night with a quick, practised ease. He did not need shelter himself. On lying down to sleep, he had simply curled up to form a protective dome around himself with his armour. From the shade of her lean-to, Hilspeth could see that the Parsinor was already awake. Sitting on a rock in the morning sunlight, he appeared to be drawing something.

The scentonomist stretched and sat up, putting on her shoes and brushing her long, thick, red hair with her fingers, before tying it back in a ponytail with a piece of string. She got to her feet and walked over to Draegar, enjoying a jaw-stretching yawn on the way. He was working on a piece of vellum, a fine, smooth bit of leather, which he had pinned onto a small board that sat on his knees. Hilspeth came around beside him, head tilted to one side to get a better look, and was surprised to see that he was working on a map. It was beautiful, with fine line drawings to indicate the terrain; trees, hills and valleys with rivers drawn in blue ink, and black lines to describe the banks on either side. Names were labelled in a flowing script and, in some places, he had drawn examples of animals to be found in the area, a few with warnings about their fierceness.

Hilspeth was taken aback by the grace and precision with which he drew. His big fingers made the quill look little more than a hair, yet he guided it across the page with an artistic skill that belied the size of his club-like hands.

'It's wonderful,' she said.

He looked up at her, but said nothing. On the map, she could see the road they had been travelling along and the grove of trees where they had stopped. There was a well in the grove behind her and that too was clearly marked.

'So,' she chirped, trying to make conversation, 'you're a cartographer.'

'I am not,' he grunted. 'Are you blind? I'm a map-maker.'

Hilspeth saw no point in arguing. She tried a different tack.

'Have you any thoughts on how to catch up on the convoy before Taya and Lorkrin?'

'Yes.'

Hilspeth waited, but he did not say any more.

'Would you care to share them?' she pressed, smiling tightly.

'In time,' he replied.

'Well, aren't we in a hurry?'

'Yes, but first we must wait.'

Hilspeth bridled at his curt tone, but she held her peace.

'I'm going to make some breakfast, then. Would you like some?'

'I've already eaten, thank you.'

Hilspeth turned on her heel and strode off. It did not take her long to find some barl root, potatoes, basil and some sausage beans. She lit a fire, and while the flames built up, she grated the potatoes, ground up the barl root and chopped the basil. She emptied the floury root powder and the basil, with the beans, into a pot she borrowed from Draegar. That all got mixed with water from the well, and would make a nice soup. The grated potatoes she made into hash browns, frying them on a pan with some more of the sausage beans. A few drops from a couple of the bottles from her waistcoat and the food was starting to smell delicious. Even Draegar was glancing over at the fire.

'Sure you won't have some?' she called.

'No, thank you.' He turned his attention back to his map.

Hilspeth shrugged, and tucked into her food. When she was finished, she cleared up and went back to watching Draegar draw. He had almost finished. The vellum was filled with a clear description of the lands around them, some of which they had passed through, some that he must have been drawing from earlier memories.

'Is that where the children's uncle lives?' she asked, nodding at a point marked 'Farm of Emos Harprag'.

'Yes.'

'He must be so worried. Where do you think he is now?'

The Parsinor dipped his quill in a small jar of water by his side and wiped it clean with a cloth.

'I don't know. But he will not rest until he finds them. Those two mean everything to him, not just because he loves them ... and he does, despite the chaos they cause, but also because their parents are the only Myunans whom he can still count as friends. He was exiled from his tribe years ago.'

'What do you mean? Is he a criminal or something? Why was he cast out?'

Draegar studied her for a moment, as if deciding what to tell her, then put the board with the map on the ground.

'It is a tragic story. Have you ever heard of the Scurg?' he asked.

'I think so. It's some kind of Myunan disease, isn't it?' Hilspeth frowned as she tried to remember where she had heard the term before.

'It was the worst plague to hit the Myunan race in generations,' Draegar rasped. 'The disease killed thousands. It would probably have killed many more, if the people were not nomads by nature. If they had lived in towns and cities, the entire race might have been wiped out.

'It is a horrible sickness, only affecting Myunans. It causes them to lose control of their bodies, the way they transform. It is an ugly, painful death. The victim starts to change shape. They stretch and swell and twist until they are distorted into a tortured wreck of what they once were. Myunans can take almost any kind of form, but they still have to drink and eat and breathe. Eventually, the disease contorts them into a shape that blocks their mouth and nose, and they die. There is no known cure. All you can do is comfort them and watch them pass away.

'The plague was already in its second year when Emos's wife, Wyla, became sick. She was standing outside their lodge one day, when she went to step forward. Her foot caught on something and she fell over. When she looked to see what she had tripped on, she discovered that her foot had grown roots. She was stuck to the ground. She called Emos, but she already feared the worst.

'They had to listen, crying in each other's arms, as the tribe's healer told them what they did not want to hear – she had caught the Scurg. The whole tribe had to be moved away at once, lest the disease spread to others. She was branded with the mark of the plague – a tattoo on her face, and Emos took their lodge down and rebuilt it around her. I could not catch the disease as I was not a shape-changer, and Wyla and I begged Emos to get away, telling him that I would tend to her. But he would not leave his wife.

'It was around the fourth or fifth day that he went away, and came back with scrolls on transmorphing. This is a kind of magic once practised among the Myunans, where they direct their shape-shifting abilities outwards, changing things around them. Transmorphing is forbidden among the Myunans, and his attempts to learn it did not go down well with the tribe. They thought Wyla should be left to die with dignity. Emos did not accept this. He practised day and night, at the same time struggling to keep Wyla comfortable as her condition got worse. But he did not discover a cure. It lasted over three weeks, and in her last days, there was nothing left of Wyla – she was unrecognisable. Even her voice had changed into something strange and horrible.

'I stayed with him all that time. He made me promise that if he showed any signs of the disease, I was to leave them both. But he never did. And when the elders of the tribe came to tell him that he had exposed himself to the plague for too long, that he was sure to have caught it as well, he was too distraught to argue. Wyla was almost dead. They branded him, too, with the mark of the plague.

'But I can tell you now, whether it was a quirk of nature, or all the transmorphing he had experimented with in the weeks of Wyla's sickness, that he did not catch that disease. But the tribe would not believe that he was safe. They thought that, even if he was immune to the Scurg, he might still carry it. He was exiled from the tribe, driven away out of fear. Only Taya and Lorkrin's parents still trusted him; their mother is his sister and Wyla was her best friend. After the years Emos spent wandering the land, sometimes with me, sometimes on his own, Taya and Lorkrin's parents helped him set up the farm where he lives now. They secretly bring the two little terrors to visit whenever they can. But he still bears that brand, the mark of the plague, and it was put there by Myunans, so he can't hide it by changing shape or colour – it always shows through. And that brand terrifies Myunans still.'

'His whole life taken away.' Hilspeth shook her head. 'I can't imagine what that would do to a person.'

'It's almost time to go,' Draegar told her, packing his things into his satchel.

Hilspeth followed him over to the well, where he peered down into the inky depths. She didn't like the look of this. He seemed to be gauging the distance.

'We're not going down there, are we?'

'Yes.'

'How is the well going to help us catch up on Taya and Lorkrin?' she enquired.

'The wells in this area are known for the purity of the water,' Draegar informed her. 'Very few people ask why. If they should, they would find the answer fascinating.'

'I'm sure I would as well.' Hilspeth laughed nervously.

'But as long as the answer lies down at the bottom of a well, I could stand not knowing.'

'Are you scared of small, enclosed spaces?'

'Well, actually, *petrified* would be closer to the truth.'

'It is the only way I know that we can catch up with your friend.'

'Couldn't we just walk very fast? Isn't there a short cut we could take?'

'Yes, there is. We're taking it. We haven't much time. Either you come with me now, or you stay here and find your friend in Noran, if you can.'

The well was a mud-brick structure about waist high, with the bucket tied to a post beside it. Draegar undid the knot and tied it around a nearby tree instead. Then he lowered himself over the side and disappeared inside, barely fitting down the narrow sinkhole. Hilspeth looked in after him, saw him sliding down the rope into the darkness and shut her eyes. How badly did she want to help Shessil? He didn't seem too unhappy with his life – a life spent imprisoned doing work that amounted to slavery. The memory of his face, his smile, gave her courage. She wanted to see his face again.

Taking out a handkerchief, Hilspeth threw her cloak over her shoulders, and climbed onto the wall of the well. She wrapped the hankie around the rope and gripped it firmly, then let herself down into the well, eyes tightly closed once more. With her feet against the wall, she half slid, half walked her way down. As she got further down, her hands began to cramp, and she had to hang from one and then the other to unclasp them and stretch them until the pain eased off. Even with the handkerchief, they were starting to burn.

Further down, her feet slipped and she hit the wall. Without meaning too, she looked down, but found that opening her eyes made no difference. She could not see a thing. The top was a bright white circle far above her. There was not enough space. She felt trapped and she began to panic. Struggling to get her feet back up against the wall, she lost her grip on the rope and fell.

She hit water with an almighty splash, and thrashed upwards even as she went under. Her head broke the surface and she screamed before drawing breath. A strong hand caught hold of her and held her up. She hugged the Parsinor until her panic had died down, and then pushed herself away, much to his relief. Looking around, she could see they were in an underground cavern, a deep stream disappearing in both directions. Draegar was holding a glass jar with a glowing liquid in it. It gave off a yellow-green light that showed Hilspeth just enough to know that she should not be here. She was trembling and she could not think. She had enough of her wits about her to be embarrassed by this. She prided herself on being able to handle most things, but she did not want Draegar to know that she was close to tears.

'Wh— wh— what do we do now?' she hissed through gritted teeth.

'We wait to be cleaned up,' came the answer.

Hilspeth wondered if Draegar had suddenly developed a sense of humour, but the odds were against it. He saw her trembling, and realised that she needed something to think about.

'The network of rivers and streams that run under this area is home to Vusquids. They do not eat. Instead, they get their energy from running water, much like a mill. To keep the water flowing as smoothly as possible, they keep it clean of mud, driftwood, people's rubbish, and anything else that might slow it down and leave them with less movement to feed off.'

'What has this got to do with us?' Hilspeth muttered, her eyes closed again.

'As long as we are here, we are interfering with the flow of the water. We had to wait because they do not travel through this section until late morning. A Vusquid will detect the change in the water and hurry down this tunnel. It will pick us up and take us to the nearest point that it can get us out. That is a day's travel in a northerly direction, near the road to Noran. Of course, it won't take us a day. The Vusquids clean very quickly indeed.'

'How do you know all this? I've never even heard of Vusquids.'

'Because a few years ago, Emos and I mapped their entire territory.' Draegar grinned, showing his bad, yellow teeth. 'That was an interesting bit of travelling, I can tell you.'

Still not sure what to expect, Hilspeth caught her breath as she heard something coming their way. It was big – of that she was sure. Peering up the tunnel, she could see the white froth of disturbed water in the poor light. It was heading in their direction. Draegar turned to face it.

'Don't worry. Vusquids are friendly. It won't harm us. It just wants us out.'

A sleek shape emerged from the water in front of them. It had four short tentacles around its flat face, with four eyes positioned just behind them. Two fins stood out from its back, two along each side, and when it moved, Hilspeth could see there were another two along its belly. It was hard to tell its colour in this light, but it appeared to be a bluish grey. It had no nose or mouth that she could see. Its tail was flat and wide, and had holes lining it top and bottom. Long thin tendrils stood out on all sides, never losing touch with the walls of the cavern. It studied them both for a moment, and then curled its tentacles around them. Hilspeth gasped, but Draegar patted her shoulder.

'It'll be all right. Just enjoy the ride.'

Before she had a chance to point out the likelihood of this, they were off. The thing stayed above the water so that they could breathe, but it tucked them in tight to its body. At first, its tail seemed to be pushing them along using a normal waving motion, but then Hilspeth saw jets of water blast from the holes along the edge and then they were rushing along with breathtaking speed.

'Beats walking!' roared Draegar, over the rumble of their passage through the water.

Hilspeth clung on tightly and waited for it all to be over.

+ + +

The soldiers marched with purpose. It was at once a frightening and impressive sight to the residents of Crickenob. The squad of twenty Noranian men and women moved in perfect time; they could march like this all day.

When the squad turned off the main street and up the road that led towards the river, people came out of their houses to see where they were going. The troops stopped outside the Moffets' house, and rumours started flying. All of the villagers knew that some relative or other of the Moffets had been arrested a few days earlier. Some knew that the man was no relation at all.

Mrs Moffet had already seen the soldiers and unlatched the door to save it from being smashed off its hinges. Instead it slammed hard against the wall when Forward-Batterer Wulms drove his shoulder into it. He was followed into the room by four soldiers.

'What's going on here?' Mrs Moffet demanded. 'There's not a door that is safe when you lot are around.'

'Where is your husband, madam?'

'Down at the river, earning a living. You should try it some-time.'

'You are charged with holding a fugitive from justice. These charges may be waived if you produce the documents he was carrying when he came here,' Wulms announced, battle-hammer held at the ready.

'I don't know what you're talking about,' she barked back.

'I advise you not to waste my time, madam,' Wulms growled. 'I don't want to arrest you, but I will if I have to. The man who attacked one of our soldiers recently was staying here. He has told us that he left notes here. We are to retrieve them and bring them to Noran. If you do not tell us where they are, then I will have no choice but to search this building, take what we find, arrest you and your husband, and burn this house to the ground. Now, where are the documents?'

'If our guest wants them, then let him come and collect them himself,' Brock Moffet snapped from behind them, having rushed back to his home. 'They are his property after all.'

'Restrain him,' Wulms said. Two soldiers pushed Moffet up against the wall beside the open door and a third fired his crossbow at the fisherman's foot. A U-shaped bolt embedded itself with a thud in the floor across his instep and pinned his foot to the floor. There was a crack as the impact broke a bone in his foot and he cried out in pain. He could not fall over because the trapped foot kept him pressed against the wall. Instead, he braced himself with the other leg and clutched the injured one to hold himself steady.

'Leave him alone!' his wife squealed. 'I'll give you the notes. For the love of the gods, just leave him be. Anything to get you bullying wretches out of our lives!'

She went to the kitchen dresser and took the leather satchel from the drawer. With an expression of disgust, she tossed it at the Forward-Batterer.

'Is this all of it?' he asked, snatching it out of the air.

'What,' she retorted. 'You think we want you to come back? Take it and leave.'

'If there is anything missing, we will come back, madam, be sure of that.'

'Why aren't you off fighting a battle somewhere, Forward-Batterer? Or are you not up to fighting alongside *real* soldiers? I expect pushing unarmed fishermen around is more your level.'

Wulms went a deep red, and looked about to hit her, but obviously thought the better of it. Waving to the others, he strode out of the house.

'Hey!' Mrs Moffet shouted after him. 'What about Brock? Aren't you going to cut him free?'

'Any good blacksmith or carpenter will manage it, given a little time,' the Forward-Batterer called back. 'Time you might spend thinking about how you should talk to officers of the Noranian Armed Forces.'

She watched them march away, lips firmly pressed together. When they were out of sight around the corner, she released a small sob and turned back to the front door of her home.

'Filliess, what's happened? What was all that about?' One of her neighbours was scuttling up the street, half concerned, half eager for gossip.

'Fetch Quilliam,' Mrs Moffet told her. 'They've left Brock bolted to the floor. He's hurt – a broken foot, I think – so we'll need a treater as well. See who you can find.'

The other woman nodded and spun around, hurrying towards the small crowd that was gathering, and shouting orders. Filliess Moffet drew in a shaky breath and went back in to her husband. He was in agony from the pressure of the iron hoop over his foot, and was struggling to stay standing. If he fell with his foot held like that, he would snap his ankle. She let him lean on her shoulder, and held his head, kissing his cheek and pressing her face against his.

'What was all that for?' he gasped. 'All that ... for some notes ... what was it for?'

'I don't know, my dear,' she hushed him. 'Quilliam's on the way; he'll have you free in no time. Just you hold on, now.'

'I don't understand these people,' he said. 'Really I don't.'

# 11 THE VUSQUID AND THE DOG-PEOPLE

Groach awoke to the sound of women singing. He opened his eyes, and was confused at first by what he saw: the large room with beautiful furniture and the morning light bursting through the stained-glass windows. He blinked and rubbed gummed-up eyelids while his thoughts returned to the night before. He was on his way back to Noran with the Prime Ministrate. They were staying overnight in a keep called Tabanark. He had never known such luxury. The bed was huge and soft, and he just wanted to go on sleeping in it. But he also wanted to know where the singing was coming from. It was sad, but uplifting, and the voices were sublime.

Jumping out of bed, he threw off his nightshirt and hurriedly got dressed. He was on his way out the door when he remembered the rubber plant. Picking it up off the bedside table, he left it back on the table in the hall where he had found it, and made his way off after the beautiful voices. He had got down to the ground floor when they stopped. He halted in mid-step, disappointed that he had missed them, but then they started to sing again, another song with a happier theme. He followed the sound along a corridor and into a huge reception room where Rak Ek Namen sat in a gilt-lined, velvet chair, listening to two young ladies and an older woman, evidently their mother, singing in the direction of a fan of delicate hairs, which moved gently with the sound of the women's voices.

The other end of the fan was attached to a device made up of brass cogs, levers and wheels, along with a mechanical hand that held a quill. A metronome kept time, and a rubber tube fed ink into the quill, which dashed across a piece of parchment in time to the women's singing. On closer examination, Groach saw that it was writing down the musical notes of the song as they sang.

The song came to an end, and the Prime Ministrate turned his attention to the young botanist.

'Good morning, Shessil. How did you sleep?'

'Like a log, thank you, Prime Ministrate.'

'The ladies of the house were just entertaining me with one of the local songs. Unfair that one family should have so much talent and beauty combined, don't you think?'

The women blushed. The mother bowed her head towards Groach.

'I hope you have been enjoying your stay in our home, sir,' she said.

'I've never experienced comfort or hospitality like it, madam. Thank you,' he replied.

'What do you think of my device, Shessil?' Namen waved with his head towards the machine. 'A marvelous invention. It cannot write words, but it can recognise any note. One of the ladies has kindly offered to fill in the lyrics for me. I collect music, you see. I spend a great deal of time travelling, and I like to bring back songs from all the places I visit.

Speaking of travelling, we must be on our way soon. The cook has fixed us some breakfast. You must have something to eat before we leave.'

'Come with me, sir.' One of the girls curtsied, and took his hand.

Groach was led into a dining room, the 'breakfast room' the girl called it, where he sat down at the head of a table that could easily seat twenty. Heavy, silver cutlery and hand-crafted porcelain plates were set for himself and the Prime Ministrate, who sat at the other end. Silk napkins were folded neatly by the side. Two servants brought out platters of food, and Groach's mouth watered at the sight of it. There were three kinds of bread, butter, cheese, plates of different kinds of sausage, slices of bacon, scrambled and fried eggs, mushrooms, kippers and fresh tomatoes.

It took some time to eat their fill. The Prime Ministrate reassured him that there was no rush. As he was cutting up some bread, Groach mentioned the rumbling he had heard in the night, and Namen smiled.

'Let's go up to the roof when you're finished there.'

They finished the meal, and climbed the stairs to the top of the keep. Flags flew from the corners and battlements lined the walls. Walking around the roof, Groach could see that the keep was situated in the middle of a lake. But that was not the only surprise. For Groach could not work out how they had got out into the middle of it. Looking down at the gates of the courtyard, he could see no bridge, nor any sign of one on the shore. And yet he was sure that they had not crossed on a ferry last night. The keep was definitely a secure place. It must be almost impossible to attack, but how did people gain access to it?

As if reading his mind, the Prime Ministrate took him over to a turret in the corner, where a guard was unlocking the door. Inside was a collection of brass levers jutting up from the floor, and some gauges on the walls between the windows. Taking a position by the window facing to the front, the man clasped the release on the lever, and pulled it towards him. The building shuddered. Groach glanced at the Noranian leader's face, but he did not appear to be alarmed, so Groach said nothing. The man pulled back another lever, and this time the keep actually moved.

Groach raced outside and saw that the entire island on which the keep was built was moving forwards towards the shore. His mouth hung open as the movement of the floor tickled his feet. He could barely believe his eyes.

'The island sits on enormous rollers,' the Prime Ministrate told him, moving up beside him without a sound. 'Rather than build a bridge that would need to be destroyed in times of attack, or have the keep nearer the shore with only a drawbridge and risk having the gap bridged by invaders, the architects built an island that could move the whole fortress away from an attack. Tabanark is one of only a few of its kind in the world. You are standing in one of the safest places in the Noranian Empire.'

Groach was amazed at how smoothly the island moved. It would hardly have disturbed life in the keep. He could hear only a deep rumbling and feel a slight, but steady tremor.

'It's time for us to leave,' Namen said to him. 'Collect your things and I'll meet you downstairs.'

The gate of the keep had connected with a bridgehead on the shore by the time they were getting ready to leave. The road ran out of the gate and onto the main highway as if the fortress had never moved. A tight join could be seen at the foot of the gate and chains were strung up as loose railings on either side of the short bridge. The battlewagons started their engines and sat warming up while the Prime Minis- trate's coach was made ready. Groach climbed in, closely watched by Cossock, whose hostile stare was as threatening as ever. The Prime Ministrate stopped to thank their hosts graciously and invite them to visit him in Noran, then he jumped lightly into the cabin opposite Groach. No sooner had he settled down, than the coach started off, guarded in front and behind by its escort vehicles.

'Do you play Pengence?' he asked the botanist, as he arranged his robes beneath him.

'Pardon, Prime Ministrate?'

'Pengence, a game of strategy and tactics. Surely you've heard of it?'

'I can't say that I have. How do you play it?' Groach asked.

'I'll have to show you. I think you'll enjoy it. It will help pass the time away.' Namen pulled out a polished, brass- bound wooden box and opened it. Inside were about forty finely shaped figures, all made from different materials. Just from where he sat, Groach could see pieces made out of ebony, oak, soapstone, tin, steel, ivory and copper. Under the tray of figures, there was a wooden castle, about the size of a large man's head, sitting in special mounts. He was struck by the appearance of the castle, for it did not seem to have a bottom. Turrets stuck straight out on all sides, the fine carving perfect down to the smallest brick. Walkways and staircases ran along the walls, doors could be opened and closed, and sections of the building could come away to reveal the interior. It was covered in match-sized holes, and

Groach watched with fascination as the Prime Ministrate took a sturdy foldaway table from under his seat, in the top of which were set four blocks of dull grey metal.

The Prime Ministrate unfolded the table and lifted the castle over it. He let go of the model, and Groach lunged forward to catch it, but stopped. To his astonishment, the castle floated freely above the table. It hung about a hand's width above the metal blocks, turning gently. This was just as well, he saw, for without the shaped mounting in the box, the model had no flat surface you could call a bottom. Whichever way you turned it, it always had turrets pointing up, as well as every other direction. The Prime Ministrate pushed down with a finger and the model flipped slowly over and over.

'The aim of the game is to become master of the castle,' he began. 'You begin by gathering wealth, exploring and taking what you can, either by force or by stealth. Every section has its own players, each made from a different material. You must win them over; you cannot kill them all. And you must overcome each type of player in a different way. Some respect force and can be beaten in combat; some respect money and can be bought. Others must be befriended or hypnotised or even married to win them over. Mark your position and those of your allies with the figurines. They fit in these holes so that you can move the castle and see what you are doing without knocking them off. To win, you must link your territory all the way around the castle, on every side, in any way you can.'

'How does it float?' Groach asked in wonder.

'The chamber in the centre is made up of the dungeon and treasure rooms. Those sections are constructed of magnets, with their negative poles facing outwards. The rest of the model is made of balsa wood – you're familiar with it, I'm sure. Light as a feather. The four pieces of metal in the base are also magnets, especially powerful ones. An inventor of ours in Noran makes them. They have their negative poles facing upwards and so repel the magnets in the model, push them away, so that with all four pushing up at once, they hold it suspended like that.'

'The game sounds a bit complicated ...' Groach started, but Namen waved his hand in a dismissive fashion.

'Learning's half the fun. Watch, you can move your pieces one notch on every go; certain notches give you extra moves. How well you fight, talk, hypnotise is decided each go with this spinner on the base ...'

The explanations went on for some time, and Groach was still trying to grasp the basics of making his pieces move, when Rak Ek Namen suggested they try a game. He found it hard to keep track of all the things going on at first, but once he got used to the rules, he began to enjoy it. He could hardly believe he was in a luxury coach, playing a game of strategy with the Prime Ministrate of Noran himself. The past week seemed like a dream now: the escape from the two shape-changers in the sewers, the night at the Moffets', being captured trying to rescue Hilspeth ... he stopped for a moment as he thought of Hilspeth, and immediately felt guilty. He had forgotten all about her. He felt a dull pain in his chest. She was still in a gaol cell somewhere. Maybe she had already had her trial and was being taken off to a prison or a workhouse somewhere.

'Prime Ministrate?' he said, clearing his throat.

'Yes?' the Noranian leader was intent on the castle.

'Sir, I have a friend, someone I met while I was ... away. She was attacked by a soldier, ehm ... and arrested when she tried to fight back. I think she is still in gaol and ... well, I'm worried about her ...'

'What's her name?' Namen asked, his attention still on the model. He hesitated for a moment, and then moved one of his pieces into the kitchens.

'Hilspeth. Hilspeth Naratemus.'

'Attacked by one of my soldiers, you say? Was it provoked? Did she attack him first?'

'It was a "her", actually. No, the soldier got abusive. Hilspeth just argued back and the soldier hit her across the head.'

'Can't have that. Your move, by the way. Breach of discipline. I'll mention it to Mungret. We'll have her released at once.'

'That would be fantastic, thank you, sir. If there's any way I can repay you ...'

'I'm not doing it as a favour, Shessil. Soldiers must learn not to act without orders. I am a hard but fair man. When my troops behave badly, when they are too violent or take power into their own hands, the people blame me. And so they should, for I command those soldiers. But I can't be everywhere, and sometimes the troops get out of line and cause harm where they should not. That has to stop. The soldier will be punished and your friend released.'

Groach sat back and congratulated himself. Here he was, in conversation with the Prime Ministrate over a game of Pengence, and he had just got Hilspeth out of gaol. He wondered if she would be impressed and found himself hoping she would. This was how you got things done. This was the way to go through life, not arguing with Hovem and the others about fertiliser or the water sprinklers. They would all listen to him, now. He had the ear of the Prime Ministrate; he was sure to be put in charge of the project. He would be famous for cracking the problem of the esh-bound bubule; perhaps they might re-name it after him. The Groach Bubule. The Esh-Bound Shessil. The Shessil Groach Bubule. He settled back into the velvet cushions and planned his next move on the castle. The Prime Ministrate was beating him, even though the Noranian leader was trying hard to give him a head start. Still, Groach thought to himself, bet he can't make a bubule blossom.

+ + +

Hilspeth was beginning to enjoy the ride with the Vusquid. It had taken her some time to accept that they were not going to slam into a rock or a wall at high speed. The creature guided itself with incredible accuracy. They were going so fast she did not have the sensation of being trapped that had always haunted her in caves and tunnels. She could have done without the rubbish though.

They had been cruising along for some time when the Vusquid had picked up a bucket. Then it had snatched a broken shovel. Then a couple of mouldy cloth sacks. It hardly slowed to make these pick-ups, and Hilspeth and Draegar found themselves at the centre of a growing pile of refuse. When it seized a wagon wheel, Hilspeth began to worry that they would be crushed under the stuff, and her claustrophobia started to reassert itself. Her breathing quickened and she clenched her hands against her eyes and tried to block out her fears. Pulling a vial from one of her many pockets, she opened it and breathed in the scent of mountain air in spring. This particular concoction did wonders for melancholy and travel sickness, but it proved little use against the fear induced by hurtling down a tunnel at breakneck speed as part of a pile of garbage.

'Yeehaaaa!' whooped Draegar.

Daylight broke over them and they were in a high-sided gorge. The light changed Hilspeth's mood in an instant, and she burst into relieved laughter. They coasted down the river towards a beach on their left. They were still moving very fast.

'Ah,' said Draegar, partly muffled by a threadbare blanket that had covered his head. 'This might hurt a little. Keep your arms and legs tucked in, and your chin on your chest. And watch you don't bite your tongue.'

Hilspeth had little time to gather what he meant before they were skidding up the beach, thrown from the Vusquid's grip and out of the water. The rubbish and debris scattered around them as they tumbled up the slope and flopped breathless in the mess strewn across the beach. Draegar climbed to his feet and brushed himself down.

'Not the most dignified way to travel, but they can certainly cover some ground those Vusquids,' he panted, checking his equipment.

Hilspeth rolled onto her belly and stared up the beach through matted, sandy hair. It rose from where they were to a V-shaped gap in the rock face, over the space of about forty strides. The sand was white, as was the rock along the base of the gorge. It was a beautiful spot, or would have been had it not been for the rubbish scattered everywhere.

'This all came from the tunnel?' she wondered aloud.

'This is only a fraction of what you'd find in there,' Draegar rumbled. 'It's amazing what people will dump into rivers. Rivers that others have to drink out of. It doesn't all go to waste though.'

Above them, figures were clambering down the gap towards the beach. Hilspeth sat up. They were dog-people. So named because they hung around like strays. Scavenging from bins and rubbish heaps, these tribes lived on the outskirts of towns and villages, and were despised by townspeople. Hilspeth considered herself more open-minded than most, but even she had to admit a revulsion at the sight of these scavengers.

'Was ist dis?' one cried as he saw the two travellers. 'Tunnel dung chucked frum the river-dog den?'

'Check your respect for the wrecked says I,' Draegar growled. 'Open hearts from the start if there is to be no vexed parting of the parties here.'

The dog-man rocked back on his heels as he heard this. He stood quiet while he measured Draegar and Hilspeth up, eyes sharp beads in his small skull. Hilspeth took the opportunity to study him. He had a tiny head, half the size of a normal man's, with a long hooked nose and protruding teeth. His scalp was bare and flaking, and his skin a yellow colour mottled with pink. His clothes were a patchwork of leather, cotton and linen with bits of metal and wooden beads sewn into them, and more made into necklaces and bracelets. He was about the same height as her, helped by a long neck rising from narrow sloping shoulders. His arms were thin, but looked to have a wiry strength to them, and he had large hands and feet. His feet were wrapped in straps of solid rubber-like gum, and when she caught a glance at the soles she saw that they had sharp stones embedded in them as grips for the homemade shoes. His six friends were dressed much the same as he was. He spoke again, this time more cautiously:

'Travelling tunnelways, clutch of the Vusquid you?'

'Clutch of the Vusquid, aye,' Draegar nodded. 'Rush with the Vusquid hustling northways Noran-bound. Any Clatterers view you?'

'Clatterers, aye,' the dog-man replied. 'Clattering northways. On way to Noran and yonder. Clatterers hand and finger one and smoketails on all.'

'He says there is a convoy heading this way,' Draegar told Hilspeth. 'Hand and finger one ... they count in fingers ... one hand means five vehicles, and finger one makes six. Smoketails mean they are all oil-powered. I think that's our boy. Taya and Lorkrin are bound to try something somewhere around here. Plenty of places to hide.'

'Has he seen them?' she prompted him.

'Pinch hand pups view you?' he asked the dog-man. 'Myunans tags and bags for kit?'

'Pups nul, but Myunans hood for good when sought,' the scavenger said, obviously pleased with the conversation. Hilspeth supposed he rarely met other people who spoke their language.

'He says he hasn't seen any, but he pointed out that Myunans are adept at hiding when they know they are being hunted. As if I needed to be told.'

Hilspeth was watching the dog-people picking among the rubbish, pointing, digging and talking excitedly as they worked. She shook her head at the sight of it.

'Don't be so quick to judge,' Draegar warned her. 'The

Gabbits are an ingenious race. They can make use of things that normal people think of as useless. The townsfolk around here will probably end up buying back some of their garbage in some form or other. Watch those two over there.'

Sure enough, two of the dog-people, or Gabbits as Draegar had called them, were attaching the cart wheel to an axle, then bowls, boards and the blades from shovels to the rim of the wheel. Holding it out over the river, they dipped its edge into the water, and Hilspeth saw it turn like a mill wheel. That movement could turn a grindstone or wind a winch. They had done this in the time that she and the Parsinor had been talking to the dog-man. They took it apart again and began packing it up. All around them, the Gabbits were nodding and chattering about objects that Hilspeth would have considered fit only for burning.

'Gabbits are offended by waste,' Draegar went on. 'To them it is a mortal sin. They don't just use garbage because they want to – they are obliged to; it is in their nature to make use of what others discard. To allow things to go to waste is an insult to their gods.'

'A very noble philosophy,' Hilspeth said, diffidently.

'Yes, but it does give them a unique smell.' Draegar smiled down at her. 'Let's go and find those wagons.'

# 12 HOW THE FERRY GETS FED

Deep in thought, Emos regarded the gouge in the mud. It smelled of Taya, but the mark in the earth had been made by a creature with a beak-like face, and was shaped as if the animal had fallen from a height. She and Lorkrin had learned to fly. That was why their trail on this hill had disappeared. It meandered back and forth, as if they had been running about, then it vanished.

A strong wind was beginning to gust across the hill, and the Myunan closed his eyes and drew in a breath. He had found their trail again in Hortenz (he was not sure he believed that they had tangled with skacks, as Neblisk had claimed). They had joined up with a woman who smelled of ... well, many things. He knew that Draegar had found them, which had offered the Myunan some comfort, but the pair had escaped his friend in some cornfields. They had been following a Noranian convoy that had set out from the town, a convoy that Neblisk had told him carried the Prime Ministrate and another man, a botanist, someone who was important to the Noranians. This seemed to be the man Lorkrin and Taya were after. Did they know who he was and what he was working on? Did he have some kind of connection with the dead man that Murris's crew had pulled up on their anchor? Emos did not want to think about what would happen to them if his niece and nephew crossed the Noranians. He was becoming more and more convinced that Rak Ek Namen was trying to start a war between the Karthars and the Braskhiams, a war only the Noranians would win. He was sure they would go to any lengths to make sure it happened, even leaving a man to suffocate to death at the bottom of the esh ... or killing two Myunan children.

Standing there in the breeze, watching ornacrids play on the hillside, he was reminded of the time his niece and nephew had come to visit during Harvest Tide. The esh had swelled and swept over his land, covering it in a wispy carpet of sessium. Taya and Lorkrin had been spellbound, scooping up handfuls of the gas and letting it drop, watching it sink slowly back to the ground.

Floating in on the Harvest Tide were the seed pods or bules which gave it its name and Emos wondered if it was these that the Noranians were after with their strange experiments. This gas-bound crop was collected by people along the Braskhiam coast, and the bules strained for their oil. Bule oil was used for everything from cooking to fuelling vehicles. The tide had only come up to his ankles that year, but it had still left behind on his land enough bules to buy a new horse. The children had wanted to ride it every day. Following the trails of the ornacrids down the hill, he thought back on what he had discovered of Taya and Lorkrin so far.

The military vehicles were bound for Noran. It was a fair guess that his nephew and niece were headed in the same direction. He could not track them while they flew, but he could find the convoy. Unrolling his tools, he started to fashion feathers over his skin.

+ + +

Groach was beginning to get the hang of Pengence now. He was still nowhere near Rak Ek Namen's standard, but the Prime Ministrate was no longer having to explain rules at every turn. He rotated the castle as he considered his next move. Namen had most of the territory, but Groach was still holding onto the ballroom and the kitchens, two courtyards and the dungeons. This meant that he could stop the Prime Ministrate from linking his territories and winning the game. He was just planning an attack on one of the Prime Ministrate's shield maidens when the coach started to slow down.

The window behind Groach opened and the driver called in: 'Approaching the crossing, Prime Ministrate.'

'Good!' Rak Ek Namen clapped his hands together and smiled at Groach. 'A chance to get out and stretch our legs.'

Groach smiled back, but did not comment that sitting in the plush cabin of the coach was far preferable to lying on bare boards in the back of a gaol wagon, as he had been two days before. He was quite happy to go on sitting there, playing Pengence for some time yet. Outside, he could see that they were travelling alongside a river with high banks, surrounded by thick vegetation. The coach slowed further and then turned out onto a pier built on some kind of rocky outcrop. They rolled to a halt, and Cossock jumped down off the back, the vehicle lifting considerably as he did so.

After a cautious survey of the dock, and a quiet word with the scouts that had driven ahead of them, he opened the door of the coach. Rak Ek Namen stepped easily down from the cabin, followed less gracefully by Groach, who leant over the wooden railing and gazed out at the wind-ruffled water. They were standing on one side of the pier, on which all six vehicles were now parked, its floor composed of heavy beams bolted to the reddish grey rock. A stunted, reptilian-looking man scampered towards them. He had bright green scaly skin, and unblinking orange eyes above a flat, wide nose. His long skull extended over his hunched back and into a striking yellow crest. His clothing was made from heavy sacking stitched with twine. The soldiers let him through, and he slid to his knees at the Prime Ministrate's feet, bowing so low his nose touched the boards.

'An honour to have you aboard, once again, Prime Ministrate,' he muttered, his face pressed against the ground. 'You grace us with your wondrous, stately presence. I deeply, deeply hope you have the most pleasant of journeys with us. What an honour this is.'

'The Prime Ministrate is in a hurry,' Cossock said in a voice like a grindstone. 'Enough boot-licking. Get us under way.'

With a snivel, the little character backed away, then jumped to his feet and jogged back up to the end of the pier. Two more men of the same race were detaching mooring chains where the pier joined the bank. The first man picked up a large net full of fresh fish and attached it to one end of a long pole. Lodging the pole into a mounting on a turntable, he swung the fish far out over the end of the pier. He then picked up a sledge hammer that was leaning against the mounting and began beating the rock at his feet while screaming at the top of his voice.

Watching this with fascination, Groach looked quizzically at the Prime Ministrate:

'Is that how he calls the ferry?'

'In a manner of speaking, I suppose, yes,' was the reply.

Groach started as he felt the ground move beneath his feet. Staggering to keep his balance, he noticed some of the guards had moved to the railings, and were peering over into the choppy water, although more out of interest than surprise. He looked back towards the little reptilian man, and his eyes bulged at the enormous head that rose out of the water, attempting to reach the net full of fish. It was the same colour and texture of the rock the pier was built on, and almost as wide. It dawned on him that this pier was not built on rock, but on the back of a bexemot. These huge creatures lived in deep lakes and rivers. He had read about them but never seen one, though he had heard there were some in the river Gullin, running through the centre of Noran. He watched as the small man dangled the fish just out of reach of the monster's jaws, and teased the creature into moving forward into the river. By turning the pole, he was able to steer the creature right and left, and Groach realised that this *was* the ferry.

He was woken from his reverie by two of the guards beside him. They were flicking the safety catches off their crossbows, and one was taking aim at something above them. Groach gazed skywards, and saw two birds circling above them. The bexemot was moving upstream, and the birds seemed to be following them. When they came a bit closer, he noticed they looked more like bats, but with long, sharp heads. The soldiers did not know what they were, and wanted to shoot one down and have a closer look at it. Groach considered this a slightly barbaric way of gathering information, but he had always been a little scared of soldiers, and the previous few days had not helped improve matters. He stayed quiet.

'I'll hit it in one, you watch,' one said to the other.

'I'm watching. I still say they're too far up. You don't have the range.'

'You watch, I'll do it.' He aimed and shot. The bolt flew nearly faster than the eye could see, shooting towards its target. It almost appeared to make it, but it slowed down and the bat thing flipped athletically out of its path. The creature dipped down and dived at them at a steep angle, dropping ever closer.

'Castig!' the Whipholder who commanded the convoy roared. 'Who gave you permission to take pot shots at birds?'

'We just wanted to see what it was, sir,' Castig, the guard holding up his crossbow, protested.

'If I see you loose off another shot from that weapon without orders to do so, you will be back shelling ornacrids in Westermare so fast, your feet won't touch the ground.'

'Yes, sir. Understood, sir.'

Just at that moment, the creature beat its wings and pulled out of its dive. A light, yellow rain fell on the guards, and Groach wrinkled his nose as a faint, but unmistakable odour drifted towards him.

+ + +

'I can't believe you did that!' Taya gaped to hide her smile as Lorkrin climbed back up towards her, fighting the stiff breeze.

'You just can't believe you didn't think of it first,' Lorkrin replied, smugly.

+ + +

Groach watched the bat, or bird, join its companion and an uneasy feeling squirmed in his gut. Memories of sewers and skacks and shape-changers flooded back to him. He was afraid that there was a reason that nobody knew what kind of creatures those were. He was afraid that that kind of creature did not exist at all. He turned his attention to the Prime Ministrate. The Noranian leader was reading a parchment, and appeared deep in thought.

He had an aura, the Prime Ministrate. Groach knew he had been very young when he had won power in Noran, over ten years ago now. Prime Ministrates were normally middle-aged, but Namen had outwitted many people in his rise to leadership. There were stories of savagery and assassinations, treachery and the exiling of his opponents; but Groach knew that there were always people who would try and blacken the name of the leader of an empire. To him, Rak Ek Namen seemed an intelligent, warm, civilised man. The weight of his responsibilities showed in the lines of his otherwise young face, but Groach felt privileged to be in this man's company, and was thoroughly enjoying himself.

'Almost there,' Namen said to him, nodding towards the shore, where there was another mooring further upriver. With no small skill, the reptilian man steered the huge beast into the shore, and two more crew waiting for them on the bank jumped aboard and attached the mooring chains to rings embedded in the quay. Groach doubted that these chains would hold the creature if it decided to wander off, but he supposed it would be less inclined to wander if it was well fed. He saw its keeper undo the net and let the fish slide out of it into the water. The bexemot sucked them in, and its head disappeared beneath the surface. Searching the skies, he saw that the airborne creatures had also vanished.

Groach was ushered back aboard the coach, and the engines were restarted and revved up to power. Namen climbed in to join him, and the convoy started off. The Noranian leader broke out lunch, another hamper. This time it was a collection of quiches, pies and pasties, cold meats and salads. There was also a selection of fruit, some of which Groach had only ever read about. Namen poured them both some wine, and Groach sat back and talked with the Prime Ministrate about the future of Noran and where science was leading the world.

They were travelling up the rocky surface of a narrow valley when the vehicles ground to a halt. Cossock swung down off the coach to talk to the convoy commander, and then came back to the door of the coach, where he explained the reason for stopping.

'A footprint, Prime Ministrate. Looks like a raspidam. We'll have to send scouts out to find it so that we don't surprise it along the road somewhere. It could pose a serious risk if it's not alone. Looks like a fully grown adult. Best to stop here until we're sure.'

Without a word, Namen got out of the coach and walked to the front of the column of vehicles. It had started to rain lightly, but the clouds above promised heavier falls before the day was out. All the engines were still running, and the soldiers were carefully scanning the slopes of the valley on either side. They were all seasoned warriors, but a raspidam was a threat that could not be treated lightly. Groach trotted along to keep up with the Prime Ministrate's long strides, holding his bag over his head to keep the rain off, and he had to skid to a halt to avoid knocking into the tall Noranian when he stopped suddenly. The footprint was as wide as the battlewagon that stood before it. It was unmistakable, a hoof with claws; there was only one animal that could leave a mark like this.

'Isn't it a bit shallow?' the Prime Ministrate asked. 'You would expect such a massive creature to leave deeper foot-prints.'

'The ground around here is bedrock beneath this dust, Prime Ministrate,' the Whipholder informed him. 'There's bare stone all around us. We were lucky to see this before the rain washed it away. It's not a good idea to be surprised by one of these beasts. I mean, they'd be unlikely to attack a convoy of this size, but you never know ...'

'All right,' Namen said in a clipped tone. 'But I don't want to be held up longer than is necessary. Find this thing or make sure the way through is safe and get us moving. I want to be in Noran by nightfall.'

'Yes, Prime Ministrate.'

As they spoke, there was the sound of rushing air, and they saw a boy with bat's wings and a long, beak-shaped head dropping straight down towards them. He swooped low in over the roofs of the battle wagons and seized Groach by his shoulders. With a powerful stroke of his wings, he lifted the slight man off his feet and into the air. Groach screamed. Cossock, standing behind the Prime Ministrate made a grab for his feet, but missed. A soldier went to fire his crossbow, but was knocked to the ground by a girl with similar wings. She carried through, making more soldiers duck, and then grabbed hold of Groach's ankles, and together the two lifted him up and away.

Another guard went to shoot them down, but the Prime Ministrate slapped the weapon down:

'No, you idiot! You might hit Groach.' The Noranian leader was absolutely livid. 'Myunans! Well, they can't carry him forever. Sound the alarm, spread the word across the area. When they land, I want troops down on their position before they have time to catch their breath.'

'That might not be so easy, sir,' the Whipholder warned. 'There aren't enough local troops to cover the area ...'

Namen moved like a striking snake, drawing the Whipholder's own sword and embedding it with frightening force in the bonewood side of the wagon behind the commander. There was time for the Whipholder's face to register shock at what had happened, before his head slipped from his shoulders and tumbled to the ground. Soldiers stepped back as his body followed it, the gaping neck spattering blood over their boots as it crumpled. The sword stayed jammed in the wall of the wagon.

'Find them, kill the Myunans, bring him back, uninjured.' Namen stepped over the mutilated body, and striding back to his coach, he called: 'There is no raspidam. Get these vehicles moving.'

+ + +

Lorkrin and Taya were tiring quickly. It was hard enough work trying to stay aloft on their own, but keeping their height while carrying a thrashing, panicked gardener made it nearly impossible.

'Let me go, you monsters!' Groach shrieked, kicking and slapping as best he could while held in the grip of the two

Myunans. 'What are you doing? Are you mad?'

'Stop ... struggling!' Taya protested. 'We're rescuing you ... stop it!'

'Rescuing me?' Groach wailed in absolute disbelief. 'Rescuing me from *what*? I'm going to fall and die in bits on the ground because you two think you're *helping* me? What kind of twisted, demented world do you two live in? LET ME DOWN!'

'I can't hold him much longer,' Lorkrin panted. 'We'd better find a place to land.'

'I'm looking. We need a place to hide ...'

'There, near the edge of the esh, those trees.'

'I see it.'

The world seemed a long way below them, and they were not flying steadily. Groach had shut up for fear of throwing up, but was still tensed up and shaking to and fro. The wind buffeted them and swirled in gusts that made it difficult to remain stable. Fields and roads could be seen beneath them, the convoy lost to sight between the hills of the valley behind them. Heavy storm clouds scudded by above and the air was becoming charged with electricity. The haze of rain around them made the ground blur.

Whirling and bucking their way through the turbulent air, they aimed for the sheltered spot they could see before them. Suddenly, a shaft of lightning arced down past them, so close they felt the heat of it in the air. It blinded them, causing the shape-changers to lose their bearings and plunge headlong towards the ground. In the tumbling confusion, Groach screamed until his throat ached.

They were almost to the treetops before they regained control and spun out of their fall, both of the Myunans crying out with the strain on their shoulders and chests as they struggled to hold onto the air. Then they were up again, swooping clear of the trees and beating on towards shelter. Ignoring her pitching stomach, Taya called to Lorkrin and nodded towards a clearing visible between the trees. He saw it, and steered them in that direction.

The two Myunans were at the end of their endurance; Groach's weight was too much for them. They sagged, and the botanist found himself whipped by branches and smacked by leaves. In a last-ditch effort, Lorkrin flung himself through a gap in the tree line and dropped to the grass as he lost control. They crashed along the ground and rolled into a sprawling mess, where they lay still. All three were moaning in pain. Taya sat up and clutched the grass on either side of her in shock as she found her legs dangling over a cliff. They had stopped just short of going right over.

Holding the grass with the claws on her wings, she lay back and flipped her legs over her head, rolling away from the edge. Lorkrin was standing up, sharing the view. Groach still lay curled up on the ground, groaning to himself.

'Wow,' said Lorkrin quietly.

'Yeah,' Taya replied. She was slunching, relaxing her body so that it slowly returned to its normal form. Lorkrin did the same. When she was back to her old self, Taya knelt by Groach and shook his shoulder. He grunted something that sounded rude. She looked over him for any sign of injuries, but apart from some blossoming bruises, he appeared to be unhurt.

'Do you think we're far enough away from those soldiers?' Lorkrin asked.

'The ones at the convoy, I think so. but there might be

others around. If the convoy sends out pigeons or smoke signals, the whole area might be looking for us.'

'Let's have a rest and then get out of here. I'm not carrying him any further, and it's a long walk back to Hortenz.'

'Sounds fine to me.'

They flopped to the ground, limbs splayed and heads back, gazing at the deepening storm clouds. It was still raining, but lightly, and the water was soothing, cold and light. As they lay there, it gradually grew heavier, and they were forced to sit up and seek shelter. Helping Groach to his feet, they trotted over to the dry carpet of twigs and scrub beneath a thick beech tree.

'We can't stay here,' Groach muttered. 'It's not safe – there's lightning coming.'

'So?' Taya frowned.

'So, lightning strikes tall things on the ground,' he explained through a tight smile, as if she were half her age. 'Things like trees. We need to get away from the trees and lie down, preferably somewhere out of the rain.'

'Come on,' Lorkrin pointed at a bank of earth nearby. 'That's out of the wind. There should be just enough shelter.'

They made their way over to the bank, heads and shoulders now hunched against the pounding rain. The wind was rising in strength and ferocity, whipping their hair and clothes about and making their eyes water. The sky was blackening and the oppressive clouds rolled threateningly overhead. They crouched under the shadow of the bank, bowed to the spray the wind threw in at them. There was the flash of lightning in the clouds and, a second later, the dull roll of thunder.

'I was in a warm, dry, luxury coach, eating wonderful food

and enjoying interesting conversation with the leader of the empire,' Groach hissed at them. 'And as soon as this clears up, I'm going right back there.'

'That's gratitude for you,' Lorkrin sniffed, huddling closer to his sister. 'We risked our lives to rescue you and this is all we get. It took us ages to make that raspidam's footprint, Taya had to walk all over me to get me into the right shape. Decided you like being a prisoner all of a sudden?'

'I wasn't a prisoner!'

'So why is it that you get locked up wherever you go?'

'I do not! What do you know about it? I was happy until I met you two. Since then, my life has gone from bad to worse. Then I thought it was all over. I was going back to Noran. I was being treated like a prince. And then along come you two again and suddenly I'm falling from the sky, getting lashed by branches, hitting the ground like a sack of bones and getting caught out in the open in a thunderstorm! Which bit should I be grateful for, exactly?'

He realised he was shouting at the boy and stopped. They were both staring at him, looking hurt and confused. He shook his head and turned away. Holding his rucksack over his head to shield him from the rain that was blowing in under the bank, he found a dry bit of rock and sat down.

Lorkrin gazed out at the dark, hazy outline of the trees, now only a shape in the grey rain-soaked air. Something caught his attention, something moving in their shadows, and he found himself looking right at a Noranian soldier. He was standing under the very beech where they had just been sheltering. The boy tugged his sister's sleeve and nodded at the man. She gasped and went to whisper to Groach, but he had not seen the soldier. She held her tongue. The man had not seen them yet. If they stayed quiet, he might miss them. But she was not sure what Groach would do. Was he serious about wanting to go back? Lorkrin could see what she was thinking, and he too was unsure what to do next. They changed colour, becoming the grainy yellow ochre of the earth behind them, melding into the background. But they could not hide Groach.

The soldier was joined by another. They were studying the ground at the base of the tree, moving carefully around it as if to avoid disturbing whatever lay there. The shape-shifters knew the soldiers were looking at their tracks. Only the force of the rain and the overhang of the bank was hiding them now; the soldiers knew they were here some-where. More troops appeared, coming through the cloak of the trees and materialising out of the rain along either side, following the edge of the esh. There were eleven, no ... twelve altogether. They grouped around the first two, and the Myunans could see them talking, but the rain and thun-der were washing all the other sounds away.

With stunning force, a lightning bolt struck a tree in the woods nearby and they all turned towards it. Groach raised his head and saw them; he was about to jump to his feet when two muddy, wet shape-changers flattened him, hiding him beneath their camouflage.

'Get off!' he wheezed from under them, pushing them away. He shoved them aside, but was too late to get the Noranians' attention. They had spread out and started into the woods in search of more tracks. The rain had obliterated all those that were not sheltered by the trees. Groach stag-gered out into the storm, calling out to them.

'Come back! I'm a friend of the Prime Ministrate's! Hello?

Hey! The Prime Ministrate is looking for me! Over here!'

'Shessil, please!' Taya begged. 'We're trying to help.'

'I don't want your kind of help!' He turned on her. 'Go home!'

Taya stopped behind him as he continued to chase after the search party. She was upset and confused. Lorkrin came up, and scowled after Groach.

'That's it. We tried to help him. Whatever it is they want him for, they can have him. He deserves them. Let's get out of here.' He put his hand on her shoulder. 'Taya, come on.'

'I still think he's in real trouble, Lorkrin.'

'Then he's in it on his own. We tried. Come on.'

As they turned to walk in the other direction, an armoured figure appeared out of the lashing rain ahead of them. She stopped when she saw them and raised a loaded crossbow.

'Run!' screamed Taya. They both sprinted in different directions, but the soldier stayed where she was. Picking her target, she aimed and pulled the trigger. Taya felt an impact in her right calf and her leg jerked clumsily. She fell, catching herself on her elbows and getting quickly to her feet. But her right leg had gone stiff, and when she looked down, she saw a crossbow bolt protruding from the back of her calf. She moaned as a searing pain spread up through her leg. Limping on, she heard the soldier behind her shouting and saw figures coming through the trees in front of her. She collapsed again, and before she could stand up, a hand grasped her hair and lifted her onto her feet. Taya squealed and tried to open the fingers that were holding her hair, but they held firm. A voice nearby called:

'We have the man. We don't want the others. You know your orders.'

A knife blade appeared in front of Taya's face.

Lorkrin did not know that his sister had been caught. He was belting along the cliff edge, trying to see through the torrent of rain to the bushes ahead of him. If he could make it to undergrowth, he could hide, become invisible among the ground cover. He became aware of thumping footsteps behind him, and glanced back to see a soldier gaining on him. But Lorkrin was a fast runner. He increased his speed, and with it, the distance between himself and his pursuer. He would make the bushes in time.

A crossbow bolt left a burning track across the side of his head and he yelped in pain. The man had given up trying to catch him. Another bolt struck the ground ahead of him and he jumped over it and ran on. He was almost to the bushes now... suddenly a soldier rose out of the foliage in front of him, and Lorkrin narrowly missed being caught, darting to one side and ducking under the man's clutching arms. He turned, stumbled, lost his footing and found himself sliding down a gravelly slope towards the edge of the cliff. Lorkrin jammed his heels in and scrabbled for a grip on the stony surface, but he failed to catch onto anything. His slide quickened until he lost control of his speed altogether, and bumped and flailed down the slope, stones scraping into his legs, bottom and back. With a scream, he went over the edge.

Groach was walking out into the clearing, with a soldier on each side. He stopped in horror when he saw another soldier, this one a woman, with a knife at Taya's throat.

'What are you doing? What's going on?' The woman hesitated, looking at her officer, who stood behind the botanist. There was a moment of stillness as the full realisation of the

situation settled on Groach before he heard a scattering of
stones, and turned in time to see Lorkrin slide out of sight
towards the cliff edge. He heard the boy scream. Groach
stood poised in indecision as he swivelled back towards
Taya again. Then he broke into a run for the precipice. A soldier raised his crossbow, but had it knocked down by the
Forward-Batterer leading the group.

The man who had made a grab for Lorkrin did not see
Groach until the botanist rammed headlong into him and
barged him aside. Groach's momentum carried him on and
he lunged into a slide down the same slope that had borne
Lorkrin down towards the esh. His rucksack dangling wildly
behind him, he slipped over the edge and fell, landing hard
on a steep incline that dropped straight down to the esh.
Trying to slow himself as much he could with his arms and
legs, Groach bounced down the stony hill and into the sea
of gas.

The Forward-Batterer ran across the clearing, but the soldier at the edge shaking his head told him all he needed to
know. He peered over into the esh and watched the wind
toss the gas into strands that threw themselves against the
cliff. The two watched for a while, but nothing came out.

'He's not coming out of there,' the officer said at last. 'The
Prime Ministrate will have to be told. He's not going to be a
happy man.'

He did not relish the idea of breaking the news to his
leader. Jamming his sword back into its sheath with some
force, he gritted his teeth and strode back towards their
remaining captive. They would at least get half this job done.

'Where are Wells and Farne?' he called.

'Still in the forest somewhere,' another soldier replied. 'I haven't seen them. Katsch is missing too.'

'Find them; we're done here,' he told him. 'And finish the girl. Kill her and let's get out of this damned rain.'

The woman with the knife pressed it to Taya's throat. But just as she did, Taya felt a thump against her back. The woman fell to her knees and keeled over, a crossbow bolt embedded in her head. Taya gasped, and looked up as a huge shape charged out of the driving rain, swept past her and swung a battleaxe over and down, cleaving the Forward-Batterer from shoulder to hip. The officer crumpled, but the Parsinor was already wading into the other soldiers, bellowing a furious battle cry. Someone crouched down by Taya and helped her to her feet.

'We have to get you out of here,' Hilspeth said in her ear.

'Lorkrin ...'

'We can't help him now. We'll come back, but I have to get you to safety first.'

Draegar fought with the axe in his left hand and his sword in his right. The remaining soldiers surrounded him, but found themselves fighting for their lives. The Parsinor had seen Lorkrin fall, and was in a blind fury. He struck down four men and two women before the others turned and fled. Sheathing his weapons, he hurried to the precipice, dropping to his knees to look over, but could not see anything but the thrashing gas. Pulling a rope from his bag, he lashed one end around a nearby tree, and began to lower himself over, knowing that if the soldiers came back, they would save themselves a fight by cutting it and sending him to the bottom of the esh.

Hilspeth led Taya into the shadows of the trees, supporting her as she half limped, half hopped to keep up. A soldier appeared out of nowhere and raised his halberd, but Hilspeth had drawn her tinderbox. Striking a spark, she tossed a burning bottle on the ground at his toes, and flames leapt up his trousers. Shrieking in panic, he dashed out into the rain.

'A little something I keep on me for cold nights,' Hilspeth murmured, and led Taya on into the darkness.

+ + +

Groach held his breath as he scrambled to a halt in the soupy gas. He could not see more than his arm's length in any direction, and Lorkrin was hidden in the thick mist. The sharp, tangy smell of the esh invaded his nostrils while he dug into his satchel, removing an oiled leather mask with glass goggle lenses and three bulky valves. He let some breath out to take some of the pressure off his lungs as he strapped on the mask, then blew out hard several times to clear it. He took one tentative breath in to check it was working, then breathed normally. The gas mask was a vital part of his botany equipment; one could not study the esh-bound bubule if one could not see it in its natural environment.

There was gloomy yellow-grey darkness down here, and Groach could feel a strong current moving around him. Every now and then, there was the dull glow from the lightning, though the sounds from the world above were muffled by the gas. He could still feel the haze of the rain as it settled over him so he knew he was not very deep, and the lack of pressure on his ears confirmed it. But he was deep enough, and the esh was not a place to be in a lightning storm. He walked over to his right, using the slope to keep track of where the shore was. Lorkrin could not have fallen far from where he had come in, so he kept around the same depth that he had landed in. Finding nothing, he started back to the left. He could hear the sounds of the esh-floaters disturbed by the storm, a high-pitched clicking and the whoosh of shoals of the creatures on the move. He clambered over some rocks and nearly tripped over something lying on the ground on the other side.

His first sight of Lorkrin shocked him. The boy's nose and mouth had disappeared, leaving a flat patch of skin where they had been. His eyes were closed. He seemed unconscious, but not dead. Confused by the Myunan's appearance, Groach stood staring at him for a moment, then came to his senses and gathered the boy in his arms.

# 13 Groach's Notes

Draegar hauled himself back to the surface to catch his breath. He had to cling to the rope to hold himself above the gusts of gas that blew around him. He could close off his nostrils, a useful adaptation to the sandstorms of his desert home, but he still needed air. This was his third attempt. Despite his efforts, he was nearly blind in the heavy gas and was beginning to lose hope. He was about to go down again for another try, when a strange form emerged from the swirling esh. Climbing unsteadily up the loose surface of the incline was a creature with round flat eyes and short stalks where his nose and mouth should be. He was carrying Lorkrin. As he came closer, Draegar could see that it was the gardener, wearing some kind of mask. He did not waste time with curiosity. Abseiling down, he scooped both of them up in one big arm and began his climb to the top.

Groach held his charge in a tight hold, trusting the Parsinor's strength as they were lifted steadily to safety. Crawling up the last bit of slope, Draegar let go of Groach and helped him lie the boy on flat ground. Groach stripped off his mask.

'His face ...' he began, but Draegar nodded.

'It's a reflex. His body changed to protect him. Watch.'

Lorkrin's nose and mouth grew back on his face and his lips parted. With a jerk, he let out a blast of breath and coughed, gasping for air. After a few laboured pants, he relaxed and lay flat, his chest rising and falling softly as if he were asleep.

'He'll be fine, but he'll need a good rest.' Draegar said. 'It was close; he wouldn't have lasted much longer.'

Groach noticed that the Parsinor was trembling, and realised the mighty creature had been extremely frightened for the boy. He wondered what connection he had with the Myunans.

'We can't stay here,' Draegar growled. 'The soldiers will come back in greater numbers.'

He picked up Lorkrin, holding him close, and asked Groach to bring the rope that he had tied to the tree. They walked to the tree line, where Draegar quickly found Hilspeth's and Taya's trail, and led Groach to their hiding place, a shallow ditch under some bushes. Hilspeth was tending the girl's wound.

'You can take the bolt out. It won't bleed,' Taya was saying.

'I think we should leave it in,' Hilspeth insisted. 'I can cut it down.'

'Take it out,' Draegar told her. 'She's a Myunan, remember?'

'Right, hold on to something,' Hilspeth warned grimly. Then, against her better judgement, she grasped the bolt and drew it out of Taya's leg. Taya wailed, and bit her lip, burying her face in her arm. Hilspeth watched with interest as the wound, free of blood, closed up almost entirely. A small hole remained, which she wiped with some water and bandaged with a strip of cloth from her skirt.

'We heal up fast,' Taya whimpered. 'But it still hurts.'

'We need to move on,' Draegar urged them. 'You two help Taya. I've got Lorkrin. Let's go.'

Bearing its casualties, the odd group made its way through the dark, dripping woods and on towards the hills, where they stood a better chance of avoiding their hunters. Above them, the storm raged on, tearing the sky and drenching the ground. Evening was falling, and what little light there was began to fade.

+ + +

The Prime Ministrate's convoy roared onwards, ploughing through the growing pools of water and mud that covered the roads. Rak Ek Namen was insisting that they reach the city-state before morning, and with their commander's body in a box in the back of a wagon, the soldiers were eager to get this journey over with. They were forced to slow down when darkness fell; the night was pitch black, pierced only by the lightning. In the curtain of rain, their lamps lit the road for no more than twenty strides ahead of them, and it was dangerous to drive faster than their light could clear the gloom.

The line of snarling, smoking, spluttering wagons carried on, upwards into the range of hills that marked the border of the city-state. Passing the regular sentry towers, where the soldiers on the tops waved their greetings, they sped up on the cobbled roads. From the tops of the hills, the lights of the city could be seen, spread thinly across the plain beneath them, gathering in more concentrated groups the closer they got to the centre and the eb-towers at the heart of the Noranian Empire.

The lights of the factories were still burning. Looking at them through the window, Namen knew they would burn for some time yet. Everyone worked hard in Noran. All day, every day, that was what he demanded. The empire kept them well fed and healthy, all they had to do was work. Those who did not work in the factories, worked on the roads, or on any number of other projects that the Prime Ministrate had conceived. Everyone working toward the same goal – that was how their leader liked it.

Still outside the main part of the city, they passed one factory after another, each one putting the latest science to work in the form of machines, weapons, new chemicals, and scores of other operations. Namen loved all these schemes, but his favourite was the Harvest Tide Project. If it succeeded, it would make his the greatest empire the world had ever seen. But the loss of Groach was infuriating. He seethed at the thought of how the botanist had been literally snatched from his grasp. And by children at that. He made a note to himself to have some Myunan tribes hunted down. Shape-changers' flesh must be useful for something. He wondered idly how well it burned.

The vehicles swept down into the shallow valley of the river, through streets of houses, shops, then warehouses and military buildings. They rumbled along the road by the wharf until they reached the base of the tallest eb-tower, turning in through the gate into the protective embrace of the walls around the massive eb-tree's base. Mungret was waiting for them. As Rak Ek Namen climbed out of his coach, the clerk ran up to him and waved a satchel.

'We lost Groach. I want him found at all costs,' Namen snapped.

'I know, Prime Ministrate. I know, sir ... but I have here something almost as good.'

'And what is that, Mungret?'

'I have his notes, Prime Ministrate. It's all here. Everything we needed. We know how to make the esh-bound bubule bloom, Prime Ministrate,' Mungret panted.

Rak Ek Namen stood stock still for a few moments, then gave one of his winning smiles.

+ + +

In the ruined walls of an old mill on a river high in the hills, Hilspeth made a soft bed of moss and leaves under the remaining piece of roof, and Taya unpacked her cloak and spread it across the makeshift mattress. Draegar laid Lorkrin down on it and pulled the boy's cloak around him.

'We need to light a fire. He has to be kept warm – he's still not well,' said the scentonomist.

'We can't do that,' Draegar replied. 'The light could give us away. He will not get any better if the Noranians find us.'

'I'm cold too,' Taya said, shivering.

'They need a fire.' Hilspeth repeated firmly, hands on her hips.

'Not as much as we need to go without.' The Parsinor stared down at her. 'I am more concerned than you are for him, but we cannot take the chance.'

Groach, who had said very little since the fight with the soldiers, had been taking in the area around them as they had been walking. He took Hilspeth's arm:

'I know how to warm this place up. Can you give me a hand?'

With another hard look at the Parsinor, Hilspeth followed Groach over the broken walls and out to the bushy hillside. The rain was still falling, but it had eased a little. Groach bent down and picked up what looked like a pine cone, but heavier and with a thin, brittle skin. He took out a small pen-knife and pushed the blade into it. Then he tossed it to Hil-speth. She cupped it in her hands.

'Hey, it's warming up,' she smiled.

'It's rotting,' Groach told her. 'It's a crumble cone, from these nocha trees around us. Pierce the skin and it rots at a terrific rate. That one will be a small piece of slime before morning. If we gather enough of these, we can get as much heat as you would from a small stove. And they don't give off any light.'

'That's fantastic ...' she held it up and sniffed it, then wrin-kled her nose. 'Ugh, that's a strong smell it's got. Like a cross between rotting meat and ... pine needles.'

'Yes, that is a bit of a problem, but they are warm.'

'Well ... I suppose it's all we've got. Let's gather some crumble cones then.' She looked at him and gave him a coy smile. 'It's nice to see you again. I'm glad you're not so keen to go back to Noran.'

He gave her a shy grin and squatted down to pick up another cone. He stayed crouching, his face pensive as he stared at it. Haller Joculeb had shown him the trick with the crumble cones when they were young, only starting out on the project. Haller, who had died out at esh during a soil survey only a few weeks before, his body lost to the depths of the gas. Haller, who had been asking insistent questions about what the Noranians wanted to do with the Harvest Tide.

After seeing Lorkrin lying there in the sessium, he had begun to wonder if Haller's death had been an accident after all.

Biting his lip, he shook his head and started to work his way across the undergrowth, picking up cones as he went. They worked together, Hilspeth using the folds of her skirt as a basket to hold what they found. Groach appeared deep in thought.

'What's up?' she asked.

'Nothing ... just worried about the boy,' he answered.

She was sure there was more to it than that, but decided not to press him. Instead, she asked him about the project, his home for so many years. He was happy to talk about it.

'I'm from Braskhia originally. I was the youngest of eight children, and when I was about six, I was sent to a monastery in Sestina because my family were too poor to feed all of us. I suppose I was upset at the time. I don't remember it much. The monks were part of a religion that believed that all the plant life of the world made up a god.'

'Everness, I've heard of him,' Hilspeth said. 'I use a lot of different leaves and moss and roots for my scentonomy.'

'Yes, Everness. The plants worked together to keep things running smoothly and all people had to do to please Everness was to learn about him through the trees and flowers and things, and to use them wisely. The monastery was a centre of learning for botany.

'I was put to work in the gardens, and I turned out to be quite good at it. I enjoyed it even though it was hard going. I was a bit of an experimenter though and I caused a few accidents along the way. The monks were tough old boys, but they were kind too. You get to be very patient when you spend your life watching things grow, I suppose. They made me an apprentice botanist, taught me a lot of stuff, how to read and write ... there was a lot of that. They made me work hard, and eventually I became a monk myself. I was a bit lax when it came to worship. I wasn't all that interested, but I had a knack for the botany.

'Then Rak Ek Namen came to power and took over the lands of the monastery. He told us we would no longer be allowed to practise our religion, but that we could continue our work. Later, he got some of us working on the Harvest Tide Project and moved us to Noran. That was nearly ten years ago now. We were joined by botanists from all over the Noranian Empire. Since then, we've worked in these huge gardens and greenhouses, never allowed to go out or talk to anyone outside the group. It still wasn't a bad life. They gave us anything we needed and left us alone most of the time. There were many rules, more than we had in the monastery ... and loads of guards too, but we were scholars – we learned how to live with it.'

'But then two Myunan children dumped you into a river and the Noranians lost track of you.'

'Yes. Since then, everything's been much, much more complicated.'

When they had a skirt-full of cones, they made their way back to the mill. The four of them then set about piercing the skins and building a pile beside Lorkrin. When the smell became too much, Hilspeth tutted, and sprinkled something from one of her bottles over the heap which deadened the odour slightly.

'What's that?' asked Taya.

'It's a concoction of mine made of rosewater, honey and quidal spit. It's for the treatment of offensive body odour.'

'You should give Lorkrin some of that when he wakes up. How do you get spit from a quidal?'

'You hold a jar over its head and insult it.'

Taya held her hands out to the warmth and eyed Groach.

'So, how do you know about all this stuff?' she enquired.

'I'm a botanist.'

'What's that?'

'It's like a gardener.'

'Then why don't you just say you're a gardener?'

'Because I'm a *botanist*.'

Having exhausted all the conversation she could muster, Taya looked down at her injured leg; she hoped there wouldn't be a scar. Scarred muscle was hard to amorph, and even harder to change colour. And besides, she was proud of her smooth skin. She self-consciously compared herself with Hilspeth, who sat across from her. Hilspeth's freckles were nice. Taya wondered how she'd look with freckles; she decided to try some when she got home. Putting a hand to Lorkrin's forehead, like Ma did when they were sick, she gazed down at him, and suddenly remembered the stolen quill. She glanced nervously to where Draegar was sitting outside.

'Here, Shessil,' she said softly. 'When you were in the sewer, we think you picked up something by accident – a quill that Lorkrin dropped. When you picked up all the stuff that fell out of your bag. It belonged to our uncle. Do you have it there?'

Groach frowned, struggling to remember what seemed so long ago.

'I left that bag at the Moffets', the house in Crickenob.'

Taya rolled her eyes and mouthed a curse.

They sat in silence for a while. Taya took some bread from her bag, and cut it into slices which she spread with honey and handed around. Groach nodded his thanks and gazed out at the sky while he ate. Taya noticed he was fidgeting a lot. He seemed to be bothered by something. She lay back and let her eyes wander across the stars visible beyond the edge of the broken roof. At one point, she thought she saw an eagle fly overhead, but she reasoned that it must have been an owl – eagles did not fly at night.

Draegar had positioned himself outside where he had the best view of the land around them. He leaned in to the rough shelter.

'We will have to move on tomorrow,' he said. 'I will keep watch. You should all get some sleep.'

Not needing any more persuasion, they all curled up under whatever cover they could and quickly drifted off. Draegar sat where he could not be seen from outside, and listened. His ears and nose would tell him what his eyes did not.

# 14 FRESHLY TURNED EARTH

Taya awoke suddenly. Sitting up, she saw that Lorkrin's bed was empty, and she got to her feet. Her leg still hurt, but she could almost walk without limping now. The storm had blown over, leaving a clear blue sky scattered with strands of white clouds. Groach and Hilspeth still lay asleep, Hilspeth under her cloak, Groach buried in some old straw. The pile of crumble cones was nothing more than a patch of brown-black sludge on the damp floorboards. Hearing movement outside, she climbed over the low ruins of the mill's outer wall, and walked to where Draegar was sitting on a tree stump, working on a map of the area. She took a quick look at the drawing, divided between envy and delight at the Parsinor's skill, and then turned her attention to the wreck of the millwheel, leaning against the riverbank. Lorkrin straddled the top of it.

'That thing could collapse, you know,' she scolded.

'I checked it out first. It's solid enough.'

Taya climbed up and took in the view from that height.

'How are you feeling?' she asked her brother.

'Okay, I was a bit dizzy when I woke up, but I'm fine now.

Draegar said you got hit with a crossbow?'

Taya undid her bandage and showed him the wound, which was now little more than a scar.

'Wow! Did it hurt?'

'Yeah, lots.'

They continued to sit there, not saying anything, just gazing around at the meadows and woods of the hills. Lorkrin broke a rotting spar off the wheel and threw it into the fast-moving water.

'I thought you were dead,' Taya said after a while. 'When you fell in.'

'Draegar reckons I almost was.'

'Shessil saved you; he had this kind of mask that let him breathe under the esh.'

Lorkrin nodded, and Taya could see he was more shaken by the episode than he would ever admit. Suddenly she threw her arms around him and hugged him tightly. Lorkrin put an arm around her, feeling a bit awkward. They pulled apart when Draegar called to them. Groach and Hilspeth were up.

'We need to get on,' he said, blowing on the map to help the ink dry, and packing the rest of his gear away. 'It would be better if we didn't move at all during the day until we get further from Noran, but we need to put some distance between us and where we met the soldiers yesterday. We'll stay under the cover of the trees in daylight, then get out onto the road at dusk. Gather your things. It's time to go.'

They climbed the slope among the tall poplars. It grew steep as they worked their way up, and Hilspeth's and Groach's calves were burning by the time they got to the top. The hill was clear of trees on the other side, and Draegar stood, surveying the land for a path down under cover. Taya and Lorkrin walked out onto the dull green moss that lined the bare slope and Taya gave a shout.

'It's mattress moss!' she cried, and began bouncing down the hill.

'Aw, yes!' Lorkrin took a running start and launched himself into the air. He landed on the spongy moss and vaulted up again, springing down the hill after his sister. Draegar sighed.

'So much for keeping a low profile,' said Hilspeth wryly.

The spread of mattress moss was like a huge trampoline; the two Myunans bounded down the slope like rubber balls, limbs flailing as they flew through the air. Hilspeth shrugged, and ran out onto the springy carpet, a giddy smile on her face as she chased the two shape-shifters. Draegar went after them at a more sober pace. Groach brought up the rear, stepping lightly, distracted by his thoughts.

Taya hit a bare patch of ground and grunted as her injured leg twinged. Lorkrin leap-frogged past her, laughing. She ran to catch up, taking strides as big as Draegar's, and feeling elated at the distance she was covering. After the events of the past few days, the mindless fun released all their tensions, letting them breathe easy again. Together they played an airborne game of catch, pestering Hilspeth until she agreed to join in. Every time they hit the moss, a light puff of dust and tiny insects exploded out of it and made it seem like the ground itself was spitting the travellers out. Draegar kept his eyes peeled for trouble. He was sure the alarm was out all over the country and many people would be watching out for them in the hope of a reward.

Taya and Lorkrin reached the bottom first and flopped on

the last stretch of moss, panting for breath. Hilspeth landed after them. Draegar loped down to them, maintaining his dignity, with Groach some way behind. The botanist was still preoccupied and hardly noticed that they had stopped.

'Let me make this clear,' growled Draegar to the Myunans. 'We are trying to stay hidden. We are trying to stay clear of the Noranians. We are trying to stay alive. If you two do not start behaving, I will tie you both up and carry you the rest of the way. Am I making myself clear?'

'Yes, Draegar,' they moaned in unison.

With expressions of mock seriousness, the two set off at a more resigned pace. The adult members of the party fell back behind them at Draegar's beckoning.

'Those two are wilful and mischievous. I expect this kind of thing from them, but we must set an example,' he lectured the other pair. 'If you have any doubt that we will all be killed, with the exception of the botanist here, then let me assure you that the Noranians mean business in everything that they do. And they mean to catch us. The soldiers are experts at hunting people down and they have skilled trackers. They will find us eventually, if we do not lose them down south.'

'And here I thought they just wanted us to like them,' Hilspeth said airily.

'This is not a joking matter,' the Parsinor retorted sternly. 'The lives of these children are my responsibility and they will not be taken by the Noranians while I am able to draw breath. If either of you endanger them further than you have already, you will answer to me.'

'I'll face Everness's wrath long before I feel yours,' Groach whispered.

'What was that?' Draegar rumbled.

'I think there is much, much worse to come,' Groach murmured.

'What do you mean?' Hilspeth asked. 'What's wrong?'

But Groach would not be drawn out and they walked along for some time after, lost in their own thoughts. At the bottom of the hill, Draegar took the lead, and they followed a gully shrouded in leafy ash trees to the banks of a river, where they turned to follow it upstream. The Parsinor chose trails that hid them from sight, sometimes keeping to the river, sometimes climbing the hillside to stay in the shadows of the foliage.

The sun was high in the sky when they came to an open space that looked as if it had been inhabited until recently. Burnt patches on the ground marked the locations of what had once been huts; freshly turned earth covered what appeared to be a burial pit, and there had been some kind of construction bridging the river, the charred remains of which could be seen on the riverbed. The odour of burnt wood and oil still hung heavy in the air.

'This was a Gabbit village, with a sundat mill,' Draegar observed. 'There would have been a wooden gantry over the river to process the skins of sundat worms.'

He examined the mess of tracks in the ground around them.

'A Noranian battlegroup was through here last night. The soldiers terrorised the villagers and burned the place to the ground. By the looks of things, the Gabbits were even prevented from putting out the fires. Their homes were completely destroyed. The Noranians beat them back, some were badly hurt. You can see where their bodies have been dragged away. And yet the people still stayed true to their beliefs. See how they've taken down the remains of the huts and buried the debris – still trying to leave the land as they found it.'

'Why would the army do this?' Taya gazed around her, trying to imagine the village that would have been here only the night before.

'Because they were looking for us,' Hilspeth muttered, and Draegar nodded.

'They would need little excuse to persecute Gabbits,' he growled. 'But this was not a random patrol. The troops didn't come from the road, but from the same woods we've just come through, and the tracks are old, from last night. Soldiers don't travel in dark forest unless something takes them there. They were hunting for us, but they were ahead of us and didn't realise it.'

Lorkrin glanced at Taya, who avoided his eyes. The knowledge that a whole village had been razed to the ground, because of them, fell like a physical blow on the Myunans. Taya felt suddenly dizzy, sitting down on a rock to avoid falling. Lorkrin rubbed watering eyes and put his hands up behind his head to ease the tightness in his chest. He had never really stopped believing that they had been living an adventure, like those he loved to hear about around the lodge's fire in the evenings. Through all their ordeals, he had been fretting over a lost quill, and how to escape their uncle's fury. But the burnt shapes in the grass – shapes that had once been homes – suddenly changed things for him. People they had never met had suffered because of them, and it awoke a profound shame in him. Looking over at Taya, he could see that she felt it too. She still would not meet his gaze, looking out over the river, and chewing on the end of her ponytail. For some time, nobody said a word.

Eventually, Draegar indicated to the others that it was time to leave, and they followed him up the slope and into the woods, away from the trail of the soldiers. Keeping well inside the border of the trees, they walked until late afternoon.

They stopped in the shade of a weeping willow, its drooping branches forming a tent around them. Groach removed his boots and massaged his aching feet and calves. He had never walked so far in his life. They had gathered berries along the way, and Taya and Hilspeth made sandwiches of them with the last of the bread and honey. Lorkrin took the canteens and went off in search of water.

Draegar sat down, and took out some parchment and a quill. He spoke as he drew.

'We're running out of trees. The next stretch is over fields. We'll walk along the hedgerows as much as possible. I want to reach the road to Brodfan by dusk. We'll make better progress once we're on the road, but we can't walk it in daylight. We'll camp in the thickets around Brodfan, then stay there tomorrow. From there on, we travel only at night.'

'I have to go back to Noran,' Groach said abruptly.

'What are you talking about?' Draegar looked up from his work.

'I know why the Harvest Tide Project is so important,' the botanist sighed quietly.

Putting on his boots, he stared hard at the ground. Hilspeth sat down beside him.

'We were never told why we were doing all that work,' he

went on. 'We were so caught up in it, we never really gave it much thought. To us, it was enough that we would be learning more about the esh-bound bubule. We believed that the Noranians wanted to farm it or something. We thought the Prime Ministrate was as fascinated by the bubule as we were.'

Stopping for a moment, he dug a heel into the ground and twisted it to reveal the earth beneath the weeds.

'We didn't know how he thought, you see – the Prime Ministrate, I mean. Noran was so caught up in learning and working hard ... we thought we were just another part of it. But we weren't; we were special. Not many projects had armed guards and high walls. I cracked the problem. I figured out how to make the esh-bound bubule bloom. That's what causes Harvest Tide, you see – that's when the esh floods the land and leaves the bules in their thousands when it recedes. The next Harvest Tide is at the end of the summer. I was amazed at how simple it was when it came to me. It was so obvious that we'd overlooked it for years. Harvest Tide happens at the end of the summer, when the esh is at its warmest. I found out that it was heat, not sunlight as we believed, that made the plant blossom. The plants soaked up heat, and then when they bloomed, they released a gas that made the sessium swell. So all I had to do was find some way of warming up the gas until it reached the temperature that made the flowers break out.'

'But how could you do that?' Taya asked. 'Fire doesn't burn in the esh. How would you manage it?'

'Several shiploads of pierced crumble cones would do it. Dump them near the bubule plains and it would take less than a day to force the plants to bloom. The only problem was that the bules themselves would be next to useless. They would give off very little oil. And the early tide killed the plants; you could wipe out the very thing you were trying to use. Force a Harvest Tide this year, you won't have one next year. No Harvest Tide, no bules. We'd explained that to the Noranians, but they didn't seem interested. That had been bothering me for some time.

'Then I went after Lorkrin when he fell into the esh. He was almost killed ... and that was when it hit me. The Prime Ministrate might not be after the *bules* at all. He might be after the tide itself. You see, when the esh floods the plains on the coast, it rarely rises above the level of your knees. Eighty years ago, though, there was a summer storm in Braskhia and the gas drove inland. It reached levels higher than the head of a grown man in several places on the coast. Some people died before they could get above it. If you heated up the esh enough around the bubules, you could create a wall of gas so high it could swallow houses, esh-boats ... everything. For anyone on the coast who did not live in the hills, it would mean certain death by suffocation.'

'Damn you and your kind,' Draegar snarled, rising to his feet. 'As if the Noranians were not capable of enough destruction, you give them a weapon that could create a disaster. Only the gods know what kind of insanity Rak Ek Namen plans. But if he can somehow make Noran stronger by killing thousands, then he will find a way to do it. Tell me why I wouldn't be making the land a safer place by killing you right now!'

Groach was hauled to his feet and found himself lifted bodily against the trunk of the willow by his throat. Hilspeth jumped up and swung helplessly off Draegar's huge arm.

'Let him go!' she screamed. 'Let him go, you animal!'

'Thggh ... haggh ... by ... notsch,' the botanist rasped.

Draegar suddenly let go, and Groach slumped to the ground. Hilspeth still hung from the map-maker's arm.

'What?' Draegar hissed.

'I told them where to find my notes.' Groach rubbed his throat tenderly. 'They probably have them by now. It's all in my notes – everything I know about the Harvest Tide.'

With a curse, Draegar thumped the trunk of the tree with one hand and shook Hilspeth off the other. Taya stood up, fearfully looking from Draegar to Groach and back again. Uncle Emos's farm was on the coast of Braskhia. She knew people out there, decent ordinary folk. Why would the Prime Ministrate want to kill them? What was it for?

'What have you done?' she asked, queasily.

'I don't know,' Groach answered. 'But I have to find out. I have to go back to Noran.'

'But they're still after you.' Hilspeth took his hand. 'We can't let you go back.'

'I have to go,' he repeated.

'Then at least let us come with you. We can't let you go on your own.'

'The children are going back to their uncle's,' Draegar said. 'And I need you to make sure they get there, Hilspeth.'

'What?' She frowned.

'This is a serious matter. Taya and Lorkrin must get home safely, but many more lives are at stake. I am going with this meddling gardener to Noran. I must find out what they intend to do with this weapon of theirs and he is my means of finding out. I need you to see the children home.'

'Forget it,' she snapped. 'I'm staying with Shessil.'

'Hilspeth,' Draegar reasoned in a softer voice. 'We cannot involve them, and I can keep Shessil safer than you could. It makes sense and you know it. If we leave the two little scamps on their own, they will follow us. And apart from all that, two men travelling will attract less attention than all five of us. Please, look after Lorkrin and Taya.'

Hilspeth hesitated, glancing at Taya, who was standing up and looking disappointed.

'All right, but you take good care of Shessil. This may all be his doing, but he's a good man. Don't you harm a hair on his head, or I'll make you sorry you were born.'

'Agreed,' the Parsinor said with a nod.

They all stood staring at one another, not saying a word. They stayed that way until Lorkrin burst through the foliage of the willow and skidded to a stop. He looked around warily.

'Why have you all gone so quiet?' he whispered.

# 15 LYING LOW AT THE LUSH OASIS

From where the column of vehicles had stopped to look at a fake raspidam footprint, Emos had tracked some soldiers to the clearing by the esh where they had caught up with Lorkrin and Taya. There was a new set of tracks, and Emos deduced that his niece and nephew had managed to rescue the man from the house in Hortenz, the botanist. At the same time, he had discovered Draegar's footprints and could tell by the Parsinor's footwork among the Noranians' boot marks that he had tackled some of the soldiers and won. The marks in the ground had been spoiled by the rain, but it told him enough. Lorkrin had fallen into the esh. Draegar and the botanist had followed and somehow got him out.

Draegar's prints were deeper when they left – he was carrying something ... and Lorkrin was not walking with them. Taya was limping, but seemed to be all right. The woman with the strange collection of smells was with them too. Having given up his search from the air, knowing Draegar would keep them under cover, the Myunan was tracking them by following the trail of scent, crushed grass and broken twigs. Along the way, he discovered another, fresher set of tracks on top of those that he was following. Noranian trackers were after them now.

Whoever this gardener or botanist was, he was important to the Noranians, and Emos was becoming more and more convinced that he possessed something the Noranians were desperate to have. He came across the mill where the fugitives had slept, and noted the sludge of rotten crumble cones. He was relieved to find that Lorkrin was walking once more.

The Noranians were closing in on them. The odd group had stopped amid the signs of destruction of a Gabbit village, devastation that could only mean a visit by soldiers. He came across a party of Gabbits further along the trail, out scavenging for materials to build their new settlement. They chattered mournfully when they saw Emos, eager to tell their tale of woe. He stopped to make some conversation and find out what he could. They had not seen his niece and nephew, but soldiers had been mobilised all over the region to search for them, and particularly for the man they had kidnapped from a Noranian convoy. The Prime Ministrate himself had ordered their arrest. After sitting down with them to a simple meal of bread and mushroom soup, Emos thanked them and left to continue his search with a growing sense of unease.

At a wide stream, Draegar had led the others in and along it and Emos lost the trail. He could see the Noranians had too. But he had noticed what they had not. The group had been picking berries to eat as they went and he searched up and down the stream's course until he found a freshly picked blackberry bush. From there he was able to take up their trail again. They were making their way south. Draegar would probably head for Brodfan, where the Noranians were not popular.

Passing a grove of nocha trees, he saw a swarm of people, nearly fifty of them, working under the canopy of the branches. They were gathering crumble cones and heaping them into sacks. Noranian Groupmasters were watching over them as they loaded the sacks into the back of a wagon. Emos kept out of sight, observing this unusual harvest. Crumble cones were not normally the kind of thing people collected. When the truck was full, it was driven off and another took its place. The labourers kept working.

Emos stopped again when he reached a weeping willow. They had rested here. Lorkrin had gone to get water, and Draegar had argued with the gardener, holding him against the trunk of the tree. He walked on and it was growing dark when he came on the hedge where their trails parted. Draegar and the other man had turned north, the others south.

Emos sat down to think. What was the Parsinor doing? What could possibly make him leave the children? It disturbed the Myunan – it would have taken something serious for Draegar to shirk what he saw as his responsibility ... It would take a matter of life and death. Had he learned something about the Noranians' plans for war?

Emos was faced with the choice of turning after the Parsinor and the gardener and getting some answers, or continuing the search for Lorkrin and Taya. He sat down to rest and leaned back wearily against the trunk of the tree. Rak Ek Namen was famous for his cunning. His forces had never lost a battle under his leadership; it was said he never started a war he could not win. It would not be enough that Braskhia and the Kartharic Peaks went to war – Namen had to be sure that he would end up crushing both countries. And he was putting all his efforts into gardening and the esh. Emos shook his head and hauled himself to his feet. It was too much of a puzzle. His first concern was finding Taya and Lorkrin.

Knowing he would have to give up following the trail when it got dark, he got up and started south after his niece and nephew. They were making for Brodfan, and he was close now. A look back across the fields stopped him dead. Just this side of the woods, someone had lit a lantern. Three lanterns. Those were not farmers; the Noranians had found the trail again.

Moving quickly, he removed what signs he could of the tracks. Then reshaping his own feet to imitate each of the different types of footprint in turn, he left a false trail leading away from the road, away from Brodfan. Let the Noranians ponder that for a while. Wrapping up his tools, he slung his bag onto his back and set out south again.

+ + +

Hilspeth, Taya and Lorkrin had left Draegar and Groach near the road, and had been walking south since sunset. The two Myunans had been arguing with the scentonomist ever since.

'But we could help,' Lorkrin was protesting. 'We can sneak into places they can't get to ... we can disguise ourselves and hide better than they can.'

'I'm not arguing with you any more. I'm taking you back to your uncle's and that's the end of it,' Hilspeth said firmly.

'You want to go too; you can't fool us,' Taya told her. 'You're worried about Shessil.'

'I said I wasn't going to argue any more and I mean it. Now, pipe down.'

'You're just scared of Draegar. He's not as mean as he seems to be, you know,' said Taya. 'Well, he is pretty mean. But he's got a nice side.'

'On the far side of the nasty bit,' added Lorkrin.

'Sort of hidden behind it ...' continued Taya.

'Well hidden,' Lorkrin finished.

'I'm not scared of Draegar. This is just not the kind of thing children should be involved in.'

'We're already involved!' Taya pleaded.

'Who are you calling children?' Lorkrin scowled. 'I'm thirteen and a half.'

Hilspeth shook her head and walked on. It was a dark, overcast night, and they could barely see the road in the gloom. Everything below the horizon was a solid black mass. They were having to follow the dim light reflecting off the puddles on each side of the road to prevent themselves from walking into hedges and ditches. Hilspeth was making her two charges walk ahead of her, and still they were difficult to see. She was convinced they were becoming darker themselves as if they were trying to disappear into the night.

The lanterns on the front of a vehicle appeared over the crest of a hill not far ahead, and the noise of its spluttering engine reached their ears.

'Quick, hide!' she cried, and they plunged into the hedges. The wagon bore down on them and Hilspeth could see it was a tractor, its iron wheels grinding the surface of the road, and pistons protruding from the massive engine to drive the six wheels. It was loud and slow. As it passed, the torches cast a yellow light over the area, and Hilspeth looked to see if Taya and Lorkrin were visible. They were nowhere to be seen. When it was far enough away, she came out of hiding and called to them. There was no answer. She searched around, wishing she dared use the light of the tinderbox, but it was useless. Instead she stood still and listened. There wasn't a sound. The Myunans were concealed in the shadows of the bushes and were not coming out.

'Fine, if that's the way you want to play it,' she said out loud. 'I can wait. I know you can hide, but if you move, I'll hear you. So, we'll just wait until daylight, waste all that time ... maybe even get caught, so that you two can make believe that you are going to Noran.'

She sat down and listened to the dark. She was not so sure she would be able to find them even in daylight. That was a Myunan's talent. If they didn't want to be found, they wouldn't be. How did you search for a person who could change their colour, even their shape at will? And they could do this every time she took her eyes off them. Even if she caught them this time, they would have plenty of other opportunities to escape her along the way. They were telling her they would go to Noran without her if they couldn't go with her. Hilspeth blew air through her gritted teeth with a hissing sound.

'All right, we'll go after them,' she sighed.

'That's more like it,' she heard Taya say, as she stood up right beside the scentonomist, the young Myunan's skin colour perfectly matched to the pattern of the long grass.

'I can't believe I'm doing this,' Hilspeth groaned.

But at least she would be there to help if ... no, when they ran into trouble.

✦ ✦ ✦

Groach and Draegar had followed the road for most of the night and now, ahead of them, were the lights of a village. Groach expected the Parsinor to veer off the road and take to the fields as they had done twice already that night, but instead Draegar strode straight down the roadway towards the village.

'There is a storyhouse here where we can get food and stay out of the Noranians' way for the day,' the Parsinor told him. 'They are no friends of the soldiers and will hide us if needs be.'

'Thank the gods,' Groach moaned. His feet were killing him and he was exhausted.

They approached a slightly tilting building that looked as if it had seen one storm too many. A sign hanging above the door read '*The Lush Oasis*'. Tiles were missing from the steep roof, the ragged remains of birds' nests hung from the eaves and most of the plaster had crumbled from its sandstone walls. The green-painted frames of the windows and doors did not seem to fit properly, and tied to railings in the yard on one side were all manner of mounts, from horses to donkeys, oxen to elmadons, tremadites to grunchegs. Three wagons and a tractor were parked on the weed-ridden gravel on the other side of the building.

'Men come here at all hours of the day and night,' Draegar said as they studied the storyhouse. 'Not every trade works during the day. This is a rough place. Don't get into any arguments and don't get in anyone's way. Places like this attract some evil types, but they won't ask questions and that's what counts for us now.'

They walked up to the door and Draegar pushed it open. Some faces in the large group of men turned their way, but most ignored them. The room was not very big, packed with benches and tables made of rough-hewn wood. The walls and ceilings were stained a greasy, brownish yellow from years of smoke, and the thick beams holding up the ceiling were hung with tankards, jugs, ladles and other serving implements. The heads of every kind of animal worth hunting stood out on plaques along the walls. There were tails, furs, skulls and bones, even the whole skeleton of a large animal Groach did not recognise adorning the stained plaster and smoke-darkened beams. Over the odour of pipes and drink, there was a faint, but pervasive stink of old embalming fluid.

Groach noticed with surprise that there was a Parsinor couple behind the bar. They were much older than Draegar, and the man was nearly a head shorter, bent deeply as if the weight of his shell were almost too much for him. His wife was taller. She wore a wig and as much jewellery as her frame could physically carry, which was quite a bit. He observed that she wore a gaily coloured dress, even though he knew Parsinors had no need to wear clothes. The couple signalled Draegar to join them at the bar.

'Draegar,' the woman purred. 'It's been too long. We haven't seen you in over a season.'

'Still wandering, Draegar?' the man enquired. 'It's time you found yourself a wife!'

'Temina, Cholsch.' The map-maker touched foreheads with each of the others in the traditional Parsinor greeting. Then Draegar handed over his weapons; clearly none were allowed to be carried in the storyhouse. Groach watched with amusement as his companion placed the collection on the bar. His battleaxe, sword and sling were joined by three knives, a small hammer, a short blowpipe, and a set of metal fangs that obviously fit in his mouth. Cholsch, the man, swept them up in his arms and placed them in a box under the counter.

'I must have your weapons as well, sir,' he said to Groach.

'I don't have any,' the botanist replied.

The storyhouse owner raised his bushy eyebrows at Draegar, who shrugged.

'He is a gardener,' he grunted. Then, leaning closer: 'The Noranians are on the lookout for him. I would appreciate it if you would tell no one about him.'

'Aye,' Cholsch said simply.

'Welcome to our home.' Temina took Groach's head in both hands and touched her forehead to his for slightly longer than he thought necessary. 'May your stay be comfortable and happy.'

'Ah ... thank you, madam,' he gave a shallow bow.

'Been harassing the Nogs again, have you?' Cholsch asked in a conspiratorial tone, looking sideways at the map-maker.

'They have been harassing friends of mine,' Draegar rumbled. 'It seemed only fair to return the gesture.'

'We look forward to hearing about it,' Cholsch said, laughing. 'But first, have a seat. Entertain our customers while we knock you and your friend up something to eat.'

'I will sit with you,' Temina said, coming through the gap in the counter to take Draegar's arm.

She led them to the centre of the room, and unceremoniously pushed two men off a bench to make room for herself and her guests. Groach and Draegar sat either side of her.

'Pay attention, you louts!' she roared and the room went silent. 'This is a dear friend of mine and weary from travel. Some of you will know him; most of you will not. But you will all discover that he is a man to admire and envy, that he is a man with stories to tell!'

Benches scraped along the floor as men came closer to the centre table to hear what Draegar had to say. The map-maker did not disappoint them. He raised his hands, palms up:

'I have travelled a long way since I was last here. I have seen rain and snow and burning sun in three lands in this last season. But it is of the witching time in the Gluegrove Swamps I must tell you now, so give me your ears and let me tell you the tale of the conjoined hags who make soup bowls from the skulls of unwary travellers!'

+ + +

Against her better judgement, Hilspeth had let the Myunans talk her into hitching a lift with a delivery man on his way to Noran. He had passed them late that morning, and Taya had jumped out of hiding and waved him down, asking him to take them as far as he could. He had been happy to help. Hilspeth had thought the better of making a scene, and had got in with the two shape-shifters. She consoled herself with the thought that the soldiers might not think to check vehicles heading towards Noran for fugitives who would be getting as far away as possible if they had any sense. The wagon was old, but big, with two rows of seats in the cab and a large flatbed with its cargo covered in tarpaulin.

'What are you carrying?' Taya called to the driver over the roar of the bule engine.

'Crumble cones,' he shouted back. 'Not my normal cargo,

mind. I carry supplies for the army mostly. Got one job where I carry big tanks of esh up to Noran. Pick them up at the coast. Very secret, that.'

Hilspeth sat in the back seat with Lorkrin, and wished Taya were less keen to make conversation. The more the driver talked, the more he would expect them to talk back.

'So, what are the crumble cones for?' Taya asked.

'Not supposed to talk about it,' he bellowed over a particularly loud belch from the motor. 'Takin' 'em to Noran. Some kind of secret plan, run by the Prime Ministrate himself. No one knows much about it. They're storing these right in the centre of the city. Very heavily guarded. They're shipping these ruddy cones in from all over the empire. I was supposed to have an armed escort myself but they couldn't spare the men.'

Taya turned and gave Hilspeth a meaningful look. The Prime Ministrate had discovered Shessil's secret, and was wasting no time in putting his plan into action. But what did he intend to do?

'Where are the cones going after you deliver them?' Hilspeth enquired at the top of her voice.

'Not sure,' the driver shouted. 'Though a drinking mate of mine says his esh-boat has been held back in the port, and is due to be sent down south with a special cargo. He couldn't tell me what the cargo was, said it was top secret, but he was asking me to hurry up with my deliveries as it was people like me that was holding his ship up.'

The driver informed them that he was under orders to drive all night. His cargo was to reach Noran by noon of the following day at all costs, and they were welcome to travel all the way with him. They could help keep him awake. He said he had a habit of falling asleep on long hauls. He added that with a bit of luck, they might pick up a military escort that evening if one of the other delivery wagons caught up with them. It was handy to have troops around you, even if they did travel a bit fast. The roads just weren't safe these days.

# 16 Ghosts are Lonely Creatures

Groach came to his senses, and for a few seconds could not remember where he was. He was in a soft bed, his head laid on down pillows, and he was wrapped up in a heavy swathe of blankets. The air around his exposed face told him the room was cold, but it just made him feel all the cosier snuggled up as he was. The bedroom was much smaller than the last one he had slept in, with rough plaster walls, bare floorboards and mismatched wooden furniture, but it was homely and comfortable and he felt safe here. Getting up, he dressed quickly, jogging on the spot to warm himself up. Spring was cold and summer came late this far north.

The bar of the tavern was no less dark in the morning than it had been the night before. The small, dirty windows let in dull shafts of light, but were no brighter than the oil lamps had been. The customers were smoking, talking, eating and drinking as they had been all night; the time of day seemed to have little bearing on life in the storyhouse. Groach looked around for Draegar, but the Parsinor was nowhere to be seen.

Stories were being traded over the tables around the

room, and Groach made his way over to one to listen. Two men moved to make room for him, one a squat Gabbit with an eye-patch and an ugly scar that extended out of it around his head, and two fingers missing from his left hand; the other a Traxen mercenary in a headscarf and camouflage paint. Groach sat down and listened quietly.

Draegar came in two tales later with Cholsch. They were arguing about something.

'There are soldiers moving up and down the main roads all the time. The last two nights there has been more traffic along this road then I've seen since the war with Sestina,' Cholsch was saying.

'Then it will be easier to conceal ourselves,' Draegar insisted. 'We don't have much time. Whatever Namen intends to do, he means to do it soon. We must get to Noran quickly.'

'Well, at least wait until this afternoon. That way you might get a night's travel out of it, before anyone gets suspicious.'

'Agreed.'

Draegar nodded to Groach as he sat down at the table.

'Another story!' the mercenary cried. 'Temina, another round of drinks, if you please.'

'I am reminded of a time ...' Draegar began.

'I have a story,' Groach interrupted quietly. After a few tankards of mead, he was getting into the spirit of things.

'Let the little man speak,' said the mercenary. 'Let's hear what he has to tell.'

Groach looked queasily around at his now-silent audience and swallowed a mouthful of mead from the tankard that was placed before him.

'I haven't travelled much,' he admitted. 'I've lived most of my life in the same place. We were not allowed out much, my colleagues and I. But our work brought us to Hortenz sometimes. We took a number of trips out on esh-boats, often spending days at a time at sail, just studying the gas and what lay beneath it.

'On a gusty day in mid-autumn, we were out of sight of land in gale-force winds. The ship was rocking violently, and the churning esh made it impossible to navigate. Late in the afternoon, one of the pumps tore loose, smashing a hole through the hull of the starboard pod and throwing four men overboard. It is said that what the esh takes, it keeps, for there is no rescue for a man overboard. He does not float and he does not swim. He falls until he hits the bottom.

'It was only by the grace of Everness that there was no fire, for a hydrogen explosion would have killed us all. The ship rolled onto its side, and all those above deck had to hold on for their lives. I was in the centre pod, below decks where we were trapped beneath the surface of the gas. The doors were jammed shut and the vessel was just barely afloat. The only hope of anybody making it to shore was for the men above us to unhitch our hull and let it fall, releasing the weight so that they could right their pod. There were five of us in my section of the hull: an engineer, a bosun's mate, two other botanists and myself. After some time, we heard the sounds of sawing and hammering, and at first we believed they were going to cut the hull free with us inside. We were horrified.

'We tried smashing a hole in the wall to get out, but we had little more than our hands and feet to hit it. The thought of falling to the bottom of the esh where we would be smashed to pieces or suffocated was more than we could bear. Soon, however, the engineer told us that it sounded more like they were cutting their way to us. They were going to get us out.

'If you can imagine, we were trapped in a small room, lying on its side so that the portholes on one side looked up through the gas towards the light of the sky, while those on the other side gave us a view of the depths below us. The whole ship rocked and pitched in the wind. We could see through the portholes the sailors dangling down on ropes, wearing gas masks to get at the hull, and they had only makeshift tools. There was also the muffled sound of voices, men trapped in another part of the pod, and we could hear work going on in that direction too.

'It grew dark and the wind continued to build. Soon, the sailors above us had to give up. They could not see, and it was too rough to work. They tapped on the hull, signalling to us that they would try again at first light. The esh at night is dark, but not black. It has a light of its own, a dull yellow glow. It is caused by algae drifting in the thicker gas, deep below the surface. So, when darkness fell, it was the turn of the portholes on the floor of our cabin to let in light. It was a strange sensation, as if the world had turned upside down and there was a yellow moon below us.

'The cabin was sealed, so we had air, but it would not last forever. We tried to rest and sleep as much as we could so that we would breathe less. Later in the night, the wind died down and the esh became very still. I was lying on the floor and gazing down out of one of the portholes when I saw something. At first I thought it must be an esh-floater. We saw them from time to time, lolling about in the gas that was their home. But this was different. It was bigger, and it moved with purpose. It took me some time to realise that it was a ship. I shouted to the others.

'We wanted to believe that it was just a wreck, or perhaps even our reflection on a lake or river below us, but we could tell from the way it moved that it was neither. It circled our position, staying far enough down to prevent us from seeing it clearly.

'Men have tried to build ships that could sail beneath the esh, but their attempts have always ended in disaster, and we could see that this was a ship built for the surface; it had sails and even a flag, which meant only one thing. This was a ghost ship, one of the thousands of vessels claimed by the esh, but one whose crew had not made it into the afterlife. We watched in terror, unable to take our eyes off it. Even when we saw shapes, figures, rise up towards us from it, we did nothing.

'But then the bosun's mate let out a scream, and the spell was broken. We started shouting and shrieking to the crew above us to get us out. We would quickly use up what air we had left, but we did not care. Ghosts are lonely creatures, desperate for others to join them. And we knew they were coming for us. In the dark, enclosed cabin, we were at their mercy. The fear drove us mad. Hammering and kicking at the wall that was our ceiling with anything we could get our hands on, we were no longer worried about the esh getting in. As long as the phantoms didn't get in first.

'The remains of the crew heard us, and must have been convinced by our screams that we feared for our very souls. They risked their lives to hang down into the gloom and tear frantically at the walls that separated us. Beneath our feet, we could hear the sound of fingernails scraping against the wood and sometimes dragging across the glass of the port-holes. I was sure I even heard the creatures gnawing at the tarred wood with their teeth. Above us, the sailors were shouting to each other that they could see things moving around the edges of the ship. The work grew even more urgent.

'I looked down through one of the portholes in the floor, and saw that the ghost ship was becoming larger and clearer. I yelled to the others that it was rising towards us. We were going to be rammed. A split appeared in the wall over our heads and a wisp of gas seeped in. An axe-head pierced the timbers, and under a steady barrage, the hole grew. Esh flowed in and we breathed deeply, readying our-selves for the moment when we ran out of air. I peered down through the gas rising around our feet to the world beyond the porthole. The dead men's ship was coming right for us.

'The last few bits of board were broken away by the sail-ors and gas gushed in as they threw a rope down. We had no masks in the cabin so we would have to hold our breaths as we climbed up to the surviving pod. I was the fourth one out. Just as the engineer grabbed the rope below me, the mast of the haunted ship smashed through the porthole and tore a gash along the lower wall of the cabin. I clambered out with the engineer close behind. With the gas around our faces, we could not see a thing, relying on the crew with masks to guide us up the rope against the side of the pod. We dragged ourselves up onto the sloping deck of the third pod and heaved in breaths of life-giving air. The captain wasted no time, yanking back on the locking levers, and releasing the wrecked pod that had held us. With a shudder, it broke free and we held tight as the remaining hull lurched back away from it and then rocked back and forth until it had settled into an upright position. We heard the hiss of the shattered pod falling down through the esh, and then nothing.

'In the swaying peace that followed, I asked the captain if they had got the people caught in the other section of the pod out in time. He told me that a team of sailors had broken through to the cabin where the others had been trapped even before they had reached us, but sailors had found only a hole in the lower side of the hull and the signs of a desperate fight. The cabin had been empty.'

Groach took a sip of his mead and waited for someone else to break the silence in the room.

+ + +

Hilspeth and the Myunans were sitting in the cab of the wagon, each of them trying to come up with an excuse for getting off that would not make the driver suspicious. Ever since he had mentioned the fact that he was due to be met by Noranian troops, the idea of walking the rest of the way had become far more attractive. Lorkrin had his tool kit out, and was doing something to his face. Hilspeth kicked him and gave him a hard stare.

'What are you doing?' she hissed.

Lorkrin had given himself boils and blisters all over his face.

'I'm going to say I've got a disease,' he whispered in her ear. 'Maybe he'll throw us out.'

Hilspeth rolled her eyes back, but she didn't have any better ideas, so she said nothing. Lorkrin was reaching over to tap the driver on the shoulder when the driver hit the brake and brought the wagon to a shuddering halt. Ahead of them was a small village – a storyhouse, and a few ramshackle houses, along with some market stalls.

'This is a rough neighbourhood,' he said over the idling motor. He looked back and his eyes opened wide at the sight of Lorkrin's face, but he quickly turned to stare ahead again. 'You'd best get out of sight. Passengers attract attention in this neck of the woods. Get yourselves under the tarpaulin and stay there until I tell you it's safe.'

Not knowing what else to say, the three fugitives climbed over the back of the seats onto the flatbed behind, and slipped under the cover with the crumble cones. Lorkrin, a little disappointed by the lack of reaction, let his face settle back to normal. The driver released the brake, and they trundled noisily down the hill to the village. They rolled through without incident and passed on out the other side into a copse of trees set on high banks on either side of the road. They were barely out of sight of the village when the wagon ground to a halt again. Peeping out from under the tarpaulin, Taya could see that there was a fallen tree blocking the road. The driver sighed and got down from his cab. He carried a wooden club in one hand as he went over to inspect the tree.

He did not appear surprised when two Parsinors wearing masks and cloaks slid down the banks on either side and drew swords. The driver, who obviously had no illusions about the speed of his vehicle, did not even try to get back into the cab.

'I'm not going to fight you,' he called. 'Take what you have to, just don't hurt me. The wife would murder me if I came home injured.'

'We only want your wagon,' the bigger Parsinor told him, and Taya's jaw dropped when she recognised Draegar's voice. 'We're only borrowing it. We'll bring it back when we're finished with it.'

'I'm sure,' replied the driver dourly.

'You have my word,' Draegar assured him. 'Go back to the storyhouse in the village and wait there. Your goods will be delivered; you can count on that. Just stay in the village and we will return your wagon. Leave the village, and we will have to dump it in a river somewhere. Do you understand?'

'Aye.'

'Good.' The two Parsinors lifted the tree out of the way and another, smaller masked man slipped down the bank on the left and climbed into the cab. With a quick glance at the tarpaulin-covered pile on his truck, the driver shook his head and started walking back in the direction of the village.

'You're not going to believe this,' Taya whispered to the others, ducking her head back under.

'We know,' Lorkrin groaned.

'Move over,' they heard Draegar say. 'You're going to have to drive.' The second Parsinor seemed to have gone.

'But I've never driven a wagon before in my life. Why can't you do it?' came Groach's voice.

'Because they don't make vehicles for Parsinors,' Draegar growled. 'How am I supposed to work the *pedals* with feet like these? Drive, get on with it. The sooner we get going, the sooner you can be back in Noran.'

There was the sound of grating gears, then Groach took the brake off and the wagon swerved backwards into a ditch. The botanist shouted an apology, shifted out of reverse and gunned the engine, throwing them forward and nearly pitching them into the ditch on the other side.

'By the gods!' Draegar roared, ripping off his mask and cloak. 'Whatever made them give up on horses?'

'I've got it, I've got it,' Groach cried out, as the truck lurched back and the engine stalled.

Cursing under his breath, Draegar got down from the cab, pulled the crank handle from its clips, and walked around to the front of the wagon, inserting the handle and cranking it until the engine started once more. Groach put it into gear and turned the large, wooden steering wheel to straighten the vehicle out on the road. Then in jolts and starts they made their way forward.

'I told you we should have kept walking,' Hilspeth murmured to the Myunans.

'He's going to have a fit if he finds us here,' Lorkrin hissed.

'I think he'll probably kill Shessil long before that happens,' Taya told him.

Groach's control of the wagon improved gradually, until he was able to make it go forwards without grinding the gears or stalling the engine too often. He did have problems keeping it out from the edges of the road, but at least they were heading in the right direction.

'Have you any idea what you're going to do when we get there?' Draegar asked him.

'I'm not sure,' the botanist replied. 'But my friends from the project are in Noran. He must still be using them. Once I tell them what they're working on, they won't take it any further. With their help, I might be able to stop Namen from doing whatever it is he wants to do.'

'It's my bet that he will use it in the Kartharic Peaks,' Draegar said. 'The Karthars are strong and a war with them would

241

be costly. With the esh as his weapon, he could kill the Kar-thars in their thousands.'

The wagon coughed and spluttered its way along the road, the afternoon sun glinting off its bodywork, and dust and pebbles spitting from under its wheels. The noise and smoke meant that keeping a low profile was impossible, but its passengers, both those in the cab and those concealed behind them, hoped that they would slip into Noran unno-ticed among all the other vehicles that were making the same journey. The flaw in this plan became apparent as they came around a curve in the road, and encountered a convoy of wagons carrying the same load as themselves. The eight flatbed trucks were being escorted by three battlewagons. Groach brought the truck to a skidding halt, but they had already been seen. The vehicles were refuelling at a bule-oil depot in the front yard of a tavern. A battlewagon reversed up to them and an officer waved them forward.

'Crumble cones? Group up with the rest. We're trying to keep as many of you together as possible, but you're coming from all over the place. Have you enough bule oil? This depot is almost out and the next one is two hours' drive away.'

'I ... I think we have enough,' Groach stammered, check-ing the gauges in front of him. 'We don't have to join up with you if it's going to cause you trouble. We're managing all right on our own.'

'We're not taking any chances with hijackers,' the Whipholder barked. 'Who's the Parsinor?'

'G— g— guard,' said Groach. 'A friend who's come along ... in case of hijackers.'

'We're much obliged, but we'll handle any problems from

here on in,' the Noranian told Draegar. 'Just stay out of the way from now on.'

Draegar nodded, saying nothing.

'Get it in line!' Groach was instructed. 'Move ahead of us and close up behind the last wagon.'

It took three attempts for the botanist to get the vehicle in gear before pulling ahead of the battlewagon and joining the convoy. Groach exchanged looks with Draegar and the Parsinor shook his head. There was no going back now. Behind them, a small hand let the tarpaulin drop back into place.

'Aw, bowels.'

'Lorkrin, mind your language!'

# 17 PHYSIOLOGY RATHER THAN BOTANY

Emos had taken to the air again, and he was incredibly weary when he landed in the yard in front of *The Lush Oasis*, but he knew he was not far behind now and he was sure he would find news of Draegar here. Both he and the botanist had come here and the vehicle that was carrying Taya and Lorkrin had passed by; all of which had left Emos tired and confused. He suspected that the Parsinor had sent the children to Brodfan with the woman, but that they had defied him. He still did not know why everyone seemed so keen to get to Noran. He slunched back into human form, shrugged the backpack from his tired shoulders and pushed the door open.

Cholsch greeted him as he walked in.

'Emos Harprag! Well, this is a day for seeing old friends! Why, you just missed Draegar. He was here only this afternoon. What brings you to our little oasis?'

'My niece and nephew, Cholsch. It's good to see you, too. How are you? How is Temina?'

'The old ball and chain? The same as always. But what's this about your niece and nephew? Why would they be in these parts?' A tankard of mead appeared as if by magic in front of Emos.

'That's what I'm trying to find out. You said Draegar had been here?'

'Yes, lit out in a hurry for Noran with some new friend of his.' Cholsch leaned closer and lowered his voice. 'Had to borrow that man's wagon. Unfortunate state of affairs.'

He nodded to a man who sat at a table on the other side of the room, well on his way to being thoroughly drunk. Emos gave him a glance and turned back to the Parsinor, who continued talking as he polished some empty tankards;

'Ol' Draegar was goin' on about the Noranians havin' some kind of mighty weapon they was goin' to use against the Karthars – said he had to get to Noran to stop them. Didn't know what he was goin' on about myself, but I helped him as best I could, settin' him up with transport an' all.'

Emos stopped in mid-gulp and lowered his mug.

'What kind of weapon?'

'That was the bit that didn't make sense. Think he's got too used to tellin' those stories of his. He said the Noranians was goin' to use the esh to kill all those Karthars.'

✦ ✦ ✦

The drive had taken them through the night and most of the following day, and Groach was congratulating himself that he had only bumped into the wagon in front of his three times. But at last the city of Noran was in sight. They rolled on past the sentry posts, down the mountain road and out onto the plain where the city grew day by day. As they drove through the streets, Draegar wrinkled his nose at the stink of too many dwellings packed too close together, and the industrial smoke that hung in the air like a fog. The convoy moved rapidly, troops clearing the streets in front of them all the way to the river. When Groach finally pulled in, they saw that the docks along the riverside were lined with vehicles, all carrying crumble cones. These were being unloaded, packed carefully into crates and hoisted aboard waiting barges. Groach was waved into a loading space beside another truck.

He and Draegar jumped down and waited until no one was watching. Then they slipped into the milling teams of loaders and found their way down one of the alleys that led between the rows of warehouses. Groach took the lead, heading for the city gardens and the area where he knew the Harvest Tide staff to be working. Around them, life in Noran carried on at its hectic pace.

The streets were busy with people going about their daily routines: market carts pulled by donkeys, horses, oxen and oil-powered engines mixed with the men and women moving between the shops and factories. The buildings were a combination of wood and brick, with gabled roofs, balconies and walkways that stretched across the streets. The houses were all clean, tidy and well maintained. The cobbled streets were free of mud and rubbish, but the air was thick, cold and humid. There were no beggars on the streets, but Draegar knew that this was only because the soldiers gathered them up and put them to work in the mines, not because there were no poor people in Noran.

Groach walked along roads, guiding himself by chimneys. He had rarely been allowed out of the buildings where he and his colleagues worked, and never without an armed guard. But he had looked out on the city so often from the upper-storey windows that he knew the roofs and chimneys of the place better than any free man. And so he was able to steer them to the compound where he knew he would find his friends.

'This is it,' he said as they stood before a high wall that extended for hundreds of paces in either direction. 'They'll all be in here.'

'How do we get in?' Draegar asked.

'*We* don't,' Groach replied. 'There are too many guards inside. I can get in, but you will have to stay outside.'

'And what happens if you can't get out, or they don't want to help?'

'If I can't get out, I'll try and get to that window.' The botanist pointed to the second storey of a building that stood inside the wall. 'I'll give you a signal ... I'll stand at the window and touch both hands to my head. If you see that, you're on your own. They have enough barges loaded to fill four or five esh-boats already. If I can get the others to help, we have fungi that will destroy the crumble cones before they even reach the mouth of the river. If I can't, you'll have to find some way to do it on your own.'

'Go, then,' the Parsinor urged him. 'And may the gods look kindly on you. I will wait here until sunset. The barges will not leave until morning. There are rocks further down river and no captain will try to pass them at night. Go ... and mind yourself, Shessil. The plants of the world would be poorer without you.'

He touched his forehead to Groach's, and the botanist shook his hand. Then the Parsinor watched him walk away towards one end of the wall. Groach strode around the corner, made his way up to the gate and waved to the pair of guards who stood there.

'By Everness, it's good to be back,' he announced, turning from one soldier to the other. 'I believe the Prime Ministrate has been looking for me.'

+ + +

The two Myunans were arguing about what to do next, when the tarpaulin was whipped aside and two hands grabbed them by the scruffs of their necks. A workman dragged them out and stared at them.

'What have we got here, eh? Two little troublemakers, I'll wager.'

Hilspeth, who had been hidden on the other side of the wagon, slipped out and crept around the back. Rushing into view, she put a hand on each of the Myunans' shoulders.

'There you are, you little scamps,' she snapped. 'How many times have I told you to stay out of the men's way? Honestly, I can't take my eyes off you for a moment. Thank you, sir, for finding them. I'm sorry if they have been up to mischief.'

'Not really, ma'am. Just playing around, I expect. Did the same when I was a lad. But you should keep them away. We're at the Prime Ministrate's work here, and it won't do to have children running about. I'd keep a closer watch on them in future, if I was you.'

'I will, of course. Sorry again. I promise they'll get a proper spanking for this.'

'I hope so. If you don't beat them, they won't learn. That's what I always say.'

'And right you are, too.' Hilspeth smiled tightly.

The workman waved to another, and they began to crate the crumble cones. Hilspeth tugged on the collars of the shape-changers, and together they escaped into the crowd.

'I'll show him "beating", that mutton-head,' muttered Lorkrin. 'I'd like to see him try it.'

'Yes, I'm sure you would,' Hilspeth said to him. 'But first let's see what's going on. It's getting dark, and I get the feeling that those boats aren't going to be hanging around when morning comes. If Shessil and Draegar have a plan, great. If not, we're going to have to do something ourselves.'

+ + +

'You escaped?' Mungret asked, with a quizzical expression.

'Well, not exactly.' Groach shrugged. 'The Parsinor was a friend of their uncle's or something like that. When he heard what they had been up to, he gave them a good shouting at and told me to be on my way.'

'But our trackers told us that you walked a good way with them. When did you get away from them?'

'I'm a bit embarrassed about that, actually. The Parsinor thought I was someone important; he was going to hold me for ransom. It took me a while to convince him I was just a botanist and not worth a lot of money. He just told me to shove off. He was a bit peeved he'd dragged me that far.'

'Well, the Prime Ministrate will be glad to have you back, I can tell you.' Mungret squeezed his shoulder. 'We would have rescued you eventually, of course. Don't doubt for a moment that you are worth a great deal to us, Shessil, a great deal indeed. Your work is vital to Noran.'

'And it's work I'm keen to get back to, sir. I'd like to join the others now, if you don't mind.'

'Ah, yes. The others. They are uh ... out on a research trip; they won't be back for some days yet. Why don't you go up to the laboratory and get on with whatever you need to do? I'm sure the Prime Ministrate will want to see you himself as soon as possible.'

Mungret nodded to a guard, and gently nudged Groach in the direction of the stairs. The soldier followed him as he climbed towards the second floor. When he entered the main laboratory, he discovered a score of people working at the tables. He did not recognise any of them. His breath caught in his throat. Had Namen decided to put more people on the project even though they had achieved what they had set out to do?

'Mr Groach!' A middle-aged man scurried across the room to shake his hand. 'It's an honour to meet you. We've been going through your notes, sir, and I must say your ideas on the bubule are quite brilliant. May I congratulate you on your studies? It will be a pleasure to work with you.'

'I ... ah, thank you. I wonder, can you tell me where my colleagues are? They are on a research trip, I believe. Have they gone back to Hortenz?'

The other man froze. Casting his eyes back towards the rest of the new team, he paused for a moment.

'Well, to be honest, Mr Groach, they have been taken off the project. Once the problem of the blooming was cracked, their services were no longer required. The project has moved onto the final stage. It is more a matter of physiology rather than botany now.'

Groach felt a tension in the place, and he took a closer look around the room. Most of the men and women here were young, and the experiments that were taking place were not those that he had been used to. Dead animals were being dissected: sheep, budgies, an ox – something he had never done, nor any of his friends.

He watched as a woman opened up a donkey's belly, cutting through creamy yellow fat, pushing it aside to slice into the filmy membrane that covered the coiled intestines. The creature was not long dead, but the guts released a pungent smell when the woman pierced them, her hands delving into the slick, snake-like organs. He turned away as she started using a bone-saw to cut through the ribcage to get at the lungs. The original project had not needed animals for their experiments. This was something different.

'What kind of work are you doing here?' he asked.

'The effects of the esh on breathing,' the man replied, clapping his hands together with a smile.

'The effects are simple,' Groach said through gritted teeth. 'It *stops* you from breathing.'

He wandered over to the large cupboard where they grew their fungi and bacteria.

'Can I help you with anything?' the older man enquired.

'No, thank you. I just need to gather a few things. Then I think I'll go to my room.'

'I can't let you take anything from the laboratory.'

Groach turned to him, some sealed test tubes in his hand.

'You can't tell me what to do. I don't know who you are, or what you're doing here, but I've worked here for years. I'll take whatever I please.'

'I am the Groundsmaster, and I say you will not take anything from here without the Prime Ministrate's authority.'

Groach hesitated. The new Groundsmaster was someone who had never worked here before. Then the others really were gone. He did not want to think about what Namen might have done to them to keep this project secret. Perhaps they had figured out what it was all for and had refused to carry on. It was all too easy to imagine what could have happened.

'All right, then. I'll do the work here. Excuse me.'

Stepping past the Groundsmaster, he walked over to one of the barred windows and sat down at the table there. The older man watched him for a while, and then went back to dissecting a donkey. The sky was bright against the horizon, the sun was setting and the ground below was in shadow. He could not see Draegar. Whatever happened now, he was not going to be able to get out of the building tonight. These new faces were loyal to Namen. They would not help him escape, and would probably warn the soldiers if they caught him trying. Groach took a piece of vellum and scribbled something on it. Separating out two of the test tubes, he wrapped the note around one, pulled out a large handkerchief and tied it around each one in turn so that both were well cushioned. The window was open. He checked that he was not being watched, and then pushed the bundle out between the bars. There was a soft thud below. Standing up, he ran his hands through his thinning hair and sighed. He was a prisoner once more.

+ + +

Draegar watched the small bundle drop to the ground, and looked up in time to see Groach put his hands to his head at the upstairs window. He cautiously checked the narrow street in both directions, then crossed and picked up the tightly wrapped package. Opening it, he found two test tubes and a note.

'I cannot get out. My friends are not here. The place is full of strangers,' the note read. 'In these containers is a fungus that will eat the crumble cones. Sprinkle some of the spores in each of the barges.

'Good luck. Shessil.

'P.S. Don't get any on clothes, shoes or any other soft material. This stuff has a big appetite.'

Draegar carefully placed the test tubes in one of his bags. He gazed up at the window again, hoping to catch sight of Groach, but the botanist was gone. He toyed with the idea of trying to go in after his new companion, but knew it was no use. He had to return to the docks or Groach's sacrifice would be in vain.

+ + +

Taya, Lorkrin and Hilspeth wandered through the melee, men with wheelbarrows and wagons and cranes clattered past them, paying them no attention. The Myunans had shed their tribal colours to appear as human children, and Taya had even changed her hair to a shorter, more Noranian style. There were more than a dozen barges against the docks themselves, being loaded up, with at least as many again waiting out in the river to take their places. In the foggy, dim light of evening, the buildings on both sides of the water were losing their detail, taking on a murky grey brown colour that melded them all into angular, featureless blocks. Stepping over mooring ropes and steering clear of gang-planks, the three investigated the docks, peering into the holds of the boats, and taking note of the soldiers who over-looked the proceedings.

They were watching more wagons arriving when a squad

of troops passed them by. One of the soldiers stopped suddenly, staring at them.

'Flivel, get in formation!' the Forward-Batterer shouted at him, but the infantryman did not move.

Hilspeth stared back at him, sure that she remembered him from somewhere. With a mounting sense of dread, it came to her. Flivel, the soldier from the courtroom. The one with bad grammar.

'That's the hag that cost me a hundred drokes,' he snarled. 'The one that was friends with that little rat who killed Grulk. What are you doing here, hag?'

He looked at the two Myunans and light dawned in his eyes.

'Hey, isn't that the pair who ...'

'Run!' Hilspeth screamed and shoved the two Myunans in front of her.

They turned and sprinted away as fast as their legs could carry them. As they passed a wagon, Lorkrin slapped the catches on the tailgate, and glanced back to watch as a pile of crumble cones tumbled into the path of the soldiers, causing the first two to stumble and fall over. But horns sounded behind them – the alarm was being raised. Taya and Lorkrin were almost invisible in the crowd, as everyone was taller than them and Hilspeth hurried to keep up, while staying as low as she could. The soldiers were hampered by the busy teams of workmen, but they were gaining on the fugitives.

'In here!' called Taya, ducking into a warehouse. They darted in among piles of tall jars, searching frantically for a way out on the other side. But the windows were boarded up and the doors were locked. They stopped to catch their breath behind a stack of jars, Lorkrin climbing up to peer over the top at the door they had come in.

'They haven't followed us,' he panted. 'I don't think they saw us come in.'

'It won't take them long to figure out where we went,' Taya whispered. 'We'll be trapped in here when they do.'

'We could turn into something nasty. Scare them off,' he suggested hopefully.

'Oh, grow up!' his sister snapped. 'That'd get us killed for sure.'

Hilspeth turned her attention to the roof.

'Do you think we could climb out of here?' she asked. 'Those skylights don't seem to be locked. It would be better than going back out the way we came in.'

They found stairs leading to a walkway that overlooked the floor of the warehouse. From there, Taya was able to stand on Hilspeth's shoulders and unlatch one of the skylights. Below them, three soldiers wandered in the doorway and started to search among the jars. Taya nodded down at them, pointing them out to the others, then she pulled herself up and out onto the roof as quietly as she could. Lorkrin followed, and once out, he slunched his feet and ankles and hooked them around a post near the edge of the opening. Hanging head-first through the skylight, he stretched far enough for Hilspeth to grab him and begin to climb up, using him as a makeshift rope-ladder. From the floor below, they heard a shout, and a crossbow bolt suddenly shot past Hilspeth as she and Taya pulled Lorkrin out. Looking frantically around, they saw a walkway leading to the roof of the next warehouse.

'They're not following us,' Taya said.

'They'll try to surround us,' Hilspeth called back as she ran. 'We need to find a way down. If we get stuck up here, they'll catch us for sure.'

Sprinting across the walkway, they scrambled up the gabled roof and slid down to the ledge on the other side. From there, they dropped onto the rooftop of a neighbouring factory. Dodging among the tall chimneys, they ran to the far end and found themselves confronted by a sheer drop to the street.

'We can make this,' Taya cried between breaths.

'How?' Hilspeth asked in despair. There was no way down that she could see.

'We slunch and drop, then you land on us. We'll soften your landing.'

'Are you mad? You'll be killed!'

'We're Myunans,' Lorkrin reminded her. 'Trust us.'

He and Taya jumped together and landed with a thump in a shapeless pile. Hilspeth moaned, and glanced behind her to see soldiers emerge from a skylight in the roof behind her. Gritting her teeth, she lunged off the ledge, falling kicking and screaming to the street below. She landed on her back on the soft cushion provided by the bodies of the Myunans and had the air knocked from her lungs. Lorkrin and Taya slipped from under her and struggled back to their normal forms.

'You could do with losing some weight,' Lorkrin wheezed.

They helped the scentonomist to her feet; she was gasping for breath. Clutching her chest, she pointed at an alley across from them. People were starting to gather to see what this unusual threesome was up to. Over their heads came the shouting of soldiers barging their way through. Taya led the others down the alley and through to the street beyond. They came face to face with Right-Speartrooper Flivel. Reaching into her waistcoat, Hilspeth grabbed the first bottle that came to hand and sprayed the contents in the soldier's face. He dropped his spear and staggered to one side, then fell over. In puzzlement, she looked at the label. It was essence of popelflower, the smell of which brought back childhood memories, but in large quantities caused complete loss of balance.

Flivel made to get to his feet again, but once up, he swayed uncertainly and toppled right over again. Hilspeth pushed him over once more as he got his feet under him, and then she ran. Lorkrin gave him an extra shove for good measure as he passed him. They did not get very far. As they watched, people moved off the street to clear the way for three soldiers who were charging towards them.

'Aw, bowels.'

Lorkrin turned around again and ran headlong into a Parsinor-shaped wall.

'You didn't make it to Brodfan, then,' Draegar growled.

He stepped past the Myunans and into the path of the soldiers, stamping Flivel into the ground. The first man threw himself at the Parsinor, who brought his elbow up and slammed it into the man's throat, knocking him flat on his back. The second made an overhead swing with a halberd and Draegar swivelled to one side, letting the weapon bury itself in the ground, before holding it down with one foot and snapping the back of his left fist into the man's face, sending him skidding back on his bottom. The third faltered, seeing his comrades beaten so easily and, as he hesitated, Draegar hooked his foot under the halberd and kicked it at him, striking him in the forehead with its shaft. The man crumpled to the ground and lay still.

'Wow,' gasped Lorkrin.

'You've just made things a lot more complicated,' Draegar told Hilspeth and the two Myunans as he led them down a narrow alley and out of the sight of the people on the street. 'Just when I don't need to be noticed, you force me to start trouble with the Noranians. Now they will be looking for Parsinors, and I have work to do on the docks.'

# 18 QUIET PRAYERS IN RUTLEDGE

The barges were moored on either side of the bases of the three eb-towers, which floated in the River Gullin, and dwarfed every other construction in Noran. Built into these enormous eb-trees were light but formidable fortresses. At regular intervals up the trunks were armoured structures with battlements that housed the government. Turrets sat on every major branch of the trees. The lower levels were occupied by the military; catapults, crossbows and archers' posts bristled from the battlements. From these positions, they could lob missiles far over the walls that surrounded the centre of the city, and the land could be watched to the horizon. Above and behind these defences, the politicians and generals languished in the luxurious rooms that squatted amongst the highest reaches of the trees. The structures were made of the same fireproof wood as the trees themselves, and each level was connected by twin spiral staircases as well as ladders and slide poles.

The floating base of each tree was the size of a small field, its rough nest of roots paved with cobbles to make way for vehicles and troops. Walls ran around the edge to provide extra security. Chains thicker than Draegar's arms anchored the trees in place in the deeper water of the river, with heavy ropes mooring them to the docks, and even sturdier lengths of cable attached to the middle of the trees to hold them steady in high winds. Stout wooden bridges led out to the gates of the three fortresses and each was heavily guarded.

Security was tight around the barges. Soldiers stood watch as dock workers carried crates of crumble cones on board. Even so, it was relatively easy for someone to get aboard ... if they could make themselves look like a crate. Lorkrin was carried on board and placed at the foot of a pile of boxes. To anyone looking at or touching him, he was for all intents and purposes, a wooden crate.

His eyes opened in two corners to check that it was safe for him to act, but before he could move, a guard appeared nearby and walked up to stand over him. It was the one who had chased them, Flivel. Lorkrin closed the eye nearest the man and held his breath, waiting for the moment when a knife or a sword descended on him. Flivel placed a booted foot up on Lorkrin's back and leaned on it, looking around. Lorkrin's fertile imagination went wild. Whatever this man was going to do to him, he didn't want any witnesses. Lorkrin was about to lunge back and start screaming, when Flivel lifted his ornacrid armour and began scratching his backside. Failing to reach the offending itch, he changed feet, Lorkrin wincing as the heel came down on what would have been his head. After a furious bout of scratching, the guard put his foot down, straightened his armour, took a last furtive look around, and walked back the way he had come.

Lorkrin let out his breath with a relieved sigh. Unfolding his arms, he held up the test tube and tapped a few of the spores into the open crates beside him. Then he shuffled to the side of the hold, hauled himself up on the gunwale, and lowered his cube-shaped body into the water. He knew that on the quay on the other side of the river, Taya was doing the same thing. Against his better judgment, Draegar had been convinced that the two Myunans were his best hope of getting the spores into the shipment of crumble cones. Still in his square shape, Lorkrin swam awkwardly to the wall and slipped out, joining the stack of crates waiting to be loaded aboard the next barge along.

+ + +

Groach sat at a table, scribbling some notes down and trying to look busy. In fact, he was listening intently to the conversations taking place around the room. He realised that these people knew far more about the aims of the Harvest Tide Project than he had, and had been recruited as much for their natures as they had for their knowledge. They knew people were going to die as a result of their work and they did not care. The fact that they were planning to cause a disaster simply made it more exciting for them.

'I think the Karthars will be affected first,' one voice commented. 'They are more used to a higher climate, thinner air. They will be breathing deeper.'

'I disagree,' another put in. 'For the very reason that they need less air.'

'It doesn't matter either way,' a third muttered. 'As long as they are standing in the way when the tide comes in.'

'What's this I hear about the Karthars landing on the coast?' the first asked.

'That's the plan. The whole army is landing on Braskhia ...

they want to trounce the Braskhiams once and for all. That's the whole point. The Prime Ministrate wants to bring them right onto the coast before we let the tide loose.'

'But the Braskhiams don't want to fight. How does he know the Karthars will take the bait?'

'Because he planned it that way, you peasant. He's been using Karthar esh-boats to attack Braskhiam ships, and Braskhiam vessels to attack Karthar ships. He wants to set them at each other's throats. The Karthar navy invades Braskhia, and that's when we launch. Then our army steps in and Noran ends up ruling both of them.'

Groach stood up, his chair scraping against the floor, and made his way over to a plans chest where the maps were kept. He took one out that showed the positions of all the esh-bound bubule plains on this side of the world. Examining it, he confirmed what he had already guessed. There were no bubules off the Karthar coast facing Noran. The only plains that could be safely reached by the Noranian fleet were off the coast of Braskhia. If Namen wanted to use the Harvest Tide against the Karthars, he would have to do it on Braskhia's doorstep. Thousands lived on the farms and in the fishing villages along the coast. He was bringing his enemies to Braskhia so that he could destroy them and cripple the Braskhiams at the same time. Crush the Karthar fleet, and drag a weakened Braskhia into the Noranian Empire, where he could have all their science and technology for himself.

Groach thumped the top of the plans chest with his fist and strode over to the Groundsmaster.

'I want to see the Prime Ministrate. Right now.'

'Do you indeed? We'll send a message to him. I'm sure he'll come running.'

The Groundsmaster waved to the guard standing at the door.

'Tell Mungret that Mr Groach has summoned the Prime Ministrate.' He smiled at Groach. 'And tell him that we will be ready for the tests on the prisoners in the morning.'

Groach heard this, and one glance at the dissection tables made his blood run cold. Turning away, he stared at the floor for a time.

'I'm going to my room,' he said, eventually. 'Good night.'

+ + +

It was not long after dawn, and Mungret was sitting at his desk in the office adjoined to the Prime Ministrate's quarters. Stacks of papers were neatly laid out all around him on the desk, on side tables and in folders on shelves. Paperwork was what Mungret did best, and he was happiest when left alone to comb through facts and figures that had little to do with dealing with individual people. He was not a people person, and resented having to cope with problems he could not solve with a pen. There was a knock on the door, and he tutted as he dipped his quill in a jar of water and dabbed it dry.

'Enter,' he said with a sigh.

The door opened, and the Whipholder in charge of security at the docks came in, followed by an embarrassed-looking soldier wearing only his armour and one boot. Mungret blinked once, then raised his gaze to the officer.

'The Prime Ministrate wanted to be informed of any unusual goings on during the loading of the barges.' The Whipholder returned the stare.

'I don't think half-naked soldiers was what he had in

mind,' Mungret snapped, picking up his quill again. 'Hardly worth wasting his time for, is it?'

'That's just the thing,' the officer replied firmly. 'Right-Speartrooper Flivel here was on duty on the docks. He was fully clothed when he went on shift. He claims his clothes dissolved.'

'Dissolved?'

'Rotted and fell to pieces, while he was wearing them.'

Mungret put his pen down again and took another look at the soldier. Flivel was standing to attention by the side of his officer, but his hands kept wandering to cover his bare back-side, his nakedness hidden at the front by his armour.

'I presume this was not as the result of careless laundry,' the clerk observed.

'My troops take good care of their uniforms,' the officer growled. He did not like the Prime Ministrate's secretary, not many of the soldiers did.

'Have you another explanation?' Mungret enquired.

'We're not sure, but the only odd thing reported was that every barge had one more crate leaving the docks than they had on their inventories. Also, a Parsinor attacked some of our men earlier today. We have search parties out looking for him now.'

Mungret stood up and walked to the window, the way he had seen Rak Ek Namen do so many times when he was deep in thought. He watched the brightening sky for a few moments.

'There was one of those desert dwellers with the Myunans who kidnapped the botanist,' he muttered. 'Alert your troops. I want every Parsinor in the city rounded up and held for questioning. Have the barges left?'

'Yes, they left before first light.'

'Get a message to the Whipholder on the boats. Have him check every vessel for anything out of the ordinary. There's something going on here. I'll inform the Prime Ministrate.'

Picking up some papers, he dismissed the soldiers and followed them out the door. He made his way down one of the staircases that wound around the trunk of the eb-tower, and climbed into a coach. Waving the driver on as he swung the door shut, he sat back in the cabin and closed his eyes. It was too early in the morning for pondering serious problems and, as usual, he had not got enough sleep that night.

It did not take long for the coach to cover the distance to the Harvest Tide Project, and once out of the vehicle, the secretary ran up the steps to the door. He was met by the Groundsmaster, who was wringing his hands with worry. There was a messenger there waiting with him. He saluted Mungret.

'Just had a pigeon from the barges, sir. They report the cargo has been destroyed.'

Mungret felt a tightness in his chest.

'What did you say?'

'The cargo's been destroyed, sir. They said something rotted it. Not just the crumble cones, either. The squad who found them said the guards and crew were naked. Not a shred of clothing between them. They reckon that whatever ate the cones ate their clothes too. Couldn't get them to come out of hiding at first – they were too embarrassed. Cargo's been reduced to slurry.'

Mungret struggled for breath, wheezing painfully.

'Have any crumble cones got through?' he gasped.

'With that lot gone, it'll just be the ones on the six barges that left early yesterday.'

Mungret shook his head and sat down. It was a fraction of what was needed, but it would have to be enough. They had no more time; the Karthars were approaching the coast as they spoke. Looking down at his hands, he saw that they were shaking. The thought of having to tell the Prime Ministrate clenched his lungs like two fists.

+ + +

Emos soared towards the town of Rutledge-on-Coast, his fake feathers ruffling in the wind. From this height he could see the headland of Noran out to his left, just on the edge of the horizon. The air was clear and there was only a light breeze, perfect flying weather. He was in the shape of an eagle, wings outstretched and tail splayed, a form he would have been relishing if he had not been utterly exhausted.

He had stopped only twice for rest along the way, and then only long enough to hear what news there was of Braskhia and the esh. The last couple of days had turned up a series of ominous rumours. Esh-boats flying Braskhiam colours had been seen far out to esh, but no one recognised the boats or the crews. Karthar esh-boats had attacked Braskhiam vessels, but some survivors had sworn that the attacking ships had been manned not by Karthars, but by humans. Emos knew now what Namen was planning, even if he did not understand how it was possible. He knew enough to terrify him, enough to hope that Taya and Lorkrin were safe with Draegar, and to turn back for Rutledge-on-Coast as soon as he had heard what Cholsch had told him. He knew that Namen intended to crush both the Braskhiams and the Karthars together, and that he planned to do it using the Harvest Tide. Somehow, he had found a way to make the esh flood the land. But for his plan to succeed, the Braskhiams and the Karthars had to be at the same place at the same time when the Harvest Tide struck.

Skirting the Braskhiam shoreline, he kept the land to his right, following its ragged edge to where Rutledge lay. Out at esh, he saw two freighters at anchor and curiosity got the better of him. It was unusual to see two such large esh-ships together. He flew nearer, and saw that they were dumping their cargo overboard. He was too far away to see what it was, but it looked like it might be crumble cones. He was reminded of the people he had seen gathering the cones under Noranian supervision, and he was suddenly sure that they were part of the plot.

Below him, he could see trawvettes pulling in their nets, and other esh-boats at full sail. It was a peaceful scene. Rutledge came into view and he circled above it, finally spotting the *Lightfoot*, Murris's boat, making its way into the harbour, bringing in its catch for the day. He dived down towards it, swooping around the sails and landing heavily on the deck, breathing hard and unable to do anything else but stand wearily while the crew gathered around this curious sight of a huge eagle with a bag on its back.

Then he slunched and stood up straight, his wings shrinking to re-form his arms, and his legs lengthening to bring him back to his full height. His beak settled back into his tattooed face, restoring his normal visage, and he turned to look around him.

'Now, that is what I call an entrance,' Murris remarked from the door to the compressor room.

'The Noranian Prime Ministrate means to kill you all,' Emos said simply.

'He's going to have to get in line,' Murris replied. 'We've just come from out east. The entire Karthar fleet is bearing down on us. It seems we are at war.'

+ + +

The Braskhiams had to get away from the coast. Emos argued frantically with Murris and others all evening as they made preparations for the town's defence. But it was proving hard to convince the Braskhiams that the esh itself could be a threat to them; they knew it better than anyone after all. The armoury near the town square was opened, and men and women queued up as weapons were handed out. Murris was the leader of a group that included several engined catapults, and was organising setting them up on the docks. His wife, Berra, was sharpening short swords on an oilstone.

'Peddar, you've got to listen to me,' the Myunan pleaded. 'Forget trying to defend the *town*; forget the town altogether. You need to get everyone out!'

'Maybe we should listen to him, Peddar,' Berra said anxiously. 'What if he's right? What if the Tide happened and we weren't ready?'

'Whatever it is you think the Noranians are up to, Emos, it will have to wait,' Murris grunted as he loaded the harpoon gun he was holding. 'We have more pressing concerns. My daughter and folks are at home, just beyond town. The same goes for everyone here. We've all got family to protect.'

'That's exactly what I'm talking about, by the gods,' Emos exclaimed. 'At least get your families as far away from the coast as possible! And make sure they get to high ground.'

Murris stared at him for a moment, then looked to his wife

and nodded. Wiping her hands on a cloth, she started moving through the defensive ranks, spreading the word that everyone not able to bear arms should flee to high ground. Emos took some comfort from that, but meanwhile every fighting-fit man and woman was gathering on the docks. Murris's team was soon in position, and settled down to wait.

Braskhiam war machines rolled onto the quays, their crews racing to get to the port in time for the initial attack. The Braskhiams gathered and waited as night fell, some lighting fires and lanterns, and preparing food for the remainder who stood with weapons at the ready, gazing out to esh. The eshtrans moved from camp to camp, giving purified air to every man and woman and blessing them before the battle. All over the docks, quiet prayers could be heard.

+ + +

The Karthars came at dawn. Emos had taken the chance to get some sleep finally, stretched out on the cowling of an engined catapult, and he was woken by the clatter of weapons being readied and bodies moving into position.

There, appearing from one end of the horizon to the other, was a fleet of fighting ships. Triangular sails drove low hulls through the gas; harpoon cannons were pressured up and loaded; soldiers stood on the decks in readiness for an invasion. The Karthars were bringing war to Braskhia. Murris gripped his harpoon gun and glared out at the oncoming esh-boats, his limbs and body trembling with adrenalin. People were running or driving in from all over the area to join the army that was forming on the dockside.

'Curse them, damn their eyes!' he snarled. 'We should

have listened to the Noranians while we had the chance. We should have put them down like the dogs they are before any of this could happen.'

Emos did not say a word. Like all Braskhiams, Murris had been trained for battle, but he was no warrior. Nevertheless, the Karthars were bringing war to them, and the Myunan knew every man and woman along that line would fight like a demon to stop the invaders. They would never give up their homes.

He looked up and down the sea wall; the rows of men and women stood on the edge of the docks, and waited as the Karthar fleet approached the mouth of the harbour. Laying his tools on the bonnet of Murris's catapult, he hurriedly began reshaping his body.

'What are you doing?' Murris asked, watching as the Myunan amorphed his arms into wings.

'The Karthars are descended from cave-dwellers – bats are sacred to them. They even breed them as pets.' Emos stretched the sides of his head into huge, convoluted ears.

'So?'

'So, I'm hoping that if I fly over them in the shape of a bat, they won't shoot me out of the sky.' He quickly finished the transformation, and, leaving his tools where they were, he struck out with his wings and took off out over the esh, heading for the approaching fleet.

The sound of the wind in a thousand sails carried like thunder, and, from above, he could see the huge snowy wake left by the spread of vessels. Spotting the lead ship by its flags, he descended slowly and cautiously towards it. Harpoons were raised and sighted on him, but no one fired. His tactic seemed to be paying off.

'I have a message for the Karthar Fleetmaster!' he cried. 'Will he hear me out?'

There was some activity on the deck, and then a Karthar in a lavish purple uniform waved him down. Emos steeled himself for what might come, and glided gently down to the wooden boards. He placed a wing against his heart and then held it out to the Fleetmaster in the traditional Karthar gesture, and the Karthar returned it, but then folded his arms and waited in silence.

'Braskhia does not want war,' Emos said, breathing heavily. 'Noran has started this, and they will finish it when Braskhiams and Karthars lie broken and dead together. Rak Ek Namen has engineered this war by attacking each side under the other's flag, and his final stroke will be the destruction of your fleet and the Braskhiams' homes. The Noranians have mastered the Harvest Tide and mean to bring it down on your heads.'

There was some laughter from the men around him, but the Fleetmaster silenced them.

'Since when did the Braskhiams use *Myunans* to deliver their messages? And what a message! Do you take us for fools? Do you think you can delay us, to gain the Braskhiam scum more time to prepare? If so, you should have invented a more believable story.'

Emos stared into the Karthar's eyes.

'Who does this war serve? The Braskhiams will lose more than they could gain, as will the Karthars. Fishing grounds are no use if there are no men to fish them. Only the Noranians will win. Ask yourself why they are not here to help defend their allies. Ask yourself what would happen if the Harvest Tide broke over your fleet while it lay off the coast.

Then ask yourself why the tide is high right now ... when it should be low.'

Some of the crew looked towards the shoreline as he said this, and saw that it was true. Any esher knew when the tides were, and what they saw did not sit well with what they knew. A sudden swell rushed from behind the Karthar vessels, running beneath them, lifting them gently and then rippling out ahead and up against the harbour wall.

'Only Rak Ek Namen wants this war!' Emos shouted to them. 'Are you willing to die for him today?'

Answered only with a stony silence, he beat his wings hard against the air and took off, rising above the sails and making his way back towards the docks. He landed by Murris's group and slunched back into his normal shape. The area was utterly quiet.

'What did you say to them?' Murris asked.

'The same thing I said to you,' Emos replied, watching the oncoming ships. 'They don't seem to want to listen. At least that's one thing you all agree on.'

With their eyes fixed on the enemy, the Braskhiams did not see the fine layer of sessium well over the edge of the wall and spread like an impossibly light carpet along the ground. Emos looked down in alarm and then cast his gaze around him, but the eyes of the Braskhiams were focused on the enemy. To the disbelief of the defenders, horns sounded abruptly, and the Karthar ships began to turn about and make for the open esh. People started to mutter among themselves. No one could understand why the enemy would come so close only to retreat again. Murris shifted his weight uneasily and wiped the sweat from his hands before replacing his grip on his harpoon gun. Emos grabbed his wrist.

'Peddar! Open your eyes, man.'

The Braskhiam glanced down; he was up to his ankles in esh. He froze. It was not the season for Harvest Tide. And even if it were, he had never seen the esh rise like this. This was something else. He called to those around him and pointed out to the sea of gas.

'She's rising! The esh is rising! Forget the Karthars! We've got to get to high ground, now!'

Everyone finally recognised what this was, and the cries of alarm were going up along the line of troops. One by one at first, then in dozens at a time, the would-be warriors dropped their weapons, turned and ran inland. Murris grabbed the man beside him and pushed him towards the town.

'We've got to get above this! he said. 'The Noranians have brought the Harvest Tide down upon us!'

'But how?' The man's voice was shaky with panic.

'What does it matter? Move!' They threw their weapons away and bolted inland. Emos gave the Karthar ships one last look, and then turned to pick up his tools. They had been moved, and were nowhere to be seen. There was no time to look for them now; the esh was up to his knees. Swearing beneath his breath, he turned and followed the Braskhiams.

The tops of the tallest buildings were already filling up with those trying to escape, so they ran on through the roads full of panicking people towards the higher land further in. The sessium was gaining on them, almost to their waists, and some of the men and women grabbed children who were running with them to lift them clear of the gas. The land in this area was flat, and what hills there were lay well in from the coast. The crowds ran for these, frantic to get above the esh before it smothered them. Murris looked desperately around for his wife and daughter, but could not see them. Emos could see the anguish on his friend's face and prayed they were already safe. The gas was up to his stomach now, and people were tripping and falling all around him, unable to see the ground at their feet. His shin struck something beneath him and he stumbled, but Murris caught him and kept him on his feet. Struggling on, they had to rely on their memory of the small town to find their way through the half-concealed streets.

The buildings around them were crowded with people taking refuge, but with all the extra bodies from the army that had formed, there was no room in the upper floors. Some people had managed to find gas masks and were helping others find their way to safety. Emos thought of the farms out on the plains. They would have no warning. Most of them had houses of one floor and no means of escaping the esh if it bore down on them. The land was higher just outside the town and the gas was still creeping up his chest. If this was a Harvest Tide, then it was going to be one of the biggest he had ever seen.

The esh made a sound like a soft wind, though there was hardly a breeze to be felt. Behind them, Emos could hear a rushing sound and feared the worst was yet to come. Harvest Tide could last for days, and the first onslaught was not always the heaviest. Looking back, he saw a churning cloud tumbling inland towards them. If it made it this far, it would cover them.

'Run!' he called out. 'Run like the gods themselves are coming after you!'

The ground rose ahead of them, and the crowd staggered to a halt at the crest of the hill. Emos and the others kept going until they had reached as high up as they could get in the crush of bodies.

'Pa! Pa! Over here!' A child's voice cried out.

There on the hill, off to one side of them, was Berra, with their daughter Bekeli in her arms. He was torn between the joy of seeing them and the fear that they were still in danger. Emos followed as Murris pushed his way around to his family; the Braskhiam kissed his wife and hoisted Bekeli onto his shoulders. Berra took Emos's hand and squeezed it, and he saw the fear in her eyes. He nodded, wishing he could offer more comfort, wishing he could have warned them sooner. The knowledge of his failure was like a weight in his stomach, as a smothering death flooded towards them.

The gas was getting as high as the adults' waists, even here. Peering beyond, they could see that the ground dipped after this hill. To reach a higher point would mean going beneath the esh. This hill would have to be enough. Facing the oncoming wave, the crowd waited with a mounting dread. Murris clutched his daughter's waist. If the esh went over his head, he would try to hold Bekeli above it for as long as he possibly could. Berra, standing behind her husband, put her arms around him and leaned her chin on his shoulder.

The wave broke as it flowed through the town, and by the time it reached the hill, there was little more than a swell, but there were more to come. Even as they watched, a second, larger crest rose over the harbour. The crowd was so absorbed by the sight, it took some time to notice the sound of marching feet. Some turned to look behind them for the source of the sound, but all they could see was a flood of esh over the land. Then, like wraiths, soldiers appeared out of the gas and strode up the hill. They were wearing masks, the kind used for exploring the shallows of the esh. A person could breathe beneath the surface with one of those masks. The crowd eyed them greedily. Those masks could save their lives, but these were soldiers from the Bonescrapers, the Noranian crack fighting force, hardened by years of war and prepared for battle.

'You there,' an officer called to Murris. 'Which way to the Karthars?'

'They've retreated, sir,' Murris replied. 'They turned about before the esh rose.'

'Retreated, eh?' the Whipholder sneered. 'We'll see about that. Move on, Bonescrapers. The enemy is out there some-where.'

Without another word, the troops followed their com-mander back into the esh, bound for the town. The crowd watched them go, and as the last one disappeared, they all gradually came to the same realisation. The Bonescrapers had come prepared for fighting in the gas. They had known that it would rise. Murris turned to Emos, who merely nodded. The Noranians could have condemned to death hundreds, perhaps thousands living in Braskhia. But the Karthars had had time to turn back; their ships had not been caught by the tide, and now the Prime Ministrate would not have his victory, even if he flooded Braskhia. Murris regarded the closing wave with a feeling of disgust. Their own allies were killing them.

The wave broke over them, and this time it went over their heads. Bekeli and the other children who were being held up were the only ones to escape. Some of the children were crying now. The surge passed and the crowd could breathe again. But another wave was already on its way. Perched on her father's shoulders, Bekeli gazed out across the sea of gas, squinting against the glow of the sun off its surface. She pointed at something.

'Ma, Pa. There's boats coming. Look.'

They followed the direction of her pointing finger, and saw Karthar esh-boats charging in.

'*Now* they attack,' Murris muttered under his breath. 'They're coming to finish us off.'

What Braskhiam boats there had been still out at esh gave chase, but they were too few and too far behind to save the people inland. Murris scowled bitterly, and Emos realised that most of the Braskhiams had abandoned their weapons at the docks. But as the crowd watched, the Karthar ships split up and made for different hilltops and buildings in the distance. Landing craft were lowered, and began taking people aboard. The enemy had sailed in across the land, not to destroy them but to save them. An esh-boat approached and its landing craft, with their cluster of small float pods, were lowered to cross the shallows under bellows power.

One drew up near Emos, and Murris and his family, and a Karthar soldier beckoned to them. With his goat-like face, grey-brown fur, and hands with their two thumbs, he was a strange sight, but a welcome one.

'We can take some of you on board, and more ships are on their way. I can take eight in this boat. Hurry, before the wave hits!'

Women and children were pushed forward, crying and calling to their fathers, husbands and brothers. When all were aboard, the landing craft pushed off and sailed back to the ship. The wave rushed over the men who remained, but they braced themselves and stayed on their feet, and the esh subsided enough for them to keep their heads clear. Emos grabbed the sides of his head and forced it upwards, stretching his neck so that his head was raised above the gas. Shorter men were lifted up by those around them.

All the men knew that the next one would be the end of them. They watched in anticipation as another Karthar ship dropped anchor nearby, and its smaller boats were lowered. A wall of esh rose up behind the town and surged across it. The men started shouting and screaming for the boats. There was no swimming in the esh; the boats had to come to them. The landing craft came close enough to reach by wading, and Emos and Murris joined the rush to meet them. Men clambered aboard; those who could not get in hung to the sides to keep their heads above the gas. Emos tumbled over the side of one and reached behind to hold onto Murris's arms. The wave lifted the esh-boats and the men clinging to them. They washed further inland, over lower ground, but the Karthar boats kept them out of the gas. Karthars and Braskhiams held each other as they rocked around in the strong currents. Murris closed his eyes and trembled with rage at what had been done to them.

By evening, the esh had started to recede, and the esh-boats, overloaded, settled to the ground before they could get back out to the harbour. The gas drew back and left a landscape littered with ships and their landing craft, Karthar and Braskhiam alike, stranded with their hulls resting on solid earth. One by one, people began climbing down and wandering around. The esh was receding as fast as it had come in, and out from its depths came the Bonescrapers. They made for the Karthar ships, but found their way barred by mobs of enraged men and women armed with the weapons abandoned on the docks, standing between them and the enemy. They would not be killing Karthars today. Faced by overwhelming odds, the Noranian elite backed off and beat a hasty retreat.

Murris watched them march away, and Emos could see that something had hardened inside him.

'The Noranians did this to us!' he yelled. 'Somehow, they did this and I want some answers. I say we go to Noran. I say we give Rak Ek Namen a closer look at this war! Who is with me?'

All around him, an angry clamour rose up. There was a reckoning to be had.

# 19 HOW THE SKACK GRUBS EAT

Groach woke up in his bed and stared at the ceiling. It was his fourth day back at the Harvest Tide Project, and he had spent most of the time discreetly searching for ways to escape again. He had found none so far. He had been questioned along with all the other scientists by Mungret and various officers, who suspected that there was a Karthar spy among them. On top of that, some crumble cones had made it through to Braskhia, and he had lain awake until late in the night before, worrying that he had not done enough to stop it. He threw the covers off and sat up, shrugging out of his nightshirt and reaching for his tunic. He was back in the work clothes of the project – the long tunic that extended to his knees, belted at the waist, and a pair of simple sandals for his feet. His beard was starting to grow back and he decided he would shave it again; it took so long to grow, and was itchy all the time while it did.

He went to the door and lifted the latch, but the door did not budge. He pulled on it again, just to be sure, but there was no getting away from it. The door was bolted from the outside. They had locked it while he was asleep. Groach sat down on his bed again. His was a basement room, with a small barred window at street level. The bars were iron and set firmly into the frame. He had already looked at possible ways of levering them out. The door was solid oak; the walls were made of stone. He put his head in his hands and chewed his lip. They were on to him.

Some time later, there came the sound of the bolt being shot, and the door swung open. Rak Ek Namen walked in, followed by a guard carrying a chair. The soldier set the chair on the floor and left, closing the door after him. The Prime Ministrate sat down on the chair and crossed his legs, placing his hands in his lap. He gazed at the botanist without a word, a tired look on his face. Groach started to say something to break the silence, but the Noranian leader raised his finger and Groach went quiet again.

'I had a dream, Shessil,' Namen said, in what was almost a whisper. 'I dreamed that the Kartharic Peaks would belong to Noran. That we would rule the Karthars and make their country our own. With the Peaks, I could have built an empire greater than the world has ever known. I've been planning this for years. Years of building my armies, years of developing weapons; I've given my life to this. I needed the Braskhiams to build me a fleet of esh-boats to equal the Karthars', but they would not, so I developed a plan that would wipe out the entire Karthar army in one fell swoop, without the need for a battle on the esh. A huge, but ultimately simple scheme. I had to make them invade Braskhia, and then I had to smother them in the esh.'

He went quiet again, and Groach shifted uncomfortably on the bed. He had never seen the Prime Ministrate like this. Gone was the charming, charismatic leader he had known before. The man who sat before him now was hard and cold, and his eyes were empty of emotion.

'You were part of that plan, Shessil. A vital part, as it turned out. You cracked the problem, made it possible to cause the Harvest Tide, and I'm grateful to you for that. But you see, yesterday, the Karthar fleet lay off the coast of Braskhia, preparing to attack. Their ships were carrying every warrior they had and I had them right where I wanted them. As it turned out, they did not land, but that should not have mattered. Because the crumble cones had been dropped over the esh-bound bubule and the Harvest Tide was coming. There should have been a tidal wave that blocked out the sky; every soldier should have been smothered, every ship swallowed up, and Braskhia should have been so crippled its people would have welcomed the chance to join our empire. I had battalions of my best troops, wearing gas masks, of course, stationed to deal with any survivors. I had drawn the Karthars right into my trap.

'But it didn't happen. Oh, the esh rose all right, but not nearly enough. No Karthar ships capsized; hardly anyone was killed as far as we can make out. Now, the Karthars have joined forces with the traitors from Braskhia, and they are on their way to Noran. They are on their way here to us. To me.'

Namen stood up and walked to the window, watching the feet pass by on the street outside.

'Our new Groundsmaster tells me there are two vials missing from one of the laboratories. They contained spores of a fungus that spreads like wildfire and eats crumble cones, among other things. It was a lab that you were working in. It is thought that the spores of the fungus were spread around the barges by Myunans. There were two young Myunans in the group that "kidnapped" you. Very few people knew what the crumble cones were for; you were one of them. I have been forced to come to the conclusion that you have betrayed me, Shessil. And at the worst possible time.'

The Prime Ministrate turned from the window to glare at Groach.

'That treachery will cost you dear, Shessil Groach. I will hunt your friends down. The two Myunan children, the scentonomist and the Parsinor – I will have them executed, and their heads will be hung from the city gates. But not yours. You will be fed to the skack grubs. You know, the children of the skacks. They have no teeth, so they dissolve you with acid and drink you, bit by bit. It will take you many painful days to die. My only regret is that there will be no head to hang alongside those of your friends.'

Namen called to the guard, who opened the door and removed the chair. As the Prime Ministrate was leaving, he stopped, standing before Groach.

'You will be fed to the skack grubs tomorrow. Do try to enjoy the rest of your day.'

+ + +

Hiding was not something that came easily to Draegar. It rankled at him that he should shy away from combat, but even he was no match for the battlegroup of soldiers who were even now carrying out a house-to-house search down the street. Backed up by an engined crossbow, the foot soldiers were kicking in doors and ransacking one house after another. Draegar's hands wandered to the handles of his weapons, but he held himself in check. Beside him, beneath the floor of a cooper's workshop, Hilspeth listened to the sounds of the boots on cobbles, and the shouts of the men and women who were hunting them.

The soldiers were sure to peer into the shadows between the stone supports where the four fugitives were hiding, but if they did, there was a chance they might not see them. Lorkrin and Taya had camouflaged Hilspeth and the Parsinor by spreading themselves over them like blankets and changing their appearance to make the huddled group look like a pile of stones.

A face suddenly leaned in to survey the space beneath the building's floor. It turned one way, then the other and then disappeared. Taya breathed a quiet sigh of relief. But then the face appeared again with another beside it.

'Better check behind those stones,' said a voice.

Draegar gripped the handle of his sword. Hilspeth fumbled for a bottle in her waistcoat, and the two Myunans held their breaths. From out on the road came the sound of a scuffle and then shouts of alarm:

'A skack! There's a skack loose!'

Somebody screamed, and the four fugitives heard doors and windows slamming shut. The catapult's engine roared, but then there came a couple of loud thumps and the noise coughed and stalled. There were some more shouts, and then a hushed silence.

The next face to lean in and stare at them was that of a skack. It hissed. Taya eyed it for a moment, and then cried out in relief:

'Uncle Emos!'

The others looked closer and saw the triangular tattoo on its face.

'A skack!' gaped Lorkrin. 'That's brilliant ...'

'Quiet.' Emos's voice silenced his nephew immediately. 'I am taking you home. I have a potato field in need of weeding, and any more trouble from the pair of you and I might have a barn to paint as well.'

The soldiers stayed hidden away in the buildings and the catapult's cab until the skack had left with the two Myunans, the woman and the Parsinor. There was a possibility that the skack itself was a Myunan, but no one seemed willing to go and find out. Once the coast was clear, the driver who had tried to run the beast down got out of his cab to see what had brought his vehicle to such a sudden halt. It did not take long to find out ... the iron rear wheels of the vehicle had sagged into folded lumps, as if they were made of butter. The man stared at them, feeling slightly dizzy. Then he got back in his cab and stayed there for some time.

+ + +

Lorkrin and Taya were squatting either side of their uncle, all of them listening to Draegar.

'He is an annoying little man, absorbed in his learning,' the Parsinor was saying. 'And he has caused a lot of what has happened. But he is a good man, I think, and he has done what he could to make up for things. The Noranians will punish him for what he has done, when they realise. I think the punishment will be quite brutal. I think we should help him escape.'

'We *have* to get him out,' Hilspeth insisted, desperately. 'They'll kill him if we don't!'

Taya, Lorkrin, Hilspeth and Draegar had spent the last few days evading the soldiers who hunted them, had seen Parsinors and Myunans being rounded up, and were now hiding in an empty water tank on the roof of a disused bathhouse. The soldiers had left the streets and were crowding onto the city walls. The Braskhiams were coming and they were bringing the Karthars with them. They had crossed the Braskhiam Gulf in an array of different vessels, the Karthars' might combined with the Braskhiams' technology. Emos, as soon as he had found his tools, had hitched a ride on Murris's boat until he was rested enough to fly again. Then he had raced ahead to Noran. He now weighed up the chances of successfully breaking Groach out.

'The children must not be involved,' he said, finally. 'But I agree. No one deserves the treatment that those animals can dish out. We must find him and help him.'

Taya peered around her uncle's chest at Lorkrin, who pulled a face. They did not like the sound of this. Shessil was their friend, and whatever trouble he was in, they were determined to help him out of it. They did not like being treated like helpless infants, not that you could expect anything else from grown-oldies. The moment that the other three were gone, they would be off on a rescue mission of their own.

'I know what you two are planning ... and I'm not having any of it,' Emos warned.

'We weren't planning anything,' Taya retorted.

'That'll be the day,' their uncle grunted. 'I'm sorry to have to resort to this. I hope your ma and pa will understand, but I can't have you running into any more danger. Hilspeth, Draegar and I will handle this. You will be staying here.'

In one swift motion, he twisted and grabbed their arms, holding them in one hand, while with the other he ran his fingers across their feet, muttering some words. Suddenly, their legs started to soften and their thighs sank into their knees, their knees into their shins, their shins into their ankles and their ankles into their feet. Their feet spread out across the damp floor of the water tank, almost filling it. Lorkrin tried to walk, but it was like having a rug for legs.

'Aw, bowels!' he barked.

'Lorkrin Archisan! Your mother would be beside herself if she heard you using language like that.' Emos wagged his finger at the boy. 'I hope you don't talk like that at home.'

'No, I don't,' Lorkrin screwed up his face in a sulk. 'And I don't melt people's legs either.'

'I'm sorry, Lorkrin,' his uncle said in a softer voice. 'If there was any other way ...'

'We'd better get a move on,' Draegar urged his friend. 'Every moment wasted is a moment too long for Shessil.'

'What if the soldiers come?' Taya protested.

'They're otherwise occupied,' Draegar reassured her. 'They've all gone to man their positions. You won't have any trouble with them, I think. Just stay quiet and stay put. We'll be back before long.'

Hilspeth offered an apologetic shrug and waved to them, and with that, the three adults climbed out of the tank and left Taya and Lorkrin alone. They listened to the retreating sounds of the scentonomist, the Parsinor and their uncle, waiting until they were out of earshot. Lorkrin turned to his sister.

'This is not fair!' he muttered. 'This ... it's just not fair!'

'He's well and truly done it this time,' Taya moaned. 'There's no way I'm going out looking like this.'

'Do you know any disenchants?' he asked desperately.

'I don't seem to remember one for stopping your legs from

becoming a carpet,' she snapped. 'We played at trying to make apples square, or tying knots in horseshoes.'

'Well, what do you remember?'

'I don't know. I've never heard about this before.'

'Me neither. We have to try something. I'm not staying here like a half-melted snowman. Maybe it's easier to undo a transmorph than it is to start one ... you know, like it's easier to keep a cart rolling than it is to get it going in the first place.'

'All right, we'll take turns,' Taya suggested. 'You go first.'

'Why should I go first?'

'You're the one who said he wanted to get out of here. Don't you want to or not?'

'Okay, okay. Right ...' He thought for a bit. Then, placing his hands on what had once been their legs, he muttered: '*Nemed qua perius.*'

The blanket of flesh started to itch, as if they were being bitten by a thousand lice.

'Agh! Not that! Not that one!' Taya cried. 'Ehmm ... *Reparicus opic trum!*'

The itching stopped, but instead, the entire swathe of flesh knotted up in a painful cramp.

'Aaaagh!' Lorkrin squealed. '*Issith trayam tangem shest!*'

The cramp faded and was quickly replaced with the unbearable tingling of pins and needles. Taya squeezed her eyes shut.

'*Teop chem querrilous!*

The tingling subsided, but was replaced with a burning sensation on their skin. Both Myunans winced and squirmed to escape it.

'*Opris tarrigus mestal crem!*' Lorkrin gasped.

The burning cooled, and then their flesh went completely numb. Lorkrin rapped his knuckles on it. The skin beneath them was as solid as the wood of the water tank.

'No wonder this stuff is banned,' Taya said, sulking.

+ + +

There was a lot of activity around the Harvest Tide Project, with messengers coming and going, and valuable records and materials being carried out, to be brought to safer locations. In all the bustle, no one noticed an extra guard walk around the corner and in the door. Even with the tattooed outline of a triangle etched on his face, he looked like just another messenger delivering news.

Emos picked up the first scroll that he found in one of the rooms, to complete the disguise, and began his search of the main building. Draegar had drawn him a portrait of the botanist and he had memorised it, but so far he had seen no one even resembling the sketch. The place was a maze of corridors and rooms, and it was not long before he was wondering if he would ever find Groach. They couldn't even plan a rescue until they knew where he was. He stopped halfway down one hallway, his attention caught by a diagram on a notice board. It was a map of the building. Whatever else you said about the Noranians, they were organised. He found the staff quarters, in the basement, and decided it was as good a place as any to find the botanist. The Myunan took the first flight of stairs he came to and made his way down.

The corridors here were darker, and many were lined with shelves holding glass cases. Inside the cases, strange, mutated vegetables were growing in a greeny brown jelly. In another corridor, he discovered walls of glass, behind which was a glowing blue fungus that lit up the hallway. He checked through the little window of each door for any sign of Groach, finding only one unknown scientist after another, either resting or reading. But most of the rooms were completely empty, with most of the staff working elsewhere.

Then he peered in another window, and there, sitting on his bed, deep in thought, was the man he was searching for. Emos tried the door, but it was bolted and padlocked. There could be no doubt about it; the Noranians knew that Groach had betrayed them. The Myunan was about to pick the lock, when he heard voices coming. Walking quickly in the opposite direction, he slipped around a corner and leaned against the wall. Taking a peek around the corner, he got a look at the three men – two soldiers and a man who appeared to be some kind of clerk. The clerk was speaking.

'Forward-Batterer, I realise you want to get to the walls and see some "action", but there is work to be done here, important work. Escorting prisoners may not be the kind of duty that wins you medals, but it is just as vital as driving an axe into the head of an enemy. This man is to be taken to cells in the Central Eb-Tower, and I ... the Prime Ministrate wants it done now.'

'Aye, sir. But then can we go to the walls? I wouldn't like to miss the battle.'

'Some would consider missing the battle a blessing, but it takes all sorts, I suppose. Yes, you may man the walls after Groach has been delivered safely to the river. Now, I need to ask him some more questions about where his friends are, and then we can get on with it. And you're to make sure he gets a cell near the skack grub pens. He might as well get a taste of what's to come tomorrow.'

Emos's blood froze. Groach was to be fed to skack grubs? He thought even the Noranians had given up that particular death sentence. The botanist was to have the most painful death imaginable. While the Myunan waited for the clerk to come out again, he got to work with his tools, listening to the sound of Groach being put in shackles. He moulded his face, sculpting the tattoo up into his hair, where it was hidden. He would have to act quickly; it would find its way back onto his face before long. The little Noranian left the room and strode quickly up the corridor. Emos was ready by the time the soldiers led their captive out. Sweeping around the corner, he approached the three men, looking for all intents and purposes like the clerk who had just left.

'The Prime Ministrate has changed his mind,' he called, mimicking the clerk's voice. 'Every soldier is to make his way to the walls immediately. We have a crisis on our hands. Leave the keys to the prisoner's shackles with me. I will take him to the cells myself.'

'You?' one of them asked, incredulously. 'What if he tries to escape?'

'Where can he run to, you idiot? We're in the middle of Noran, with every gate guarded, and the enemy on our doorstep and he's in shackles. Stop thinking with your axe and use your head for a change. Now give me the keys and go.'

The soldiers looked at one another, shrugged, and the Forward-Batterer tossed Emos the bunch of keys. Then they shouldered their weapons and hurried off to join their comrades.

'Shessil, take no notice of my face. My name is Emos,' he told the botanist.

'Lorkrin and Taya's uncle?'

'That's right. I'm here to get you out.'

'But how?'

'We're going right out the front door. As far as anyone is concerned, I'm escorting you to the Central Eb-Tower. All we have to do is head towards the river and then lose ourselves in the back streets. Are you ready?'

'Ready as I'll ever be. Let's get out of here.'

They passed through the hallways and up the stairs, Groach shuffling as fast as his leg irons would allow. As they headed for the front door, a coach was drawing up outside. Groach slowed down, but Emos egged him on.

'We're almost there,' he muttered as they walked out.

The door of the ornate coach opened and the Prime Ministrate leaned out.

'Ah, Mungret, there you are. And Shessil too, I see.' He motioned to Emos. 'Get in, and bring our little traitor. I have some more questions for him before we send him to the skack grubs. I need you to fetch me the plans for a siege defence. The Karthars and Braskhiams are closing on the outskirts and we're going to have to close off the gates soon. I need those plans.'

Emos hesitated. They were surrounded by the Prime Ministrate's escort. There was no chance of escape. Thinking fast, he nodded and shoved Groach in the direction of the coach. They climbed in and sat down opposite the Noranian leader. The door was closed behind them and the coach started off.

'You're not looking yourself today, Mungret,' Namen commented. 'Lungs at you again?'

'Just all the excitement, Prime Ministrate,' Emos wheezed, hoping the Noranian would not notice the difference in his voice. His head was starting to itch. He had spent years learning to hide the Myunan plague brand under his hair where it could not be seen, but it was cursed always to find its way back to his face so that all those who came into contact with him would know what he was. Now he could feel it edging towards his hairline. Holding it at bay took enormous effort.

'Yes, well we'll soon show that scum what it means to betray Noran. And if the Karthars want to fight us on our home ground, they can pay the price too. I'll cut down every last one of them.'

# 20 A BEXEMOT HUNGRY FOR LOVE

On the river, the three eb-tower fortresses were being stocked up for a siege, with food, water, ammunition, and other supplies. The huge trees with their turrets, platforms and heavy weapons emplacements were a hive of hectic activity, so nobody noticed two extra barrels appear out of nowhere to join a stack that sat on the docks. They were picked up and carried past the guards, and onto the island-like base of the centre eb-tower. Every now and then, a pair of eyes would open on one of the barrels and glance around. Taya and Lorkrin had undone their uncle's transmorphing. It had taken a lot of effort and a few near accidents to do it. They had suffered aches, stinging, swelling, numbness and dizziness, but they had finally managed it, and now they were determined to break Groach out. With no idea where to start looking, they had made their way to the eb-towers. Because they were tall and important-looking, and because Shessil said he worked with plants. For once, luck was on their side.

A coach led by an armoured wagon pulled past and stopped inside the gates leading onto the base of the huge tree. A man who had to be the Noranian Prime Ministrate got out with a smaller man in tow, followed by Shessil Groach. They heard the Noranian leader order the second man to take the prisoner up to his quarters. Namen wanted to speak to the officer in charge of security for the eb-tower.

The two barrels sidled out of sight behind a pile of flour sacks and slunched back into their normal forms. Taya unwrapped her tools, and began to mould her skin into the texture of bark. Her hands trembled, slowing her down. The atmosphere was heavy with the threat of looming battle, but she blocked it out as she worked. Flushed with the thrill of the rescue, her mind was filled with their tribe's tales of romantic adventure. She would show Uncle Emos that they were no longer children. The sound of alarm horns burst out above them, making her start. Cursing men's stupid love of war, she gritted her teeth and added the finishing touches to her camouflage with a routing comb.

'Where do you suppose they're taking him?' Lorkrin asked as he did the same.

'The Prime Ministrate said his quarters. They're probably really high up, near the top. That's where I'd be if I lived here.'

'We'd better check the windows as we go up, all the same. You never know.' He twisted his head right around so that he could see as he worked on his back.

It did not take them long to complete their new forms.

'Are you ready?' his sister prompted.

'Yeah, let's go.'

Moving slowly until they reached the first branches, so as not to be noticed, the two Myunans began to climb. Their fingers and toes were long, and ended in hooked claws that could grasp any small crevice in the tree's surface. Their camouflage made them almost invisible against the dull brown bark, and they were careful to stay in the shadows wherever possible. Bit by bit, they made their way up the towering eb-tree. When they reached a ledge, Taya stopped for a rest, and gazed out over the city. Beyond the walls, past the factories and houses, she could see a dust cloud rising on one whole side of the city. Within it, there were hundreds – no, thousands – of soldiers and vehicles, an army moving in a wave towards the centre of Noran.

'There's going to be one almighty fight,' Lorkrin whispered beside her.

'Let's make sure Shessil isn't here when it happens,' she replied.

They both went still as a guard strode around a walkway above them. He carried on around the trunk and tramped down some stairs. All about them, men and women were busy preparing for the siege. Weapons were being loaded and buckets of water positioned to put out fires. People ran back and forth carrying things and shouting to one another. There was a feeling of adrenalin-charged urgency in the air. Lorkrin had always wanted to see a battle. Like every other boy he knew, he had played at war with his friends. Now he was seeing it as it truly was, and his heart was thumping in his chest, his stomach knotted with excitement and fear. His scrape with death when he fell in the esh had changed him, and for the first time, he had been faced with the knowledge that people could die for stupid reasons, without noble last words, or some heroic last stand. Death was fickle. And today, in this battle, everybody would be facing down fate. Something in Lorkrin got a sickening thrill from that knowledge.

They had to stop again when they were blocked by the floor of a heavy crossbow emplacement. There seemed to be no way around. There was a turret filled with soldiers to their right and a walkway to their left, with people stamping up and down it in a constant stream. They had reached a dead end. Taya pressed herself as flat as she could. Her camouflage was good, but hanging here as they were, their shapes could be seen against the curve of the tree by anyone who looked hard enough. She swore silently. They might have to give up and head back down.

Lorkrin bit his lip, feeling the strain starting to tell down his arms and shoulders. He was suspended from his claws and his toes were beginning to cramp. He stole a glance at Taya, and could see that she was also struggling to remain still.

'We're stuck. We'll have to go back down,' Taya hissed.

'Wait!' Lorkrin tugged her arm. 'We can get up that way!'

Out along a branch was a rope ladder that hung from a platform where a winch sat for hauling up supplies from the base of the tree. The platform was well above the level of the crossbow emplacement, and they would make a lot of headway if they took that route. There was no one at the winch. It would mean climbing out in full view, but it was less risky than taking the stairs. They walked out on the branch, balancing precariously, Lorkrin reaching the suspended ladder first. He checked below them, to make sure that there was nobody climbing up, and then started his ascent to the platform. Watching him go, Taya prayed that he was not seen. Disguised as he was, he looked like a thin, dead tree stump making for the sky. Even the dumbest soldier would be bound to get a mite suspicious.

He crawled onto the platform and waved her up. She took the ladder in both hands and scaled it quickly. Up by the winch, there were coils of thick rope and harnesses of various kinds. A gurney was slung from a cable between the platform and the tree trunk, and together they jumped on and slid the length of the cable to the relative cover of the trunk. Here, they stepped off the walkway and clung to the heavily ridged wood, continuing their climb, peering into windows as they went up, looking for signs of Shessil or the Prime Ministrate.

+ + +

Draegar and Hilspeth found their way to an outdoor kitchen that served tourists to Noran. He had to keep a low profile as Parsinors were being arrested all over the city, but she was relatively free to wander and find out more about what was going on. While she stood waiting for her soup, Hilspeth talked casually to the old woman who was serving. Draegar sat down at the table in the corner, keeping a wary eye out for soldiers.

Hilspeth joined him with the food, pushing the soup and some bread towards the Parsinor.

'Apparently the Prime Ministrate is raging. He has the word out that we are to be executed when they find us. All the Myunans and Parsinors that they've found can't tell them anything, so the Noranians are threatening to execute them if we're not captured.'

'Damn their rotten souls! Any word on what's happening beyond the walls?'

'The Braskhiams and the Karthars are almost at the outskirts of the city. They've smashed their way past the sentry posts in the hills, and have sent word that they want the Prime Ministrate himself or they will sack the city.'

'They could do it too, if they could take the eb-towers. Listen, I've been around this area before. I used to sell maps to the Noranians. We need to cause some chaos, give Emos the chance to break Shessil out, and maybe do some damage to the eb-towers into the bargain. If we can distract the Nora-nians' attention, Emos can save Shessil. I know how he thinks. This is what we need to do.'

After he had explained what he had in mind, Hilspeth nodded.

'I know exactly how to do that.'

+ + +

Emos followed the Prime Ministrate up the stairway, keep-ing Groach ahead of him. This was not going according to plan. While they were surrounded by soldiers, there was little hope of getting the botanist out, and his head was starting to itch intolerably. It was all he could do to stop from constantly scratching it. The brand would show on his face before long, and then his disguise would be useless. Cossock, the monstrous bodyguard, stayed close behind him so he was unable to say anything to Groach. After a seemingly endless climb, they reached the Prime Minis-trate's quarters. Namen gestured Emos and their prisoner into the main study.

'Pull out everything we have on siege strategies while I'm gone. I must see to the defences. I'll be back soon.'

With that, he left and they were alone together.

'What are we going to do now?' Groach asked.

'I'm thinking,' the Myunan replied. Walking to the

window, he looked out and wondered how far down it was to the river. Too far, he decided.

Rak Ek Namen went down the steps three at a time with Cossock at his heels. There was so much to deal with and so little time. He was convinced Groach's friends were Karthar spies, and that they must be found before they could cause any more harm. Then there was the battle ahead. The opposing army was strong, but they were tired from travelling and would not be well supplied; he was sure he could defeat them.

He nearly ran into Mungret, who was climbing up the steps towards him. Namen stared at him.

'I thought I told you to ...' He paused, frowning.

'To what, Prime Ministrate?' Mungret enquired, knowing trouble brewing when he saw it.

'Grab him!' Namen shoved the clerk at Cossock and raced back up the stairs.

Emos was listening at the door. When he heard the Noranian leader running up the steps, he turned and cast his eyes around the room. There was no time to amorph into another disguise. In the shadows between two bookcases, there was a stand holding an array of antique spears and swords. He stared at them for a moment.

+ + +

Taya looked up and shouted a warning to Lorkrin, hugging the trunk as some spears fell past her. They narrowly missed her brother, who swore in fright.

'Bowels! They're onto us!'

'I don't think so,' Taya shook her head, gazing upwards. 'I don't think that was meant for us.'

'What, you think they chuck spears out of windows for laughs up here?'

+ + +

Rak Ek Namen burst into the study, closely followed by Cossock and a nervous clerk, and found only a slightly bemused Groach standing in the middle of the room. His face a mask of controlled rage, the Prime Ministrate looked around the room, and then strode forwards and peered out each window. Cossock checked behind the door, and searched through the official robes hanging in the large, ornate wardrobe.

'Where is he?' the Noranian leader demanded.

'Who?' Groach replied, pointing at Mungret. 'You mean him?'

+ + +

Draegar and the scentonomist left the kitchen, and walked along the back alleys to the docks. Hilspeth stayed ahead of the Parsinor, checking that the coast was clear before he followed. They hurried across the loading areas to a bridge that spanned the river above the eb-towers. Climbing down, they slipped into the water underneath, and vanished beneath the surface.

Hilspeth had always been a good swimmer. She had grown up in an area on the shores of a great lake, and she and her friends would often spend summer days playing in the clear waters. The water of the River Gullin was in stark contrast to that lake. It had a mud bottom that was constantly disturbed by the current, making it murky and full of silt. Pollution from the factories gave it a dank smell, and something in it was stinging her eyes. Draegar touched her arm and pointed. Below them, partly buried in the mud, was what they had come to find. It was a bexemot, sleeping on the bed of the river. Draegar had told her that they were enticed here by the Noranians, who used them for moving the eb-towers into deeper water when the river level dropped. This was one of at least five that he knew were in this area. Letting some air out through her closed lips to take the pressure from her lungs, Hilspeth held her nose and popped her ears as she dived deeper.

If there was anything that Hilspeth knew a lot about, it was smells. And when you knew a lot about smells, you learned a lot about noses too. It was all part of the job. Even unusually large noses like that of a bexemot. Actually, studying the inside of a bexemot's nose was essential to a scentonomist's training. How else was one to get such a close look inside a working nasal passage?

She swam down to the head of the monstrous animal, and worked her way along to one of its nostrils. Then she ducked inside. Just inside was a large hollow, big enough to hold an air pocket at the top that she could fit her head into. She exhaled as she hit the air and heaved in a few breaths. The nostril was the width of a respectable wine barrel, and its walls were lined with a slimy mucus that made it slippery. There was no movement in the passage. A sleeping bexemot could hold its breath for weeks. She felt uneasy being in such a confined space, but she had a job to do, which was enough to keep her wits about her.

Digging her feet in to hold her head in the small air space, she reached into her waistcoat and pulled out a vial. There was almost no light in here, but she knew most of her bottles by feel. Holding her nose, she unplugged the cork and let the contents empty into the water around her. It was essence of timbleleaf. For humans, it was a treatment for jealousy: for bexemots, it was a powerful love potion. There was enough in that vial to make even the most unfriendly bexemot go looking for romance. She was not sure how fast it would work. She had her answer before she could get out of the nostril.

The world about her shook and there was a rush of moving water. She felt the pressure change, and was almost sucked farther in as the creature's head broke the surface and it took a deep breath. With an almighty explosion of air, it sneezed, blasting her into the sky as high as the roofs of the buildings on either side of the river. She sailed through the air, arcing down the river and landing on her back with a smack that stung her from head to toe. She skimmed the surface, bounced and slapped the water hard again. The wind was knocked out of her, and she sank beneath the glassy ripples. With a few frantic strokes, she clawed her way up to the surface again, fighting for breath. She paddled weakly until a heavily muscled arm encircled her waist and guided her to the shore. Draegar pulled her out under the cover of the bridge and watched her until he was sure she had recovered.

'Never seen that before,' he told her.

The bexemot was wide awake, and could be seen with its head and back rising out of the murky water. It swivelled slowly this way and that, then found a scent and started moving.

'I wonder if it's a boy or a girl,' Hilspeth mused.

The enormous animal swam past the bases of the eb-towers, snagging anchor lines and brushing against the thick roots on which the trees floated. The tall floating fortresses swayed violently back and forth, starting to pull at their moorings as their suddenly unanchored bases began to move with the current. The mooring ropes pulled taut, and the huge trees shuddered, held in place only by the ropes and the long cables that ran from the ground to the higher branches to hold the tops steady.

The bexemot continued on its way, determined to find love. It dragged some anchor chains with it, and was hardly slowed when they jerked taut and snapped, shaking the towering fortresses to their roots. Horns were sounding the alarm, and soldiers and dock workers ran to help secure the eb-towers. But nothing could be done while they rocked from side to side; men and women were tossed across the roots and thrown from the branches into the river; loose ropes and chains whipped around and knocked people to the ground. Hilspeth winced as she saw one soldier hurled towards the bridge by a pivoting tree.

'I think we may have overdone it,' she grimaced.

'They'll be all right.' Draegar was unsympathetic. 'A good swim never hurt anyone. At least it'll draw attention away from Emos. He should have got Shessil out by now.'

+ + +

Groach cowered as the Noranian leader advanced on him. Suddenly the room lurched and they were all thrown off their feet, with the exception of Cossock. Namen jumped up, but the tower shook again and he had to grab a table to steady himself.

'Find out what's going on!' he shouted to Cossock.

The bodyguard dragged Mungret out with him and charged down the stairs. Namen stepped over to the stand of weapons between the bookcases, glowering at Groach as he reached for a sword.

'You're up to something and, whatever it is, I've had enough of you.'

His hand failed to grasp the weapon. Turning in surprise, he found that the narrow space between the two bookcases was filled with some solid shape. There was only the image of the weapons' stand, as if painted onto a wall. He gasped in surprise, but recovered in an instant and grabbed a letter opener from the bookshelf, driving the blade into the image before Emos could regain his shape.

Emos cried out, but lunged out of his hiding place. And now he had the knife embedded in his shoulder, he held it to him. The room shuddered and Namen stumbled. Emos slunched back into his normal form as he threw himself for-wards, knocking the Noranian to the floor. Tossing the knife away, he swung his fist hard against Namen's jaw. Namen got his foot against Emos's chest and kicked him away. The Myunan rolled and flipped onto his feet, but Namen was already up. Groach charged at him, wrapping the chain of his shackles around the Noranian's shoulders. Namen was snared long enough for Emos to get another punch in before the Noranian leader blocked him and landed a fist right across the Myunan's nose. Emos let his face go soft, and Namen's hand left an imprint. The Noranian swivelled and caught Groach with an elbow in the ribs. He shrugged out of the botanist's grip and swung an uppercut that cracked against Groach's chin and sent him reeling backwards. He collapsed unconscious against the wall. Namen stepped outside Emos's next punch and drove his foot into the Myunan's midriff, hurling him back across the room.

+ + +

Taya pulled herself onto a deck where she could hold on, helping Lorkrin up as the tower pitched back and forth violently. They had almost been thrown off when it had started moving, and now it was rocking like a ship in a storm. Lorkrin panted as he crawled to join her at the post where she was clinging on tightly.

'By the gods,' he gasped, wrapping his arms around the post. 'This is getting to be a bit much, really. Maybe we should try taking the stairs from here on up.'

'Well, at least it's giving the guards something to think about,' Taya replied.

Anchored to the post were two heavy ropes which were pulled taut, acting against the movement of the tree. She reasoned that they must be linked to the ground, stabilising the tower. Her eyes followed their length down through the branches, and she found herself looking straight into the face of a soldier on a walkway below them. His face changed as he saw her.

'Intruders!' he roared, pointing up at them.

All of a sudden, there were four more Noranians at his side. They snarled at the Myunans and grabbed the ropes. Climbing hand over hand, they made their way up the cables towards the two shape-shifters. Lorkrin pulled his bag off and rooted about inside. Drawing his knife, he started sawing through one of the ropes.

'What are you doing?' Taya exclaimed.

'Getting them before they get us!' he grunted.

The fibres of the rope parted under his sharp blade, and the tension of the rope pulled it apart. It snapped, nearly catching Lorkrin across the head as it whipped away, sending two soldiers tumbling down through the branches below them. The eb-tower, already fighting the current of the river and the collision with the bexemot, shuddered, and the strain on the other rope increased. He and Taya began to cut at it, and this one gave way almost immediately. The remaining soldiers fell kicking and flailing into the foliage.

'They could be killed,' Taya said, anxiously.

'Nah, they're bound to hit something on the way down.'

The gigantic eb-tree turned to hang from its last anchoring lines, but the strain was too much now and one by one, they snapped like whips as the huge tree tore loose.

The eb-tower spun and swayed, its wide base giving in to the current that it had stood firm against for so long. With the extra weight of its turrets and buildings, its top rocked about, the Myunans clinging to the post for their lives. Slowly, but with unstoppable force, it began to move down river.

+ + +

Emos twisted out of a headlock and swept Namen's feet out from under him. The Noranian fell back, staggered and hit the wall. His hand found a battle axe mounted by the window and he yanked it from its brackets. The room trembled again, and he was forced to hold on until it died down. Emos used the time to become a shorter, squatter shape and lengthen his arms. Punching a Myunan master was like thumping putty, but there was no doubt that Rak Ek Namen was the better fighter, and Emos was already weakening from his wound. If the Myunan did not use every advantage he had, he and Groach were both dead. By making himself smaller and stouter, he was better able to keep his balance on the rocking floor, and if he could keep the Noranian at arm's reach, he had more of a chance of surviving this. As long as he had the longer arms.

The Noranian closed in on him, brandishing the axe. Emos ducked and stepped to one side as the blade swung at his head, then leaned in and slammed a fist into the Prime Ministrate's belly. Namen coughed and doubled up. Emos went for another punch, but Namen straightened up suddenly and drove the butt of the axe handle into the Myunan's chest. Emos grunted but stayed standing, side-stepping Namen's next strike and rolling away across the floor out of reach. The chamber pitched again and Namen wobbled on his feet. Emos leapt at him, wrapping his arms around him in a bear hug that trapped Namen's arms.

Taya appeared at the window as the two men crashed to the floor.

'Uncle Emos!' she screamed.

Emos slunched and linked his arms into one band that held the Noranian leader fast. Looking up, he saw Lorkrin follow his sister through the window. Namen snarled as he recognised them.

'Get Shessil out of here!' Emos bellowed.

'But you ...' Taya started.

'Do as I say, girl! Get out now!'

Turning towards the window, Lorkrin's face dropped and he grabbed Taya's shoulder. The tree was heading straight for one of the other eb-towers.

'OH BOWELS!' Taya cried.

The eb-tree groaned and leaned hard over, the top of the

other tree filling the view in the window. Gripping the sides of their mouths, the two shape-shifters slunched and each pulled their mouth open wide enough to swallow a water melon. Then, seizing Groach under his armpits, they pushed him through the window and followed him out.

Moments later, the tops of the two eb-towers smashed into each other. Wood and metal, furniture, weapons, doors and windows were all pulverised as the enormous trees collided. The two trunks tangled on each other's wreckage, tipping both over. Then they tore apart and rocked back up, their heavy bases bringing them upright.

The three friends fell, branches and leaves sweeping past them as they hurtled towards the river far below. Opening their gaping mouths, the two Myunans let their entire bodies go slack, and the whistling air rushed up into their throats, shaping them and hollowing them out. The air filled them to their toes, expanding them until they were no more than billowing bags of flesh. Their fall slowed as they caught the air, their bodies stretched to their limit ... but it was working. The wind caught them and they swooped further down the river. Like a pair of paper bags, they floated down, dropping Groach into the water before settling in themselves, deflating into loose folds. They tried to pull the botanist towards the shore, but they were too weak and clumsy. His unconscious body started to slip beneath the surface. They heard the sounds of splashes and felt hands grab them. They were hauled ashore and laid out on the ground. Lying in a stunned sprawl, and with his wide, flat head lolling about, Lorkrin saw armed men and women all around them. They were outside the city walls, but were surrounded by troops and machines. Groach was lying still beside them. It did not matter. The soldiers had caught them after all.

A familiar face appeared above Taya, his head tilting from side to side as if trying to imagine what she would look like if her features were closer together. His eyebrows lifted as he recognised her.

'What are you two doing here?' Peddar Murris asked, a concerned look on his face as he studied the two Myunans in confusion.

Too weak to answer, Taya let out a deep, deafening belch, and flopped helplessly on the wet grass. Tears welled in her eyes as she thought about her uncle, caught in the Prime Ministrate's chamber when the eb-towers collided. There was no way that he could have survived. She felt a hand flapping against her foot and heard Lorkrin's feeble voice:

'Look ... look up.'

She blinked, turning her head as best she could to look skywards and saw what appeared to be a sheet of paper floating down towards them. As it sailed closer, she could see that it was shaped like a man, but the size of a boat's sail. It was Uncle Emos. With most of his body stretched out as thin and flat as sailcloth, he was riding the wind like a kite. He spiralled lazily down until he came to rest nearby. Then crefting back into shape, he got stiffly to his feet and walked over to kneel between his nephew and niece, holding their stretched, baggy hands. Taya sobbed again, but this time with joy, and Lorkrin sniffed back some tears. Whatever happened now, at least they had their uncle back.

# EPILOGUE

Lorkrin and Taya were wrinkly. They had resumed their old shapes, but were covered in sags and folds that betrayed their day's adventures. Exchanging glum looks, they turned with pleading expressions to their uncle. He smiled at them and spread his arms, shrugging.

'You overstretched,' he said simply. 'You'll return to normal eventually.'

'But how long will it take?' Lorkrin asked.

'A few weeks, perhaps.'

'Weeks!' Taya burst out. 'I can't walk around looking like this for weeks!'

'Well, maybe with a bit of effort, you will fix up in a day or two,' he reassured her, barely suppressing a laugh. They were obviously upset, but they did look very funny.

The three Myunans were standing near the river in a camp of Braskhiam troops, Sestinians and others who had joined the march on Noran. With them were soldiers from the Kartharic Peaks, mixing, talking and sharing food and drink with the people who had been their enemies only days before. Tents, weapons and vehicles were scattered all around them, positioned for a siege on Noran that had never happened. When the eb-towers had collided, the fight had gone out of the soldiers still loyal to Noran as they realised they had lost their leader. Emos had been thrown clear when the towers had crashed together, leaving Rak Ek Namen caught in the chamber as the two huge trees demolished each other.

'Couldn't you do something?' Lorkrin begged. 'I bet you could fix us.'

'Oh, no. I don't think so.'

'I bet you could,' Taya repeated.

'Give me a couple of days to think about how to do it,' Emos told them.

'Uncle Emos!' they wailed in unison.

'In the meantime, you two can think about how this found its way to the study of the Noranian Prime Ministrate.' He held up his quill.

'What's that?' Lorkrin raised his eyebrows, in an attempt at ignorance.

'Looks like a pen, or something,' Taya chirped. 'Is that yours, Uncle Emos?'

The discussion was interrupted by the sound of an engine drawing near, then a skid and the clang of metal on metal.

'Sorry, sorry,' came the sound of Hilspeth's voice. 'By the gods, these things are harder to drive than they look.'

The three Myunans turned to see the wagon that Draegar had hijacked, resting against an engined catapult, its front bumper dented. Hilspeth and the Parsinor were getting down from the cab, and Hilspeth whooped when she saw Groach sitting, having his head tended by one of the Braskhiam healers. She ran over and wrapped her arms around him, kissing him hard on the lips. He was taken aback at first, but then he kissed her back tentatively.

'You made it!' she cried, as she pushed him back to get a good look at him.

'Most of me.' He gave a pained smile. 'It seems I owe my life to just about everyone.'

'You'll just have to live a quieter life from here on in.' She hugged him again.

'I'll certainly try my best.' He dropped his head, and then raised it to meet the gazes of the others. 'Thank you. Thank you, all of you.'

There was an awkward silence while everyone tried to think of something to say.

'I have a wagon to return,' Draegar spoke up. 'I must head south soon and make what amends I can to the driver. I can only hope his stay at the storyhouse has been pleasant. I'll need somebody to drive the thing. I still can't get my feet on the pedals.'

'I'll drive for you,' Emos offered. 'These two are overdue back at their parents'.'

'I'm not sure what I'm going to do,' Groach muttered.

'The farmers in Braskhia will need all the help they can get to save their crops after the Harvest Tide,' Murris told him. 'I'm sure they could find a use for someone with your expertise.'

'That sounds like a good place to start making amends,' Groach smiled. 'There's a fisherman and his wife in Crickenob to whom I owe a debt as well. South it is then.'

'I'll need to get back to work down that way too,' Hilspeth said. 'We can all go back together.'

'A recipe for further disaster, I'm sure,' grunted Emos with a wry smile. He rubbed his hands together. 'I look forward to the journey. For now though, I think a good meal is in order.'

'A feast more like,' Murris cried out. 'I feel a party coming on. You must all stay until you are stuffed to the gills and we've danced 'til we've dropped. I think it should be the last act of this war to go out to music. I do love a good dance.'

Suddenly, Taya grabbed Lorkrin's saggy wrist and nodded towards the river. Emerging from the water was a huge, scarred, yellow-skinned man with weapons draped about him. In his right hand, he held a spiked iron ball hanging from a chain; in his left, a viciously sharp axe. He had murder written on his face.

'Cossock,' Groach whispered.

The Barian advanced on them, ignoring the rebel soldiers on either side. Draegar drew his sword and his battleaxe and took a stance before him. Cossock measured him up, and then growled to the group of friends:

'Make your peace with your gods. I will feed the grass with your blood before I am killed.'

Emos put a hand on the Parsinor's arm and faced Rak Ek Namen's bodyguard.

'If it's a fight you want, you'll get it, friend. But don't think that you will get the honourable death you're looking for. We will not fight to kill you. But if it's embarrassment you are after, I can guarantee it. I am a master of transmorphing. Just one touch is all I need to give you ears like a donkey, or feet like a duck, or perhaps just turn you bright pink. You can fight to kill me, but I will fight to humiliate you. Just one touch, whether you kill me or not. And then every man here will descend on you. So, win or lose, you will die a laughing stock. Now, was it a fight you wanted?'

Cossock stood stock still, unsure of himself. It was the Barian way to fear nothing, to fight and kill and die with honour. Nothing in his experience had prepared him for an opponent who would make a clown of him whether they died or not. This was not the kind of combat he knew; it did not seem fair. More people had gathered. Hundreds were watching. This was not how it was supposed to be. He bared his teeth and hissed, but nobody seemed impressed. They were all waiting for the moment when he grew duck's feet and turned pink.

For the first time in his life, Cossock blushed. With a roar of disgust, he threw his weapons to the ground, and walked back to the river, his head in his hands. Stumbling into the river, he dived into the current and swam away. The crowd relaxed. Lorkrin was secretly crestfallen that there hadn't been a fight, and even Draegar looked a little disappointed.

'Could you really have done that?' Taya asked her uncle.

'Well, no. It takes a bit more than a touch to do it. It would have taken a little work.'

'Then you lied?'

'Exaggerated, dear. Better than somebody dying, don't you think?'

'Oh, yes.'

'This definitely calls for a celebration!' Murris was still determined to have his party. 'A Barian embarrassed into defeat. Now that's a story that will travel! Somebody make some music!'

+ + +

Later that night, as Groach, Taya and Lorkrin were sitting together, taking a rest from the joyous mayhem that was going on all around them, Taya looked up at the botanist and took his hand.

'I just want you to know that we don't blame you for everything that's happened.'

'Oh ... good.' Groach nodded uncertainly.

'But just in case it was all your fault,' Lorkrin continued. 'You will let us know if you get in any more trouble? It's been loads of fun.'

'Yeah,' Taya laughed. 'Much better than Uncle Emos's farm. Promise us you'll keep in touch. We'd miss not having you around.'

'Taya, I can safely say that my life has not been the same since I met the two of you. If ever I am being hunted and attacked and imprisoned, you will be the first people I think of.'

'We're sorry about the sewer ... and making you lose your beard.'

'Well, at least I can say I came out of this looking better than you two.'

Taya pulled the folds around her neck up over her face to stifle a snort of laughter.

Lorkrin chortled and slid his loose scalp down over his eyes. Deciding it was a good time to join Hilspeth in the dancing again, Groach excused himself, stood up and disappeared into the crowd.

The Myunans' giggling was lost in the noise of the singing and the stamping, dancing feet.

# COMING SOON

## ALSO BY OISÍN MCGANN

# UNDER FRAGILE STONE

## THE ARCHISAN TALES

Taya and Lorkrin's shape-changing tribe faces an invasion by Noran, whose rulers want to mine the valuable iron ore from the sacred mountain, Absaleth. But the mountain is haunted and every attempt to dig into it is met with super-natural resistance.

Then a mine tunnel collapses and the miners are trapped. With them are Taya and Lorkrin's parents, Nayalla and Mirkrin, who had been searching for their unruly children. Taya and Lorkrin are terrified for their parents. But help arrives in the form of a man who knows these mountains better than anyone – their Uncle Emos. He and his friend Draegar tell the Noranians that there is one chance for the trapped people – another entrance to the caves far back in the mountain range in an area inhabited by the violent, inbred Reisenicks, who hate outsiders.

A rescue party sets out as the mountain starts to collapse in on itself and the land all around threatens to pull itself apart ...

## ALSO BY OISÍN MCGANN

# The Gods and Their Machines

*Two worlds. Two different lives.*
*Divided by hate and violence.*
*Thrown together by chance.*

Chamus's nightmare begins when he survives a massacre. Suicidal assassins from neighbouring Bartokhrin are terrorising his country, Altima. How do you fight someone who isn't afraid of death?

Across the border, Riadni is no ordinary Bartokhrian girl; she dresses like a boy, fights like a boy, spits and rides her horse like a boy. When the Hadram Cassal set up camp on her father's land, she is drawn to these rebels who are prepared to fight – and to die – for their homeland.

A crash landing in Bartokhrian territory forces Chamus and Riadni together and they find themselves on the run, hunted by killers, danger and death closing in on them from all sides ...

# CONOR KOSTICK

# Epic

*#WELCOME TO EPIC:*
*PRESS START TO PLAY#*

On New Earth, Epic is not just a computer game, it's a matter of life and death. If you lose, you lose everything; if you win, the world is yours for the taking. Seeking revenge for the unjust treatment of his parents, Erik subverts the rules of the game, and he and his friends are drawn into a world of power-hungry, dangerous players. Now they must fight the ultimate masters of the game – The Committee. But what Erik doesn't know is that The Committee has a sinister, deadly secret, and challenging it could destroy the whole world of Epic.

# STEPHANIE PEARL-McPHEE CASTS OFF

## The Yarn Harlot's Guide to the Land of Knitting

Storey Publishing

The mission of Storey Publishing is to serve our customers by
publishing practical information that encourages
personal independence in harmony with the environment.

Edited by Deborah Balmuth and Elaine M. Cissi
Art direction and design by Mary Velgos
Text production by Mary Velgos and Kristy L. MacWilliams
Cover and interior illustrations © by Jamie Hogan
Cover photograph © by Adam Mastoon

© 2007 by Stephanie Pearl-McPhee

The information in this book is true and complete to the best of our knowledge. All
recommendations are made without guarantee on the part of the author or Storey
Publishing. The author and publisher disclaim any liability in connection with the use
of this information. For additional information please contact Storey Publishing,
210 MASS MoCA Way, North Adams, MA 01247.

Storey books are available for special premium and promotional uses and for custom-
ized editions. For further information, please call 1-800-827-8673.

Printed in the United States by CJK
10 9 8 7 6 5 4 3 2 1

### Library of Congress Cataloging-in-Publication Data

Pearl-McPhee, Stephanie.
    Stephanie Pearl-McPhee casts off : the yarn harlot's guide to the land of knitting.
        p. cm.
    Includes index.
    ISBN 13: 978-1-58017-658-3 (pbk. : alk. paper)
    1. Knitting—Miscellanea. 2. Knitting—Humor. 3. Knitters (Persons)—Miscellanea.
    I. Title.
TT820.P3747 2008
746.43'2—dc22

                                                                        2007003975